D1348319

Please return/renew this item by the last date shown. Books may also be renewed by phone or internet.

🖥 www.rbwm.gov.uk/home/leisure-and-culture/libraries

☎ 01628 796969 (library hours)

☎ 0303 123 0035 (24 hours)

www.rbwm.gov.uk

Royal Borough
of Windsor &
Maidenhead

Windsor and Maidenhead

95800000209892

# After Paris

ALSO BY NICOLE KENNEDY

*Everything's Perfect*

# After Paris

## NICOLE KENNEDY

An Aria Book

First published in the UK in 2022 by Head of Zeus Ltd,
part of Bloomsbury Publishing Plc

9 7 5 3 1 2 4 6 8

A catalogue record for this book is available from the British Library.

ISBN (HB): 9781800240162
ISBN (XTPB): 9781800240179
ISBN (E): 9781800240193

Cover design: Helen Crawford-White

Printed and bound in Great Britain by
CPI Group (UK) Ltd, Croydon CR0 4YY

Head of Zeus Ltd
First Floor East
5–8 Hardwick Street
London EC1R 4RG

WWW.HEADOFZEUS.COM

For Cara, Jemma and Katie

# 1

## Hôtel de Crillon, Paris, 1999

'She's disappeared!' Teddy huffed, and Alice arranged her mouth into a smirk. Unease had restructured his already exquisite features, rendering his face pensive and brooding; his cerulean eyes glazed sulkily, his full berry lips pouting. It was so unfair that he looked *so good*, all the time, even now as his distress escalated. She didn't *fancy* Teddy – Lordy, he was practically her brother – but she could appreciate fine art when she saw it and Teddy Astor, with his fine-boned nose and sharp-lined cheekbones, was a subject worthy of the Old Masters. Pity he was such a pain.

'I'm sure she'll turn up. She's hardly going to miss *le Bal*,' Alice replied, a yawn in her voice, as though Teddy's problems were just so *tedious* to her and there wasn't a delicious justice in him being stood up at the society function of the year. Chunky, he'd called her. *Chunky*. And she hadn't forgotten it.

'She might. She's French,' he said, as if that explained everything.

Around them the lobby bustled with activity – women dripping with pearls, the press dripping with long-lens cameras. 'There must be someone high profile here,' Alice observed. The list of debutantes was always a closely guarded secret, adding to the mystery and glamour of the event. Teddy ran a hand through his hair nervously and the effect was so enthralling Alice had to look away. She was fortunate she was impervious to his charms. 'What are you doing out here, anyway?'

'Avoiding your mother,' he answered, sombre. He signalled to the barman for a drink, a gesture that seemed to transform him from a boy to a man. *When had he started doing that?* Alice put a hand on his arm.

'Well, I can't argue with that, but there's no time for a drink. Come on, let's get this over with.'

'This is all your fault, you know. Why couldn't you have debuted in London like everyone else? Always got to be different, haven't you?' He looked skyward, as if praying for something. Divine intervention from tonight, perhaps.

Alice had been asking herself the same thing. She'd liked the idea of being more anonymous in Paris, of not feeling like she was being sized up against her contemporaries when she'd spent her whole life doing that herself. And of course Mummy was thrilled with the suggestion, immediately tapping into her extensive network of influential friends to secure her, and Teddy, an invitation – but rather than making her feel less visible, as she'd hoped, the new surroundings were having the opposite effect. At least she knew where she was in London. At least she could chatter her way around the room, outrunning her nervousness, and duck off somewhere with Lulu and talk about how unflattering her pale lilac-blue lace dress was and yes, Lulu often made her feel a hundred times worse, but at least the whole scene would be *familiar*.

She wouldn't feel the rising sense of being adrift that she was experiencing here.

'She's wearing yellow, apparently. The Frenchie. Nina Laurent. So she shouldn't be too hard to spot.' His mouth formed a line of distaste, as though he'd eaten something sour. Alice didn't answer but obviously she hoped Nina Laurent was a total bitch and ugly to boot. Her mother's wish had been for Teddy to be her *cavalier*, but Alice had prayed for the formidable Madame Chapelle, *le Bal*'s imperious organiser, to allocate her someone else and her prayers had been answered, in the form of a tall, fair, serious-looking Swiss count. 'Sounds delightful, doesn't she?'

Alice shrugged.

'I met the count earlier,' he added, in a teasing tone and with a look on his face which said: *lucky you*. She rolled her eyes. She'd already had her fill of jokes from her father, whose only contribution to this evening, beyond attending as a lord himself, had been a steady stream of puns: *I bet you're* counting *down the days! You can* count *on it!*

Their attention shifted as another debutante crossed the lobby. Alice looked around furtively, nervous of reproach from Madame Chapelle if they were spotted. The debutantes weren't supposed to be out here, they were meant to be tucked away, hidden like precious jewels about to go up for auction, but every now and then a gem escaped, gliding across the lobby to speak to a parent or whisper something to a sibling. Alice wished she had a sister here to talk to. Not Teddy, whom her mother had taken under her wing when his parents died ten years earlier.

Alice watched Teddy's eyes follow the young woman. She was wearing a long pale-pink gown that snagged on her hip bones, a tiara atop her blonde hair, which fell in glossy curls around her shoulders. Lordy, how Alice wished something would snag on *her* hip bones. Most of the debutantes looked like supermodels and Alice cursed herself again. *You can't disappear in a place like this.* As Teddy's eyes tracked the girl in pale pink around the room, Alice felt a deep ache tugging in her chest. Would anyone ever look at her that way?

'She's out of your league,' she said, and smirked again. Why did she always smirk so much around Teddy?

He cocked his head as though considering this. It had been a while since Alice had last seen him. It was the previous summer at The Hurlingham Club (with the unforgettable chunky incident: she'd beaten him at tennis and he'd attributed this to her chunky thighs, making her four brothers roar with laughter). He'd spent October half term in Hong Kong with a cousin, rather than with them as sometimes happened. She suspected he was steering clear of her mother, who was keen for them to coordinate their gap year plans, but he needn't worry; Alice had no intention of travelling with Teddy Astor. She and Lulu already had a rough itinerary, although the thought of being in a bikini next to Lulu brought her out in hives.

'I think being at *le Bal* puts me exactly in her league,' he said finally and as Alice caught his eye, she realised he too understood that his stock had recently gone up. Teddy Astor, hitherto a gangly, awkward teen, but now on the cusp of being a man, was *gorgeous*.

It was lucky she despised him or she'd be in serious trouble.

$$\star\,\star\,\star$$

4

In the lobby of the hotel, perched awkwardly on a circular leather banquette, a copy of *The Economist* pressed against her lap, Julia Frey was doing that thing she always did after talking to a boy. Running and rerunning their exchange in her head, cringing at the things she'd said, admonishing herself for the witty, interesting things she *could* have said. Why was speaking – such a basic, perfunctory thing – so difficult sometimes? Julia rarely said much, even though at any given time thousands of words galloped through her mind, a fizzing backdrop of linguistic opportunity and regret.

*Valentin*. Even his name was French and sexy. The things she wished she could say to him. She couldn't even blame the language barrier, since his English was excellent and that was how they mostly conversed, to her annoyance and relief. Julia was an almost straight-A student. The only subject she struggled with – the only subject that might lower her International Baccalaureate points and scupper her chance of studying maths at Cambridge – was French. So when she had to make plans for a work experience placement, she'd convinced her parents to allow her to do hers in Paris. She'd requested a 'business' opportunity but had wound up in a pharmacy, which seemed not so bad when she met Valentin on her first day. But that was two whole weeks ago, and today had been her last day. There'd been no signs he had even noticed her until this afternoon and then of course she'd blown it. Now he thought she was some uber-posh rich kid. Which she wasn't. Middle-class, but not posh. Comfortable, not rich. The only reason she could attend her school was thanks to her academic scholarship and a reduction in fees because her mother taught English there. That's how she'd wound up doing the IB, and not A Levels, as she'd have preferred. Oh, why did she tell Valentin she was coming *here*, to *le Bal*?

'Okay,' he'd said, with an awkward grimace.

She hadn't realised he was about to invite her to the bar he was heading to with the others.

'You have friends there?' he'd asked, surprise and disdain in his voice as he appraised her again, making a fresh assessment of her family and economic circumstances: her smart black suit trousers, her pin-striped shirt, the delicate pearl earrings gifted from her godmother, which she now regretted wearing.

'Hm, sort of,' she'd shrugged. Not wanting to lie, nor to tell the truth.

She cursed herself again, as she scanned the lobby, her fingers tightening around *The Economist*. The truth was, people-watching was a hobby of hers. She loved to observe people when they thought no one else was watching. Enjoyed overhearing conversations and imagining the context, the stories they divulged. And nowhere was better to people-watch than the annual *le Bal* at the Hôtel de Crillon. When Julia had realised she'd be in Paris for it, she'd marked it in her diary in capitals and underlined it. The people she could watch! Like the couple over there. A tall, handsome boy in white tie, with a pretty, slightly chubby girl in a blue, lace dress with capped sleeves and a full, tiered skirt, cinched round her waist with a wide satin sash. She was trying her best to tease him about something, but the flush on her cheeks and the way she kept angling her body towards his was giving her away. They were looking around them, for a parent perhaps, or a friend. What were their worries right now, she wondered? Was he bored? Roped into this by a relative? Perhaps she had a boyfriend – because it seemed to

Julia as if everyone else in the world had a boyfriend except for her – but she liked this boy better?

Across the lobby, she noticed a hotel manager watching her closely. She'd arrived after work and in her smart attire had walked straight inside, but that was a couple of hours ago and the lobby was beginning to fill with photographers and guests. She sensed it was time to leave. She wasn't sure how much more she'd be able to see anyway; she could hardly sneak into the ballroom where *le Bal* was held. Would it be weird if she joined Valentin at the bar in Le Marais now, turning up late when she'd told him she had other plans?

She stood quickly and made her way to the restrooms, but a queue had formed. She continued walking, in no rush and enjoying the buzz around these people who were, in theory, quite close to her world – she was at one of the best independent schools in the country, after all – but in practice were aeons away. Someone like Julia would never be able to gain entry to an event like this. If only Jennifer, her best friend and the other scholarship pupil in her year, could see her now. Jennifer was obsessed with the London socialites, poring over *Tatler* the same way Julia did the *Financial Times* in preparation for her future secondment interviews. She had a clear career trajectory mapped out: Cambridge and then financial analyst at one of the large investment banks in the City.

She found a restroom away from the main lobby, tucked down a small corridor. It was quiet, an oasis of calm compared to the melee in the central atrium. She peered at herself in the mirror, evaluating her face from different angles and frowning. It had been two hours since she'd left the pharmacy and last applied make-up in the cramped cupboard toilet at the back, and some shine was creeping in. Sometimes she feared she was destined to spend the rest of her life at her dressing table, staring into her vanity mirror, charting the rise and fall of empires on her face: the blackheads on her forehead, the whiteheads around her nose, *the lurkers*, small angry lumps beneath her skin that lay like dormant volcanos, hot to the touch but offering no sign of release. She wrote everything down in her diary, hoping that this scientific approach might someday provide an explanation for what she referred to internally as *the state of her face*. She could have been beautiful, that was the huge injustice of it. Her hair was long and blonde, her body toned and taut from hockey and barely eating. *A body like* Baywatch, *a face like* Crimewatch. That's what she'd heard a boy in her Duke of Edinburgh's Award group say as the others laughed. *Fuck you*, she would frequently think. *Fuck all of you*, when I'm earning enough to have my skin lasered, or whatever advancements lay ahead. Until then she applied make-up. Lots and lots of make-up. She needed her toolbox, she thought, reaching for her hefty bag, glad to have this bathroom to herself.

*Oh.*

She started at the unmistakable sound of crying. She considered leaving – tearful situations were not her speciality. She was practical, concise. She could explain the law of indices or accurately predict a chemical equation. She could not dissect a text message from a boy, or console a friend while they tearfully complained about their mother. It was for this reason some of the girls at school branded her 'cold', or sometimes 'frigid'. She hated that word, with its Miss Havisham undertone, as if all the other girls were gamely shagging or dishing out blow jobs every night after school

– she wasn't more frigid than anyone else, surely? They were seventeen and at an all-girls' school! And then there were her clothes; whatever she tried, she always seemed to get it wrong, the other girls laughing that her outfits were 'too loud' or 'too clashy'. It was why she was wearing practically a uniform today, so she couldn't get it wrong. She did as she always did. Told herself it didn't matter. Because it didn't. She was bright and she was focused and she'd get out of that school and she'd get a good job and she'd make enough money to fix her skin properly and she'd be a success. She felt certain that of all the things she couldn't control, her success was a surety. But she was feeling a little different tonight. There was something about being here for *le Bal*, in this beautiful hotel, something about knowing Valentin had invited her to join him and the others. She felt emboldened. She felt like maybe she could have something to add sooner than she thought.

She approached the closed door, her heart tap-dancing in her chest, and rapped her knuckles against the wood.

'*Est-ce que ça va?*' she asked – *Are you okay?* Not knowing what she would do if the occupant replied in rapid-fire French.

She stood there for a moment, excited to have stepped out of her comfort zone but apprehensive, silence permeating the space. She tapped over her forehead gently, moved her fingertips in small circular motions over the hot lumps before realising she'd need to press powder on to them again. She couldn't have known this moment would change her life and yet she was holding her breath.

'*J'ai besoin d'aller dans ma chambre,*' the voice replied tearfully, in staccato, faltering French. The voice belonged to someone young, perhaps a similar age to Jules. As she translated in her head – *She needs to go to her room* – her sense of intention dissipated. *Why am I getting myself involved in this?*

'Okay…' she said aloud, thinking through her response. Behind her she heard someone else enter the restroom. She glanced over her shoulder, distracted, and saw the girl in the ruffled blue dress. *The deb!* Oh God. She hated speaking French in front of other people. *Mortifying.* 'Um… *avez-vous*…' She closed her eyes, heat flushing her entire face. She'd really have to go to town with the powder after this. 'No. Um, *desolé*. I mean… Um…'

'Can I help?' the deb asked, appearing beside her, a keen, interested look on her face. She was beautiful up close, with soft creamy skin and arresting sapphire eyes. She smelt of roses and hairspray, her chestnut-brown hair swirled and secured around the nape of her neck, a thick wave of fringe curving over one side of her perfectly clear forehead. 'I speak French.' *Of course you do*, thought Julia, picturing chateaus in France and al fresco dinners at long tables laden with fresh flowers and red wine.

At their interaction, a gasp erupted from behind the door. 'You're English?'

'Yes!' Julia said, turning back and placing her hands on the closed door. 'You too? Are you okay?' she called into the wood.

She heard a loud sniff and nose-blowing from inside the cubicle. 'Can you help me? I need to get up to my room, without anyone seeing me, and I don't have my room key. I've made a mistake. Un *gros* mistake! Oh dammit,' she muttered. 'Why am I slipping into French? I've been trying to speak French all week and I can't!'

\* \* \*

Alice was trying not to look too excited by this exchange. She'd only popped into the loo because she needed some air before the ceremony, but now there was this poor girl crying, and this other girl, who was dressed like a middle-aged accountant but appeared to be around her age, seemed out of her depth. She was tall, her face blotchy, red heat battling with a thick layer of make-up and winning. She had oval eyes that glowed a pale green, their rapid movement reminding Alice of dragonflies darting over the lake at her family's estate in the summer. Her anxiety was palpable.

'What shall we do?' Alice whispered. 'I'm Alice, by the way.'

'Julia,' the girl replied, and she stuck out her hand as though they were concluding a game of lacrosse. Alice didn't know why but she suspected Julia would be very good at lacrosse; as well as her height, she was lean, and had an officious, confident air. 'I don't know,' she said, looking around quickly as though the baroque bathroom might provide an answer.

Behind the door, the sobbing had resumed. 'A big, big mistake,' the girl repeated.

'Who are you here with?' Julia asked, in a clipped, demanding tone.

'My... dad,' said the voice uncertainly. A soft London accent that Alice was unable to place.

'You're going to have to find him and get a key,' Julia said, forthright, as though it were simple, but Alice was conscious that if it were, this girl wouldn't be hiding in the restrooms of Le Crillon.

'Unless it's him she's trying to avoid?' Alice mouthed.

'I can't,' the voice sobbed. 'I don't know where he is. It's been like this all week. He dragged me to Paris and then—'

Julia gasped.

'*He dragged you?*' Alice exclaimed.

'No, not literally. But he made it sound like it would be fun. And it's not. It's not fun at all.'

Julia exhaled quickly and Alice was torn between being secretly pleased she had a genuine reason to leave and disappointed she couldn't stay.

'I've got to go…' she said quietly, peering at Julia's watch and frowning. For the first time, she noticed Julia's shoes: electric blue with a large satin bow, entirely at odds with the rest of her conservative look.

'Don't go!' Julia whispered, her tone almost aggressive.

'I have to!' Alice said, gesturing at her dress, and Julia gave a reluctant nod of understanding.

'Won't they recognise you at the front desk?' Julia asked, turning back to the door and wishing she'd never intervened. The scene was too highly charged, her ability to be of any use too limited. 'So you can get a key?'

'I guess so, but I can't go out there. I can't leave this room.'

'Why ever not?' asked Alice, astonished, halfway to the door but desperate to stay.


Inside the toilet stall, Nina pressed more toilet paper beneath her eyes and took three deep steadying breaths. 'Dammit,' she muttered, her voice muffled in the confined space. She had her hands on her hips, a small silver purse her grandmother had lent her dangling from her wrist.

'Because I'm dressed like this…' she said. She opened the door, wobbling on her high silver sandals, not the floral Dr. Martens she usually stomped around in, and gestured at her canary-yellow dress. With its tight structured bodice, flared feathered skirt and a fluffy feather trim lining the top of the corset and adorning her wrists, it combined Big Bird with Abba.

'Wow,' Alice and Julia said in unison as she stepped out of the cubicle.

'That's quite the look.' Alice felt suddenly grateful for her own dress. 'I saw you earlier, in the lobby. You were wearing dungarees? You had a guitar?' She didn't add, *I noticed you because I thought, no one should look that good in dungarees.* And no one should look that good in that dress. 'You're a deb?' Her face betrayed what she was thinking: *Who is she? Why don't I know her?* It was practically impossible to be a deb in Paris – that's why Lulu was so annoyed she'd got in – and there were no other British debs on the list. It was, she suspected, the first time her parents had invoked her title, in their supplications (discreet of course) to Madame Chapelle, and it had given her a weird little jolt to see it on her invitation: *Lady Alice Digby.*

'Well, yeah, I am and I'm not.' Nina scratched her nails through her hair and Alice realised it wasn't pinned up under her feathered headpiece as she'd first assumed. She had a pixie cut. *A pixie cut! A deb with a pixie cut and dungarees!* She was slim, too, halfway to a Kate Moss waif, with huge hazel eyes and perfectly arched eyebrows. What was *she* doing *here*, crying in the bathroom of Le Crillon at *le Bal*? 'I mean, I… Samir Laurent's my dad.' Nina shrugged, to imply nonchalance, but the way she said it was like she had something stuck to her tongue and she was trying to extricate it.

'*Samir. Laurent.* Is your *father*?' said the official-looking girl – did she work at the hotel? – sounding impressed. 'How old are you? How old is *he*?'

'Seventeen. I know, right? Fuck. What am I doing here?' She removed a cigarette box from under her arm, flicking it open with a thumb and withdrawing a cigarette using her teeth. Alice couldn't help but think it was the coolest thing she'd ever seen.

'Do you think I can smoke in here?'

'You're a deb and your father's a film star.' Alice shrugged. 'I think you can do as you please.'

A cloud passed over Nina's face. She looked as though she might be sick. 'When in Paris, eh?' she said, leaning an elbow against an ornate mirror as she took a drag on her cigarette. She offered Alice and Julia the box. They both shook their heads. Nina shrugged and the whole exchange seemed so perfectly sophisticated and French that Julia practically swooned. She felt entirely out of place, as she often did, but for the first time it felt enthralling.

'I only just found out. He's my dad, I mean. Well, six months ago, when he invited me to this.'

*She's a deb with a pixie cut and dungarees and an estranged movie-star father.* Good grief, thought Alice, this was getting better by the second.

'But I don't know why he bothered, to be honest. I've hardly seen him. I've mainly had awkward fittings for my dress – everyone's annoyed at having to leave it so late, and the fuss over these stupid feathers – with my grandmother, who keeps trying to speak to me in French and looking annoyed when I

can't reply. I thought this would be exciting, but instead it's…'
She stubbed out her cigarette against the porcelain sink, her
words juddering to a halt as she fought back tears.

'What's the problem with the feathers?' Julia asked,
surveying them. She avoided adding, *apart from the obvious*.

'They're… jaunty,' Alice supplied, struggling for something
positive to say.

'Last-minute addition,' Nina said, 'after my grandmother
spotted my tattoo.' She winced and turned her back in their
direction. If you looked properly, an aqua-blue shape was
just visible above the springy feathers. 'I am literally half-
ostrich right now,' she said, deadpan and Alice had to stifle
a giggle.

'Is that a… dolphin?' Julia asked, if anything so Nina
didn't notice Alice, who was fanning her face with a rolled-
up hand towel, overcome. She shot her a quizzical look over
Nina's shoulder: *what?* But all Alice could do was shake her
head and gulp. She shouldn't be surprised, she'd assumed all
debutantes would be affected. Mind you, even Julia could see
that Nina didn't appear to be your usual deb.

'Where are you from?' she asked.

'East London. Mile End,' Nina replied, her voice rising at
the end as though she wasn't sure it was the right answer.
'My mum's Irish though…' She trailed off, distracted. 'I got it
first, you know,' she added, an edge of irritation to her voice
as though this was something she'd said many times. 'Before
Mark Owen,' she added, to Julia's blank look. 'The dolphin
tattoo.' Julia was totally flummoxed.

'I didn't have you down as a Take That fan,' Alice said in a
small, squeaky voice as though she was struggling to contain
herself.

Nina slid on to the floor, tucking her legs beneath her. Julia shot her another look and asked if she was okay.

'I stopped telling people my dad was a film star when I was ten. Even then, I could tell people thought I was mad… I assumed it was a family rumour that had been blown out of proportion. Like, my dad was really a blue coat at Butlins or something. But it turns out it's true.' Julia fell silent, and Nina couldn't tell if she was sympathising with her or judging her for not appreciating her luck. She'd called her cousin, Erin, earlier, to tell her how awful everything was, but all Erin could say was 'it sounds *so cool!*' And it wasn't, it really wasn't. For years she and Erin had speculated on her paternity. Gorged on snippets gathered via her Aunty Niamh. *Could it be real? That Joanie had a brief fling with a fledgling movie star? That he scarpered as soon as she told him she was pregnant?* But the older Nina grew, the odder it seemed, and it started to make her feel strange when she thought of it; light-headed and unsettled. As though there was a tiny dark spot in her chest, a pinprick, widening into a gap, and if she thought about it too much she had the dizzying sensation that the dark hole might get bigger and bigger until it was all that was left of her, so she stopped talking about it and put it to the back of her mind. She kept busy: baking with Niamh, playing her guitar, drinking in the park with Erin, because as long as the balance was right, and the dark hole was satisfied, and her brain was left with no time to consider the alternative, things felt good. And then one day the invitation came.


Alice recovered herself as the silence stretched between them, the mood downbeat as Alice and Julia joined Nina on the floor. 'So you're Nina Laurent,' she said. She shook her head gently. She was beautiful and cool and her father was Samir Laurent. This was *so typical* of Teddy. But she couldn't stay cross, because there was such a fragility to Nina. If you had told Alice she was about to meet a movie star's beautiful French debutante daughter, she would never have pictured the girl standing before her. She seemed *normal*, aside from the haute couture custard dress.

If Alice felt out of place here, she could only imagine how Nina was feeling; but Alice could help, they could stick together, Alice instructing her on what was happening and pointing out who to avoid. She did a quick calculation in her head: yes, if Nina didn't go and Teddy was stood up, it would be gratifying; but perhaps if she and Nina spent the evening together, it could be even better – maybe they could become friends? 'Look, if you're a deb, we've got to go,' she said. 'The ceremony starts any minute.'

'I'm not going,' Nina said decisively. 'I can't. I can't wear this dress. I can't waltz. Especially not with Samir, pretending everything's okay. I don't know what I'm doing here.'

'But you have to,' Julia said. 'It's *le Bal.*'

Nina blinked rapidly, the eyeshadow the make-up artist had applied heavy on her lids. The metallic shade brought out flecks of amber in her hazel eyes. *She glows*, thought Alice, and she guessed Julia thought so too, judging by how often she touched her fingertips to her own face and glanced longingly at the sink, where she'd left a bulging make-up bag.

'So?' Nina shrugged. Her face betrayed what she was feeling. She swallowed. 'The truth is, I don't think Samir invited me here with the purest of intentions. I thought we'd spend the weekend getting to know each other, ambling around Paris. I didn't know about *le Bal* or what it meant, having an escort, or *cavalier*, or whatever...' Her hands flew around theatrically, until she ran out of steam. 'I dunno, the whole thing makes me feel grubby, which I don't really understand since I'm in possibly the most beautiful hotel, in the most beautiful city, in the world. I've always wanted to come to Paris...'

Nina began to cry again, and Alice slipped her hand into hers. She understood. She hadn't been able to articulate it until now, even to herself: she'd joked about it with her father; finding a husband at her deb ball and being married off (the historical backdrop to these events, even though these days they were more about getting dressed up and raising money for charity), but she couldn't shake off the feeling that she was being put on display, and in her case, the exhibit was lacking. That's why she was in Paris; she suspected the sting of rejection, of not being the darling of the ball, would be a little softer here. It mattered less, since she knew no one other than Teddy and now Nina. *The Count didn't count.* She smiled in spite of herself.

'I don't want to go either,' Alice said softly. 'Why don't we go together and get it over with?' She squeezed Nina's hand and then stood, shaking out the full skirt of her dress and pulling Nina up too. Beside her, she was aware of Julia, now in front of the mirror, prodding her face.

'Why are you going if you don't want to?' Nina asked, confused.

'I don't know. Because my parents want me to, I suppose. And it's what everyone does.'

Nina looked horrified. Alice cursed herself; she bet

Nina Laurent didn't set much store in following society's expectations.

'*Alice!*' Teddy hissed suddenly by the door. '*What are you doing? Everyone's looking for you.*' His face wore an angry grimace, until Nina stepped out from behind Alice. *Is it possible to hear the sound of a jaw dropping?* Alice thought.

'Hi,' Nina said, and she felt the moment. The moment where her world slipped and slid. The moment her eyes locked with Teddy's.

'This is Nina Laurent,' Alice said, and Nina wondered why she said it so emphatically, like Teddy was supposed to know who she was. 'This is Teddy Astor,' she said, turning to Nina. 'Your *cavalier*.'

'Nina O'Connell,' Nina corrected, frowning, a ruse to mask her embarrassment because she'd seen the man before her earlier: rushing into a lift, a burst of action and a musky scent that had left her breathless. She was jacked up on hormones and paternal abandonment, she'd thought, and then scribbled it down in the notebook she always carried with her: song lyric ideas. She hadn't imagined *he* might be a *cavalier*, she'd been picturing someone far less handsome, someone old.

Alice looked between the two of them, their attraction unfurling like caramel, and felt instantly panicked.

'We're not going,' she announced to Teddy, her arms folded.

'What?' Nina exclaimed as Teddy snapped to attention.

'What do you mean, you're not going?' he asked, working hard to shift his eyes away from Nina. 'Alice, it's *le Bal*. Thousands of girls – hundreds of thousands – would give their right arm to be here right now. You *have* to go. Imagine if you don't!' Alice did imagine it. She imagined walking out right now, head high, a cool girl, like Nina Laurent, or O'Connell, whatever her name was, not one beset by tradition and expectations and uncomfortably fitting dresses. The whole event was so *old-fashioned* and *showy*. 'Your whole family will be out, Alice. Your children won't be able to debut.'

'That's all the more reason not to do it!' she cried, feeling revolutionary. 'Tell my mother—'

'You are joking? There's no way I'm telling her anything. The count's already one surplus *cavalier* with you not there. If you're both ditching,' – his eyes found Nina's again, hesitant but full of expectation – 'I'm coming with.'

'No!' groaned Alice, but she could see how he was looking at Nina. She could already see how this would play out. The two most beautiful people in a room always find each other, don't they? 'Why do you always have to…'

'Always have to what?'

'Nothing,' she tutted. She knew she was being childish but all her life it felt like Teddy was always there, commandeering her things: her brothers, her mother and now Nina Laurent. *She'd* met her first, not Teddy. Oh God, why did she sound like such a child? She was seventeen! *Time to grow up, Alice,* she seethed to herself silently.

'Are you coming?' she asked, meeting Julia's eyes in the mirror.


Julia had been watching them as she discreetly reapplied her make-up, using a plethora of tubes and brushes and powders. She felt sorry for Alice; could sense that things were not unfolding in the way that Alice had hoped.

Julia had come to *le Bal* to people-watch; to be invited to join some *le Bal* runaways was beyond her wildest dreams.

These were exactly the sort of people who wouldn't give her a second glance at school; who didn't register her, with her lowly teacher parent and acned skin. Imagine, when she told Jennifer, and word leaked to the cool set. And yet she couldn't, could she? She was so different to them all. What did she know about being a debutante or having a movie-star father? But she felt connected to them all the same. She didn't believe in fate, she believed in science, and yet even to her it seemed particularly serendipitous that it had been her who had found Nina Laurent; it's not every day you meet a movie star's daughter in the bathroom of Le Crillon, is it? And there was something captivating about Nina Laurent. There was a restlessness to her that Julia recognised. Besides, isn't this partly why she'd come to France? For so long, she had felt like she was waiting for her life to start and now here it was, slowly spinning into action. She was at *le Bal*, with two debs and a *cavalier*. Why not? Why not join them? Julia was tired. Tired of always having to weigh things up, tired of being a bystander and not a participant. She had this growing sense that it was time to *live*. If not now, then when?

'I do know a bar we could try...' she said.

While the others hid from sight, Julia convinced the short man with the reedy voice at the front desk to give her a key to Nina's room. It was her no-nonsense tone and utter unflappability that compelled the concierge to hand it over. 'I'm Nina Laurent's personal assistant,' she repeated imperiously, *Economist* slapped on the counter, 'and it's imperative I get that key.'

A short time later, Alice, Julia and Teddy gazed around

Nina's room in amazement. Even by Le Crillon standards, this was really something. In the distance the Eiffel Tower shone gold against a cobalt-blue sky. Nina scrambled around grabbing things and went into the white-marbled bathroom to get changed.

'If we're doing this,' Teddy said nervously, 'we need to do it quickly. Won't your father come to look for you? Your mother definitely will.' He shuddered in Alice's direction.

Teddy shed his waistcoat, jacket and tie as Alice removed the sash securing her dress so the lace flared loosely. 'Could I borrow this?' she called to Nina, lifting a denim jacket from where Nina had slung it over an armchair earlier. *Much better,* she thought, holding out the capacious skirt in pinched fingers as she twisted and turned before Nina's full-length mirror. Julia took in the room and her new acquaintances' clothes and once again had a rush of feeling that she was out of her depth. She was dressed for work in a pharmacy, not an exciting night out with three *le Bal* escapees in Paris. As if reading her mind, Alice came over. 'Look, undo that button, oh and that one too, and—' To Julia's alarm, Alice lifted her hair up, away from her face, pulling it into a high pony as she weighed up her new look. Julia's thick blonde hair was a barrier between her and the rest of the world. She had never worn it up.

'No, no, no,' she said quickly, pulling back, her curtain of hair resuming sentry. She noticed Alice's eyes trailing over her skin and offered up a quick, silent plea that she wouldn't comment on it.

'Sorry,' Alice said simply. 'How about... a hat? Or a scarf?

Or, I know! Teddy pass me your waistcoat and bow tie.' She helped Julia into the waistcoat, leaving the buttons undone, and draped the bow tie around her shirt collar. Instantly, Julia's smart trousers and pin-striped shirt had added cool: a *Le Smoking* effect. 'Do you have any blue eyeshadow in there?' she asked, motioning at Julia's large bag. A few minutes later she stood back gratifyingly, nodding as she surveyed the effect, Julia's electric-blue pumps popping – along with her eyeshadow – now too. 'When in Paris!' Alice grinned.

Nina emerged from the bathroom, her dungarees back on with a neon-pink crop top underneath, and she'd kept on her yellow headpiece and silver, feathered heels. '*Très chic, non?*' She laughed nervously, her East London accent just below the surface of her carefully enunciated French.

By nine o'clock, Julia – or Jules, as she was now – had Valentin's arm resting lightly on her shoulders, having recently broken off their kiss to smile at one another nervously. Julia's brain was screeching *Yes! Yes! Yes!* She had long ago accepted that she would likely start university not only a virgin, but one who had never been kissed. They reached for each other again, delicious kisses growing deeper in the dark, sweaty bar. For the first time in about five years, Julia wasn't thinking about her skin. Alice had hooked up with one of Valentin's friends, Jean-Pierre, and had to bite her lip to stop herself giggling, it reminded her so much of her French textbooks from school. Nina was being spun around the dance floor by Teddy, her eyes alive, her headpiece precarious, bits of feather and lace in danger of cascading over her face like flowers trailing down a wedding cake.

When 'Spice Up Your Life' came on, Jules and Alice joined them on the dance floor and they all shook it to the left and slammed it to the right, including Teddy, belly-laughing. They swung their arms around each other, singing at the top of their voices, jumping up and down as a new track came on that they all knew. They devised silly dances. 'I call this *Le Tour Eiffel*!' Alice shouted, making a triangle shape and then moving her hands around like flashbulbs. 'I do this, on the hour!' she said, and each time the clock crawled on to the next hour one of the others would grab her and shout '*It's time*!' There was an attempted lift, *Dirty Dancing* style, which resulted in Alice and Nina in a heap on the floor, laughing. 'Amateurs,' scoffed Julia, because she'd spent hours watching other girls doing this during their gymnastics lessons at school but had felt too afraid to try herself. 'Come on, Nina, I've got you…' she said, grounding herself to the floor and tensing her thighs. Nina stepped back, further back still at Julia's command, and then she was running and flying and swooping over the dance floor in her dungarees and heels and her stupid yellow headpiece, before she and Julia also ended up on the floor, the three of them crying with laughter.

'You are dazzling,' Teddy whispered into Nina's ear a short while later, looping his arms around her and gently spinning her round. In a shadowy corner of the dance floor, he kissed her, his hand on her neck, eliciting shocks of stardust down her spine, and their bodies pressed together, magnetic. Nina felt suddenly grateful to her movie-star father for inviting her to Paris.

\* \* \*

By 1 a.m. they were all at Valentin's flat in Montmartre. Julia and Valentin were in his bedroom, snogging, and Alice, not used to drinking, had fallen asleep in his small sitting room.

'I want to show you my favourite place in Paris,' Teddy whispered to Nina. Since leaving the bar they had sobered, grown awkward around each other with Julia and Alice close by. It occurred to Nina that the others didn't know they had kissed, even.

'We shouldn't leave Alice.'

'We won't be long and she's soundo. Jules seems pretty happy in there.' He gestured in the direction of Valentin's bedroom door and grinned. The cold air hit them afresh as they stepped outside and Teddy raced back up to the apartment, returning with a blanket. He wrapped it over both their shoulders, securing it in place with his left hand and holding Nina's hand with his right. They navigated cobbled streets, laughing when Nina's heels got stuck, pressed side by side for warmth. 'I come here whenever I'm in Paris,' Teddy said, pulling Nina up an uneven flight of stairs.

By 3 a.m., Nina was sitting on the top of the steps outside Le Sacré Coeur with Teddy and he had shared with her how both his parents had died when he was young, in a house fire. How they'd managed to bundle him in a blanket and pass him through a small top window to a neighbour. How difficult it had been since. How in every city he visited he would find a church and light a votive candle for them both, the only way he could think for them to still travel together. At some stage he'd abruptly changed the subject and made a joke, and they were drunk enough for their conversation to snap like elastic on to lighter matters. Soon they were shooting lines from their favourite films back at each other.

She laid her head on his shoulder and he wrapped his arms, and the blanket, around her. It was almost freezing, but beer and lust kept them warm.

By 5 a.m., they returned to Valentin's flat to retrieve Jules and Alice and the four of them wandered through the streets of Paris back to Le Crillon, singing 'Disco 2000', swapping stories and promising each other – swearing on the *Bow Tie of Fun*, which Julia was swinging around her head – that they would do this every year. They would meet back in Paris. (And they would get matching dolphin tattoos – even Teddy.)

'Let's meet here! At the fountains!' they whooped as they reached Place de la Concorde; pointing at the huge Fontaine des Fleuves, illuminated arcs of water creating crescent-moons of gold, lambent droplets falling like shooting stars over the tritons and mermaids; swinging from lamp posts as they passed them, feeling like every movie, every moment, was seeping into their skin. This was their city. This is where it felt like their lives had finally begun.

'Let's do it though,' they said later, as the sky began to lighten, 'let's really do it,' their fingers cold, their backs wet with dew as they lay on the grass of the Jardin des Tuileries, sharing the blanket and Nina's cigarettes, the hum of the city beginning around them, the imposing architecture of Le Crillon behind them. 'Let's meet up here every year, whatever happens.'

Twelve hours in Paris. That's all it took to cement their futures. They would often wonder in the years ahead: what if Jules had never come across Nina in that bathroom? What if Alice and Teddy hadn't been there at all? Where, and who, would they all be now?

# 2

## Twenty Years Later

### Friday a.m.

*Nina*

Nina was humming a Florence + the Machine song as she scanned the busy concourse for a place to sit so she could rearrange the various items she was juggling: magazines were slipping from her underarm and bulging paper bags from La City Pâtisserie were digging into her wrist on one side, while the other hand dragged along her suitcase and the song in her head told her to Shake It Out.

Jules had a problem with earworms – songs she couldn't forget that burrowed in her brain – so these days, whenever it happened, she sent a voice note of the song in question to her friends. The subsequent flurry of messages was usually a successful antidote and as Jules said, even if it wasn't, there was comfort in knowing the three of them were now listening to – or in Nina's case, humming – the same tune.

That's what had happened this morning, when their messaging group, *When in Paris*, had been particularly active:

My Uber driver is SO FIT! He looks like Keanu Reeves.

Young or old? I would take either tbf.

Lordy, I think I just wet myself running for the train!

Nina loved the preamble to a weekend away; the joy of it was all part of the experience for her. It was three years since they had last all been in Paris together and Nina sensed they needed a few days there now more than ever. She certainly did.

From the corner of her eye, she thought she saw Alice. She squinted as she approached. *Was that Alice?* She had her look: flippy skirt, chunky jumper and boots, wavy shoulder-length ombré hair, her slender frame and protruding cheekbones, toned by the demands of parenthood; but it was hard to tell, hunched as she was, head in hands. It was only when Nina was practically on top of her, and could see the small symbol of the Eiffel Tower etched in delicate black lines on her neck, that she was absolutely sure. She glanced down at her wrist, red-lined by the takeaway bags, to her own matching Eiffel Tower tattoo: they had got them together to mark their thirtieth birthdays (deeming the Eiffel Tower more fitting than a dolphin). Jules's was on her hip, discreet and not discernible in her work attire. *Nine years ago*, marvelled Nina with a smile.

The wish-washy feeling in her stomach she'd had since last night had intensified as she approached but she recognised her nervous system calming as she sat down, reaching an arm around Alice in hello, grateful that she still doused herself in rose perfume and hairspray. It was reassuring; it made Nina feel like things would be okay.

'Morning!' she chirruped. She wasn't a natural chirruper – it broke the gentle, melodic rhythm of her voice, honed through hours of yoga and mindfulness – and it came out high-pitched and forced.

Alice started, reflexively shrugging off Nina's arm, her dark blue eyes blinking, as though she hadn't expected to see her there even though they were due to meet by the Eurostar entrance in twenty minutes. 'Oh, Neen,' she said, pulling her into a hug, not seeming to notice the mini baguettes that must be poking into her ribs.

'Are you okay?' Nina asked, pulling back, putting a hand to Alice's upper arm. She looked tired and anxious and for a moment Nina forgot her own problems. She had been sure, as she tried to sleep last night, as she was in the shower this morning, as she slipped her passport into her bag before she left home, that with one look her oldest friends would have it figured out, but she realised – with a mix of gratefulness and guilt – that Alice had too much on her plate to notice how tired and anxious Nina was herself this morning.

'You're early,' Alice said, miming intense surprise.

'I do that now,' Nina said, grinning good-naturedly. Sometimes she found comments like this from Alice or Jules annoying – sure, for the first ten years of their friendship she was usually late, but for the last ten, and definitely since Alice had had three kids and Jules had been doing her thing in the City, she was the only one on time – but today she was so grateful to be here with Alice it didn't bother her at all. She glanced at her watch. She had time to tell Alice, before Jules arrived. She took a deep breath and was about to tell her everything when she noticed Alice's eyes, puffy and bloodshot, her face pale.

It took a moment for Nina to realise Alice was crying. 'What's wrong?' she asked, wrapping her arm back around her. This time Alice collapsed willingly into her shoulder.

'They'll be okay?' Alice sobbed, burying her face in her hands. 'Won't they?'

'The kids? *Of course.* They'll be *fine*.' She pulled Alice closer into her, trying to ignore an intense rush of nausea as floral notes invaded her nostrils, and weighed up what to say. When it came to Alice's children, and Charlotte especially, it was easy to say the wrong thing. 'They'll have a great time with Ted.'

Nina felt Alice flinch and swallow beneath her embrace and she looked skywards and sighed. *Motherhood, man.* She often thought of how much of herself Alice had willingly handed over to her family. She felt a quiver of fear.

'I can't do it,' Alice said finally, and she raised her head, chewing on her bottom lip, and there it was: a glimpse of her old self. The Alice threaded with determination; the one who could make a split-second decision – like skipping out on *le Bal* – and stick with it. 'I'm going home,' she declared. *Oh no. No, no, no.* This wasn't the thing she wanted Alice to take a stand on.

'You can't,' she said, and it came out more pleadingly than she expected. 'Jules needs us.' And she wasn't sure if that was true, but she could see the resolve in Alice's face, could hear it in her voice, and she began to panic and wonder, if Alice was going, could she leave too?

'I don't know what to do. I really want to come but... I can't say this in front of Jules, Nina,' – Alice's eyes darted around furtively – 'but it's *so hard*. This stuff with Charlotte... I don't know how Ted will cope.' She threw her hands up. '*I can't go away for the whole weekend!*' She said it in the same way as you might declare you can't go to the moon, or embark on a solo sail across the Atlantic, not to spend a couple of nights away in Paris with two of your oldest girlfriends.

'But *Alice*,' Nina said. 'You've been saying how much you need this. You *deserve* this. What was Charlotte's teacher warning you about? ASD-parent burn out?'

But all the mention of the wise words of Mr Hough did was seem to push Alice over the edge. '*What was I thinking?*' she cried, her cheeks burning red as she gathered her things, and Nina's heart began to pound: there was no way she could get through this weekend without Alice.

She hated to say it. She didn't want to get involved. But equally, she needed Alice to stay. 'I thought Charlotte was better with Ted?' she asked awkwardly.

Alice frowned. It felt like battle lines had been revealed and Nina now inadvertently found herself on the wrong side of them; on Ted's side. She tried to back-pedal but Alice was immediately incensed, ranting, 'Is that what he's said? He has *no* idea! She masks! She masks with Ted because she doesn't feel comfortable with him!'

'No, he hasn't, honestly,' Nina said, her voice strained, because Ted had in fact tried to draw her in to a number of conversations on this, but she had steadfastly resisted. 'But *look*, if that's how you feel, maybe a weekend alone with the kids will do him good? It's forty-eight hours. *Two nights*. You need this, Alice. We all do.'

She saw Alice's eyes flicker up to her, caught the slight raise of her eyebrow, the unspoken *What do you need a break from,*

*Nina?* Did she have time to tell Alice now? Perhaps if she told her she wouldn't feel as sick to her stomach, perhaps the calm she'd felt when she first sat down beside Alice would return? For Nina, this weekend in Paris had come at the perfect time. She needed a break from London, and Flynn, to decide what to do. She needed the restorative effects of two days in the company of her oldest and best friends, the women who knew her best. 'Listen, Alice, I need to tell...'

'Oh, sugar,' Alice said, waving above them.

Nina broke off as she clocked Jules descending regally down the central escalator, turning heads even with her eyes glued to her phone. Jules was wearing her 'off-duty' uniform, as dictated by her personal stylist: a pearly pale silk shift dress with a blazer, a large grey leather tote bag, Chanel flats. Her skin gleamed, her hair shone. Nina swallowed the words on her lips, and waved.

'When in Paris?' she called as Jules approached, holding her bags of coffee and croissants aloft, her voice rising at the end like perfectly fluted piping. She ignored the stars that seemed to whoosh round her head like a crown, the dizzying sensation of life spiralling out of control, as she stood. She caught the irritated look that passed over Jules's face before it converted into a polished, practised smile. She never used to smile like that, Nina thought. She used to smile properly, goofily, before she was rich and successful and obsessed with ovulation and fertility and overpriced herbs.

'Oh, girls,' Jules said as she reached them and hugged them in turn. 'You do not know how much I need this weekend. Let me just finish this.' She waved her phone in her hand and moved slightly away from them, tapping furiously.

*She needs us*, Nina reminded herself. *She's having a really horrible time.* And that's why they were here; to support Jules, before her final round of IVF after years and years of heartbreak. Nina often wondered how Jules had kept on going. Dusted herself off each time. She knew that was intrinsically Jules: to keep going, to keep working, to keep moving forwards, but it must have taken its toll. She felt her own problems pale into comparison and as she met Alice's eyes, she saw it on her face too. This was it, this was Jules's last shot, thanks to Paul, and all they had to do was spend a weekend with her in Paris, helping her relax, reminding her that whatever happened they were there for her.

Nina could see the turmoil on Alice's face. She lowered her voice and put her hands either side of Alice's shoulders. 'Come on, Alice, you need this too. A weekend just the three of us. When did we last do that? Visiting our old haunts, eating nice food, drinking nice wine…' She had Alice in an awkward embrace now, sort of swaying the two of them from side to side, Alice snotty and smiling in spite of herself, removing evidence of her smudged mascara from her cheeks as Nina thought *Oh shit, I can't do that, can I? I can't drink nice wine? And aren't there foods you shouldn't eat?* She made a mental note to investigate on the train.

As Jules returned, Nina tried to ignore the flare of emotion that shot through her chest like a distress signal, as she gathered everything she had to fix a bright smile firmly in place. These were her two best friends in the world and right now, this was exactly where they should all be. She gathered up her bags and looping arms with Jules, they ambled over to Departures. They were going to Paris.

★ ★ ★

*Jules*

The train doors closed, the click of the electronic locking mechanism audible, and Jules took a sharp intake of breath. This was really happening. She was getting away. She shoved her phone to the very bottom of her bag, breathed out slowly and relaxed back into her seat, the visions of Paul charging along the platform and storming the carriage, demanding she come back home, receding. That was the last time, she told herself.

It was always the last time.

She meant it this time. That was it. She'd had enough.

Her second sigh raised the eyebrows of her friends. 'Work's bonkers at the moment,' she said, by way of explanation. 'And I want to get as much done as possible so I can rest up a bit during my... treatment.'

'Has anyone clocked yet?' Alice asked.

'Nope,' Jules said. 'I almost wish they would. The subterfuge is an added layer of stress I don't need.'

'Maybe it's time you told them? Take some proper time off?'

'If you worked with women, someone would have noticed years ago,' Nina mused. 'Not kept fast-tracking you and giving you more to do.'

'But what if it doesn't work?' Jules bristled, as she always did when it was suggested, usually by her mother, that it might be her job, rather than her *hostile uterus*, that was preventing her from having children. Yes, she worked long hours. But do you know what she didn't do when she was working? She didn't smoke, she didn't drink, she didn't do drugs. She *did* work out, in the company's top-floor gym, she did jog around the City when she'd done an all-nighter and needed a shower anyway. She did earn enough money to live in a nice house in Strand-on-the-Green in Chiswick with a little red sports car parked outside it, which a child would be extremely fortunate to grow up in. That's what she told herself, anyway. '... I'll be off the leadership programme and still no baby. I've made so many sacrifices, I can't give up everything.' She swallowed, her eyes filling. Every now and then, raw pain still took her by surprise. 'And this is it, isn't it? This is my last shot. Paul says he can't do it any more and I do get it,' she said carefully. 'I do...' She sniffed and trailed off, her lips pursed.

Beside her, Alice put her head on her shoulder. Opposite them, Nina, dressed for spring in a voluminous rainbow-striped cropped mohair jumper (except it probably wasn't mohair, likely something more ethical), was producing all manner of things from her various bags: sticky, still-warm pastries, a huge flask of the coffee she was famous for and chunks of juicy fruit. Her friends had dispensed with the platitudes of infertility some time ago, at Jules's behest, and she was grateful for it. These were, after all, her longest, most solid friendships. These were the women who knew her best. Having them beside her was enough.

'I got you *The Economist*...' Nina beamed, waving a stack of magazines, and Jules didn't have the heart to tell her she'd stopped reading that a long time ago. She wished she had the time. 'And these...' She put three of her signature coolers on the tabletop: grated seasonal fruits (strawberries, rhubarb and elderflower this week), mixed with crushed ice and rose-scented water.

'I love these!' Jules said, her cheeks warm with pleasure.

Flashes of green and grey shot past the window, the distance between the train and London growing ever wider. She took in deeper and deeper breaths, her body flexing, straightening, broadening, no longer curled in on itself as it had been since last night.

'Only the best for you two,' Nina winked, but her smile wasn't quite as wide as usual. Jules could spot an undertone a mile off, but of what she did not know.

*Alice?* Alice was chewing on her lip and staring out of the window and Nina shared a half-grimace and a shrug with Jules: something to do with the kids, Jules imagined. She took a napkin, some chunks of mango and melon and a small silver fork with a pale ceramic handle and delicate floral etchings that complemented the napkins.

'These are gorgeous,' she said, the fork in the air. 'You're so lucky you get to do stuff like this.' She supposed this was the sort of thing you had time for when you were self-employed and – she glanced at Alice, who looked tired and washed-out – didn't have family or fertility worries.

'Like what?'

'You know, coordinating napkins and handles and...' She gestured over the spread; the table looked fit for a magazine shoot. 'Making things look nice.'

'It is my job,' Nina said lightly as she took a photo.

'Oh, I know,' Jules said quickly. 'I just mean it's a perk of doing your own thing.'

Nina could have pointed out that since Ted's firm had invested in La City Pâtisserie, which was on the cusp of launching a string of patisseries nationwide, the free rein she had previously enjoyed to 'do her own thing' and 'make things look nice' had dwindled significantly, but she let it go.

She was used to Jules's awkwardness, her ability to say the wrong thing even when well-meaning.

'You *do* know what I mean?' Jules said, concern wreathed around her face. Most of it anyway: her forehead remained smooth and wrinkle-free.

'I do.' Nina grinned. 'Botox?' she asked.

Jules nodded a yes. 'You've always been good at making things look nice,' she said pleasantly, keen to ensure she hadn't offended Nina.

'I have,' Nina agreed genially, enjoying, as she always did, the flow of conversation between them. 'Thank you. I'm glad you noticed.'

'I do. I notice you. I appreciate you.' Their eyes danced together. One of the benefits of Nina's years of therapy was the knock-off second-hand therapy the other two had gotten via her. They were getting better at being honest with each other. To a point.

Alice looked between them. 'You got Botox?'

'Oh, ages ago,' Jules said. 'Can't you tell?'

Jules and Nina both angled their faces directly at Alice and she surveyed their crease-free skin.

'Mine needs redoing, but I'm waiting until after...' Jules trailed off again. She'd been living on this line, the before and after line, for too long.

'You won't shave your legs but you got Botox?' Alice said to Nina, her head cocked to the side in astonishment.

'One woman's beauty standards are another woman's... something or other.' She grinned and gestured her hand around vaguely. 'Oh, I don't know,' she shrugged. 'It takes ages to shave your legs. Did you go to Dr M?' she asked Jules.

'Of course,' said Jules.

'Who's Dr M?' Alice asked, increasingly feeling like a left-out child at a party.

'Dr Maryam. She's the go-to Botox person on Harley Street and she runs a clinic in the City,' Jules explained. 'Renowned for her needle-jabbing precision.'

'Why didn't you tell me?' Alice frowned. 'Look! I'm frowning at my frown lines!' she exclaimed to laughter. 'Book me in too, next time.'

'I only had mine done a couple of weeks ago, it's still not properly set,' Nina said. Then asked suddenly, 'Should you not have Botox when you're pregnant?'

'It's not advised,' Jules said. 'Obviously. Or if you're trying. If I were pregnant, I wouldn't take any chances.'

Nina nodded and started rooting around in her bag for her phone.

The smell of the pastries made Jules's stomach flip: cinnamon rolls laced with orange curd and a honey glaze, rose and cardamon threaded croissants. She had been following a strict clean-eating regime devised by Flora, her fertility doula (the best in West London), but even Flora had agreed she should take this weekend as an opportunity to relax. Could she risk a pastry? It felt so decadent. So indulgent. 'Did you go to the café this morning?' she asked.

Nina nodded, humming with an almost manic edge, as she looked something up on her phone. Jules recognised 'Shake It Off', the song she had sent to her friends this morning, and smiled. Of all the things that had gone wrong in her life, her friends were where she had gone right.

'Just to pick up a few bits,' Nina said.

'Definitely not to check up on Luca,' Jules said.

'Absolutely not. That would imply some sort of

control-freakery of which I'm not sure I'm capable,' she laughed. 'No, seriously, the managers are so good in there now, not even Luca needs to be there really. We've got a brilliant team. I woke up early so thought I'd grab some decent breakfast for us.'

'Is Luca the perfect man?' Alice asked. 'Handsome, reliable, funny and gay.'

'I think he might just be,' Nina nodded.

To Jules at least, Nina had the perfect set-up. She ran La City Pâtisserie by day and her close friend and flatmate, Luca, ran it as a wine bar and charcuterie by night. They lived in a huge warehouse conversion apartment together with Luca's partner, Kai. Sundays were 'family days', the three of them trawling a market, heading back to the flat to cook lazy Sunday dinners, other friends dropping in, including Jules and sometimes, when he was in the mood, Paul. For so long Nina had seemed lost but now she seemed complete, in a way Jules couldn't recognise. She longed to be happy and fulfilled with her life, the way Nina was. To feel child*free* like Nina, not child*less*. What was different about them? 'Is the divine Flynn providing any competition?' she enquired instead, surprised to notice Nina's cheeks immediately flush.

'Flynn and I are on the same page. We have a lot of fun together and that's it,' Nina said firmly, to envious looks from her friends. Jules couldn't imagine a life that wasn't riddled with complication. Was it really possible, no-strings-attached sex?

'Does he have a gig this weekend?' Alice asked.

'Yep. Edinburgh, I think,' Nina said vaguely. Jules sensed she seemed keen to shut the conversation down.

'I *love* spoken word! Can we go to see him sometime?' Alice asked eagerly.

'Mm hm,' Nina said unconvincingly and Jules, taking the hint, returned to Luca. 'I messaged Luca to say thank you. I'll pick him up something in Paris. Does he still love macarons?'

'It's no big deal, honestly. And I do need to learn to let go a bit. There's so much other stuff going on with the expansion. I can't be in there every day. But it's hard to let go when it's your baby.' Something flickered across her face then, her countenance briefly jolted and Jules felt a flutter of irritation: Nina didn't usually censor every conversation slip around her. She resisted the urge to sigh as Nina moved and shifted things around on the table, topping up both Jules's and Alice's coffees even though neither had taken a sip yet.

'How are things going with the expansion?' Alice asked. 'Ted's working flat out.'

Jules tuned out her friends' conversation and gazed down the aisle. She considered a walk along the carriages just for something to do. She drummed her thumbs on her thighs, her phone still in her bag. How long had it been since she'd last checked? Twenty minutes? Thirty? She dared not look.

Needing to satisfy at least one impulse, she reached for a rose and cardamon croissant, pink sugared petals scattering artfully over her napkin. Everything about Nina's products was perfection: the flavours, the presentation, the culmination of years of her friend's hard work. Nina had started with patisserie and pastry but later, due to popular demand, had introduced a lunch menu too. Jules delicately tore apart the layers of flaky pastry, delighting in the streak of blush pink within. She was practically drooling now as layers of butter and rose – and almond? – sunk on to her tongue. At

Flora's instruction, she'd trained herself out of eating sugar and fat over the last few years. Along with caffeine. Alcohol. Anything that had been processed. Not that any of it had made a difference.

She knew that was the point of this trip: to let loose, to relax, before her final round of IVF, *her last chance...* but to enjoy Paris she'd need to be deprogrammed; all the information she had read and digested about fertility and optimum conception conditions somehow wiped from her highly retentive brain. She could tell you the calories and fat content in virtually any foodstuff; the pH level of a banana, the mercury content of tuna. When Jules took on a project, she took on a project and this one – the baby project – was the only one she'd failed to complete.

She gingerly chewed small fragments of the croissant, enjoying it less and less, half listening to Alice, who was now relaying how she'd had to check – double check, triple check – that Ted knew Charlotte's routine, knew where Phoebe's cricket kit was, wouldn't forget Wilfy had a birthday party to attend on Saturday afternoon and the gift was wrapped and hidden in the pantry of their beautiful Oxfordshire home.

Jules often thought that Alice's home was a perfect reflection of her: it had an old romantic feel, with its crumbling, ivy-clad walled garden, a stream running along the end banked with daffodils in the spring, but with a contemporary edge; the extension they'd worked so hard on, joining the old house with their renovated barn, made entirely from glass. Inside, the colours were bold, like Alice had been when they first met at *le Bal*: deep indigo blues, striking shades of plum and emerald, always shot through with a dash of something you wouldn't expect – tangerine or lime or steel – but after seeing it couldn't live without.

For a long while, Jules had tried to emulate the same look. She'd often experienced the opposite problem: the things she wore or selected for her flat in Clerkenwell, before she lived with Paul, should have worked, but they didn't. She could never tell why, didn't realise until she showed someone else the dress and shoes, or sofa and rug, and read their reaction, figuring out if she'd made a hit or a miss. It was tiring and eventually she'd employed a personal stylist who'd ripped through her wardrobe ferociously, throwing most of its contents into sacks for the charity shop and providing her with the perfect capsule wardrobe and hints (instructions, really) on what to pair with what. She couldn't bear to bring them to the charity shop so instead they resided 'in storage': the fitted wardrobes in the guest room.

'He'll never remember it's in the pantry.' Alice was eye-rolling and Jules had to suppress the urge to eye-roll herself. Surely Ted could figure this stuff out? He was a partner in a venture capital firm. He could manage the weekend calendar of a twelve- and two eight-year-olds respectively, couldn't he? Yes, he'd secured the role through family connections rather than stellar intellect, but he had more than two brain cells to rub together. She felt her stomach clutch as she thought of how attentive Paul was with her appointments and schedule, his precision with her hormone injections. She just knew that he wouldn't be that sort of parent, that she wouldn't need to fawn over the tiniest of achievements. If only he were given the chance.

The thought of Paul shot a dart of sickly nausea into her throat. The guilt began to billow in her chest. Each time it happened, she told herself not to feel guilty. She told herself it wasn't her fault. She told herself she hadn't done anything wrong. But it always caught up with her eventually.

'I saw the link to the autism charity auction is live,' Alice said suddenly. 'Thank you. You're a good friend, Julia Frey-Jackson.'

Jules waved her thanks away. Her fund's charity department was constantly looking for new causes to champion, ideally ahead of their rivals. Besides, Jules suspected she'd spent most of her university days and working hours surrounded by high-functioning autistic men; they were excellent at their jobs, technically able and highly focused. It only took her an evening to set up the charity auction and their clients were more than happy to contribute lots; private dining experiences and boxes at the O2. It was something extra to add to their Corporate Social Responsibility reports, after all. Since Jules had arranged it and not the fund, they could apply match-funding, doubling whatever was raised.

'It went live at 9 a.m. and last time I checked the bids were already over £5,000,' Alice was telling Nina.

Jules reached into her bag, retrieving her phone, hoping they were by now at least forty minutes nearer to Paris, and felt disbelief that only *fourteen* minutes had passed since she'd put it into her bag. How could time be moving so slowly? She wanted to be safely in Paris. Safely back in a city where she knew who she was, with her oldest friends. She craved just a few days in that Paris bubble. It would restore her to herself, the old Jules. It would stop her making so many mistakes. She knew that's what Paul was hoping for too.

Notifications were listed in groups on her phone screen, as was usual. But one stood out from the rest. Paul. Her fingers began to tremble. She had to fight to keep the small, glistening squares of almond and rose pastry in her stomach. She was grateful Nina and Alice were now locked in a discussion about the mums at school, because they didn't notice the sweat accumulating around her hairline, didn't see the red-hot waves of fear emanating from her face.

She opened the text and bit hard on her tongue to stop herself from crying out. It was worse than she feared. A single line, but enough for her to know that her life, as she knew it, was over:

'You did it again, didn't you?'


*Alice*

'I know it's basic, but it's such a time-saver.' Alice cringed at herself even as she spoke, waves of shame washing over her as the train sped towards Paris. *What had she been thinking?* She wasn't even sure what *being basic* meant, or if she was using it in the right context, it just came out. Was it basic to buy three pairs of jeans in the exact same cut because they fitted you perfectly? Hiding your muffin top and lifting up your bottom? More than ever, she felt like the frumpy old mum next to her more glamorous counterparts. Nina, as usual, looked impossibly chic in that subtle, fresh-faced French way she had inherited. Her dark hair was bobbed with a tousled fringe, and she had a pale pink scarf knotted through it. When did they both start getting Botox? She'd assumed their bright-eyed looks were to do with the absence of little people in their lives waking at all hours, but now she felt cheated. Why hadn't they included her? Or told her about this *Dr Maryam*? How had it happened that *their* go-to place was Dr M and *her* go-to place was a trampoline park?

'That's not basic, I always buy more than one of something if I like it. I've got ten Huda lipsticks in different shades,' Nina said, and Alice thought to herself that that wasn't quite the same thing.

She attempted another sip of coffee and winced. 'So good,' she muttered, and cursed herself inwardly again. Why wasn't she honest? Why didn't she say how she felt around them these days, why did she pretend to like things she hated, like the strong, bitter coffee that Nina kept winning awards for? Give her a cup of tea or a jar of instant any day. She wasn't sure she was even that excited about Paris any more. When she thought of Paris, she thought about feeling young and vibrant and vital. Would she still belong there now?

At this introspective turn, she had a stern word with herself as she gazed out of the window. *You're with your two best friends, Alice, on your way to your favourite city. If anything is going to make you feel more like your old self, it's this.* Even Mr Hough, the delectable Mr Hough, who was all warm, freckled skin and sun-kissed dirty blond hair, had told her to go when she was having a wobble about it yesterday morning. Warning him that Charlotte might be off-kilter today with Alice going away. 'Take some time for yourself, Alice,' he'd reiterated, his sea-green eyes burning into hers. At least he'd finally dropped the Mrs Astor. 'Alice, please.' 'Alice, please.' 'Alice, please.' She'd said it so many times she almost let out a happy squeal the first time she finally heard her name fall from his soft, pink lips. *Oh God, she'd fallen for him so hard, why did she have to send those text messages last night?*

She put her head in her hands and collapsed her shoulders

around her neck, immediately eliciting comforting rubs and squeezes from her friends, soothing words – *Oh Alice, don't worry about the children, you'll be back before you know it!* – which only made her feel worse. She didn't deserve their sympathy. There's no way she'd be on this train if she hadn't wanted to escape, albeit briefly, while the sting of embarrassment still burned on her cheeks. *Texting her daughter's teacher!* What had she been thinking? She'd got carried away by thoughts of Paris and romance and the bottle of red she'd cracked open and sunk listening to her favourite French Chill playlist while she packed last night.

She'd been so thrilled she fitted into the black lace dress from Sandro she'd bought in Paris over a decade ago, she'd danced around her room. *When had she last danced?* She'd applied red lipstick and pulled up her hair, giddy and excited to be going away. She looked in the mirror and for the first time in a long while, she didn't feel depressed at what she saw. Feeling like a teenager, she took a selfie. It was unfortunate timing that a few minutes later she received an innocuous text message from Mr Hough: 'Just to let you know I've sent back those forms. Hope the packing's going okay!'

She replied: 'Thanks so much, really appreciate it. A' And then without thinking, she sent the photo and the message: 'I'm all set!'

And then the worst possible response. A series of dots… a series of dots… a series of dots… and then nothing.

She wished she could roll back time. Now she was whizzing on her way to Paris, away from her children, away from Ted, who didn't seem to listen to a word she said when she repeated the children's routines, and away from Mr Hough and a very embarrassing text message.

She wondered what Mr Hough was up to now. Was he in the staff room, wincing and telling the other teachers about tragic Mrs Astor? He'd have to explain they'd exchanged numbers – entirely innocent, since there was a constant barrage of forms and assessments relating to Charlotte and her application for an Education, Health and Care Plan, but which would be frowned upon, nonetheless.

Could she mention it to the girls? Would Nina tell Ted? She doubted it, Nina had become too therapised to breach a confidence like that. But what if she thought she *owed* it to Ted? Or owed it to herself to not have to carry the weight of the secret? She stole a surreptitious glance at Nina. Carefree, happy, successful Nina. She envied her, she realised. Envied her freedom, her independence. Envied, if she were being really honest, the way Ted spoke about her. Had always spoken about her, but especially recently, La City Pâtisserie on track to be a hugely successful strategic investment for his firm. All the more galling since it was Alice's idea that he invest in it. She had to talk him into it, talk both of them into it. And it was going better than any of them could have predicted, and all the times Ted seemed in awe of Nina, Alice felt herself shrink back a little bit more in comparison.

'How's *your* new business going?' Nina asked, catching her eye, and the way she said it – so respectful and sincere, as if Alice's business was any match for her own – made Alice's heart catch. She felt so *seen* when she was with Jules and Nina. It had always been this way. She wasn't just a mum to them now, wasn't just a posh deb then. She was Alice and that meant something. She resisted the urge to groan aloud. To throw her head back down on the table and cry, *That's a total mess too!*

'It's not really going,' she said instead, purposely not looking towards Jules. 'It's been so hard to find the time. I need to work on my portfolio, finish my website, post more on social media…'

'The photos of Elliott Mantel's place looked amazing!' Nina enthused.

Beside her, Jules said nothing, no doubt racking her brains for something positive to say to make Alice feel better, and Alice felt the weight of the silence.

'Hmm,' she murmured vaguely, trying to think of a way to divert the conversation to something new, but her mind had become fogged with hot disappointment.

Elliott Mantel, along with her wife, Aki, a hotelier, was a well-known financier and philanthropist and close friend of Paul, Jules's husband. They were so impressed by Jules's home when they visited that they insisted she share the details of her interior designer, who was none other than Alice. It was a recent career move, interior design, her work at the auction house after her history of art degree not compatible with small children. She was used to compliments on her interiors and Jules and Nina had convinced her to give it a try. She'd worked on Jules's place for free, to build up her portfolio, and was ecstatic to have the chance to work on the Mantels' nursery renovation. It was a dream project, their space allowing for a bedroom and separate playroom, and their brief – *a modern take on their American and Japanese heritage* – fitted Alice's style perfectly: playful and bold. The Mantels had seemed delighted when she finished, thanking her and saying they would recommend her and be in touch with further projects – would she be interested in trying her hand at some of Aki's hotels? – but she'd never heard from them again. And, most importantly, she'd never been paid. Her first commission, and her work clearly hadn't been good enough.

'It was a great project to work on,' she said, turning to Jules, hoping to smooth things over and remove the elephant from the room, but Jules's eyes were closed. 'Oh!' she said to Nina. Then whispered, 'She's asleep.'

All the better, to avoid an awkward conversation. Alice felt too new to the design world to ruffle the feathers of such a high-profile couple. Better to go away quietly and hope she hadn't blown her chances for any further work with Paul and Jules's friends and clients. Their West London circle was a gold mine of opportunity for interiors work and she knew how to fit into their world. They liked her. Just not enough to pay her for shoddy work, evidently. That's the problem with people like that. High expectations. Accepting only the best.

Hadn't the same thing happened with Jules? She'd kept saying she had to pay her for all her hard work, but it never materialised, which was unlike Jules. She was so generous with her friends, gifting them tickets to shows and insisting on picking up dinner after a bonus. But perhaps with this she didn't want to mismanage Alice's expectations? Maybe her ideas were too high-concept; playful and bold but not liveable. The sort of schemes that give you a headache after five minutes. She wondered if the mural – a joyous explosion of colour: mountains and national parks, iconic landmarks and spring blossom – on the Mantels feature wall was being repainted right this moment?

'I fancy a nap myself,' Nina said. She appeared to be reading something, frowning and then making notes on her phone. 'Do you remember when we used to have a power nap before going out?'

Alice chuckled. 'Maybe we should do it when we get to the apartment.' She could so easily fall asleep too, if she just closed her eyes. She felt her face move into a smile at the thought of Nina's apartment: the many times they'd got ready to go out, sequins and champagne littering the room, how they'd sat in Nina's bed together eating ice cream and watching *Sex and the City* on her laptop as, outside, the streets of Paris busied around them. She knew it meant a lot to Nina too, having been her grandmother Sylvie's. On their last few trips to Paris, Nina had seemed at home there, grounded in a way she hadn't been when they were younger. Light streamed in through the train's window, bathing them in a wash of gold, warming her skin.

'Thanks so much for letting us all stay,' she said.

Nina shifted in her seat, looking uncomfortable. She glanced at Jules, whose face had relaxed into sleep. Nina seemed to be weighing something up.

'Paul booked it,' she mouthed.

'I know,' Alice nodded. Paul had said he would pay for their travel and accommodation when he presented the weekend as a gift to Jules at her birthday dinner a few weeks ago. He'd had someone mock up a train ticket for her inside her birthday card: '*A weekend in Paris with your girlfriends!*' it had said. 'He's smooth, isn't he?'

Nina pulled a dubious face at that and then said in a low voice, 'No, I mean he booked it without telling me. He got his secretary to do it, so her name showed up, and I accepted and he paid for it and *then* he messaged me to explain and check it was okay. Which was a bit, "after the event", you know? Like, what if we were busy, or couldn't make it or something?'

Alice paused, thoughtful. She'd assumed Paul and Nina had come up with the weekend away plan together, that Nina had volunteered the apartment.

'Oh,' she said. That was different. She'd never shared with Nina her concerns about Paul. She'd been dazzled by him when they first met, a tall, handsome, smooth-talking Bermudian. He was charismatic and charming, as well as thoughtful. But in the last few years he seemed to have grown aloof, sometimes not turning up for things at the last minute, Jules seeming distracted when asked where he was. She'd assumed it was just her who had noticed, but from the look on Nina's face now, she wasn't sold on Paul either.

'It's a bit weird, isn't it?' Nina said.

Alice nodded, checking again that Jules was asleep. Her mouth was parted slightly now and her breathing was deep and regular. She looked like she needed to sleep, as if she'd been up all night working, which she probably had. She would never say it to Jules but she secretly thought that her job, with its demanding hours and late nights, couldn't help with her fertility quest.

'It's nice though, too?' she said, thinking how elated she'd be if Ted took the time to elaborately plan a weekend away for her with her friends. If he noticed her at all.

Nina cocked her head to the side, shrugging. Alice knew it was that sort of thing that put Nina off relationships. She loved her self-sufficiency. She didn't want to be doted on, or to have someone plan what she was going to do. Neither did Alice, in principle, but she was so body-wearily tired, the idea of anyone doing anything for her held an appeal. Unexpectedly, her thoughts shifted again to Mr Hough. The only person who had recognised, like her, that Charlotte was struggling at school. That she wasn't being 'naughty' or 'difficult' or 'manipulative', nor was it 'weird' that she mainly chose to communicate through Dimples the Unicorn, but there was something else going on. It was thanks to his encouragement that they'd got a diagnosis – for Autism Spectrum Disorder and Attention Deficit Hyperactivity Disorder – at all. At the reminder of Mr Hough and last night's messages, her face flooded with heat again.

She wished she could tell Nina. What stopped her? It wasn't really because she worked with Ted; Alice knew her bond with Nina ran far deeper. Until working together recently, Nina and Ted had barely been in touch, their friendship petering out more than a decade ago. She supposed it was because she knew what she was doing was dangerous. Saying it aloud, even to Nina and Jules, would require her to acknowledge that something was wrong. Her marriage was in trouble. Instead, she sat back in her seat and forced down more of her lukewarm coffee. '*So good,*' she murmured.

# 3

## Paris, 2003

Nina and Alice were back in the Jardins des Tuileries, on their annual pilgrimage, walking through the park and past the fountains at Place de le Concorde. Jules had got caught up at work and was joining them later. They had maintained their promise to meet every year – although not always in November – and, for obvious reasons, Hôtel de Crillon was no longer their centre point. They wound around the city in circles, a large part of their time spent walking and talking, catching up on each other's lives and what had happened in the intervening period since they'd seen each other last. The first couple of years they'd stayed in a hostel near the centre, the last couple they had availed themselves of a rarely used flat in the 5th owned by Alice's godmother. Nina had marvelled, again, at how much easier life was when things like weekends in Paris were granted so easily.

The year after they met, Jules had followed her dream and studied maths at Cambridge. She'd graduated with a first and a heap of job offers to choose from: the first time she'd found herself in demand. She was now on a graduate programme at

Austen Miller, a large American bank with headquarters in New York. Nina, still undecided on what she wanted to do and determined not to ask for a penny from Samir, had taken a year out, working in Virgin Megastore to save for university, and eventually, with the encouragement of Jules and Alice via MSN Messenger, working up the courage to apply to study music at the Guildhall. Alice had taken a gap year of a different sort, travelling to Thailand and Australia with her friend Lulu, before starting history of art at St Andrews. She was now on an Erasmus programme, spending a year studying in Paris, sharing a flat in Le Marais with another student. There was already talk of her working at Sotheby's, via a great-aunt, when she finished her degree. Although Nina loved Alice, she couldn't help the recurring thought: *This isn't how normal people live.*

Alice and Nina crossed over the Seine and began the long walk along rue du Bac to Sylvie's apartment. One of the highlights of Nina's weekends in Paris was the chance to see her grandmother. When Nina had first met her, Sylvie had seemed stern and disapproving, but she soon realised that was directed towards Samir, not her. Sylvie had been furious when her only son publicly shamed Nina in the papers for humiliating him at *le Bal*, and she compensated by making sure Nina knew she was welcome in her life any time she chose. Soon their relationship was flourishing, Nina teaching her grandmother how to speak English and, in return, Sylvie showing Nina how to cook the food her own grandmother had made her in Morocco: grilled meats and vegetables and huge plates of steaming rice, tinted yellow with saffron and scented with cloves.

Nina had never met her Irish grandparents, Joanie's parents

having disowned her when she fell pregnant, and she bathed in the contentment she derived from this relationship, like a cat in the sun. They rarely spoke of Samir, which suited Nina just fine. Nina was looking forward to lunch with Sylvie today, but for one thing: she hadn't told her grandmother that Samir had contacted her in London out of the blue and had promised – over drinks at the Savoy – that he would help with her music career as an apology for being a useless father. And she hadn't told her yet that she'd dropped out of her music degree as a result. She knew that Sylvie would be disappointed; would tell her that Samir couldn't be trusted to look out for anyone except himself. And Nina knew that was true, but she was racking up enormous debts as a student already, and her most likely destination after her degree was tutoring some poor kid who didn't want to be there. The thing about people with money is they always assume everyone else has it too; not just Sylvie and Samir, she'd seen it with Alice and Jules. While Nina would never ask Samir, or Sylvie, for money, she knew Samir was right about one thing – if her demos were ever going to reach a music executive, she'd need a connection. She'd have been mad not to say yes.

Perhaps she was delaying telling Sylvie, but as she passed Le Bac à Glaces with Alice, she couldn't help but stop and peer through the glass at the counters beyond: sesame and pistachio, caramel and salted butter, honey and pine nuts... they all sounded so good. 'Shall we get an ice cream?'

While she waited inside to order, Alice securing them a table outside on the pavement, she wondered whether to talk to Alice about Teddy. Her relationship with Teddy was one of the few things Nina didn't discuss with her friends. Her open heart, her exposure to him, felt too raw and vulnerable.

But it had been going on so long now, this impasse, she was beginning to wonder whether she had misread the situation.

Nina and Teddy had met up a few times in London after *le Bal*, but things seemed different there, a holiday romance transported. Nonetheless, the romance started with promise: terse kisses and hands held, frequent phone calls. He had even visited her at home, his eyes scanning her small terraced house in Mile End earnestly, like a foreign exchange student weighing up their new surroundings. They'd kissed in the bedroom she shared with Carey, her little sister (a half-sister technically, though Nina never thought of her that way) Nina laughing off the soft toys and fairy lights, Teddy grimacing awkwardly, but later that afternoon, on a bench in Tredegar Square, her cold hand on his warm back as they kissed, he suddenly sprang apart: 'I can't do this,' he said. 'I like you too much.'

She remembered her response. *Okay... Please elaborate.* She was trying to be stand-offish and aloof, to pretend she didn't care as much as she did. She'd removed a box of cigarettes from her coat pocket, lit one with shaking fingers and turned her head in the opposite direction to exhale, needing those few seconds to regain her composure.

'I'm going travelling soon,' he said. 'So this can't work out and... you know... I don't want our friendship to end when it all goes wrong.' She felt stung by his assumption that they couldn't have a relationship long distance, but was too embarrassed to tell him so: a cool girl wouldn't care, right? A cool girl would be finalising her own plans for the next year.

'It's fine,' she said instead. 'Don't worry about it. It was just a casual thing.' She turned her face again as she smoked so he wouldn't see the look of distress she wore at how easily he gobbled up her lie and agreed: 'Yes, that's what I thought too. Just a casual thing.' They parted awkwardly at Mile End station. He sent her emails from his gap year – *Hello from Koh Samui! Getting out of the outback!* – and initially her responses were curt. But by the time he was at university – economics at Exeter – their correspondence had evolved, smelted into something precious, a trail of gold. Now it ebbed and flowed, their banter bouncing off the page, the boundaries jagged – *were they friends or something more?* When not studying or working, she wrote songs about unrequited love, surrounded by her sister's Care Bears. She would laugh about this to Teddy during their long phone calls, minus the bit about the unrequited love, although he had asked her what she wrote about and she ad-libbed with, 'just life, and stuff, you know'. Beside her, she'd scribbled in her notebook: *Life in general and love in particular.* It was going to be the name of her first album.

Only Teddy knew how painful Nina had found the sale of her childhood home – where she had grown up with Joanie, her Aunty Niamh, Uncle Seamus and her cousin, Erin – last year. It made sense: Joanie had married, an electrician called Liam whom Nina liked, and had Carey, who was at preschool already. The house had grown too small for them all and – fortunately – rocketed in value. Joanie had worked long hours as a nurse when Nina was young and not wanting to miss another daughter grow up, had sold the little terraced house in Mile End and moved to Essex to open a floristry. Nina tried to be happy for her, and for Carey, but she confided in Teddy about the tiny little sting, like the graze of a thorn, she felt at the belatedness of her mum's decision. At the way her life had felt upended: she'd moved with them to Essex but she didn't know the area, it wasn't home, and she missed her extended family – Niamh and Seamus and Erin – who had bought a large house in Ireland with their share from the sale. She tried not to mind. Reminded herself on the Tube and train journeys between central London and Essex that it was only temporary: one day, she would live with Teddy, and it would be her music playing on the radio.

Finally, the queue moved and the mustachioed server snapped her out of her reverie with a wave of his ice-cream scoop. She ordered for herself and Alice and carried the laden tubs outside, her mouth watering, Teddy still on her mind.

'I wonder how Teddy's been getting on in Aix,' she said.

'You can ask him! He's arriving soon,' said Alice, missing the shock passing over Nina's face.

'He's coming *here*?'

'Of course! To see everyone,' said Alice, but this didn't make sense. It was the girls' fourth time meeting in Paris, and Teddy had been absent the other times. The skin on Nina's face tingled gently as she fought against the smile building. Her stomach fizzed. *He was coming to see her.*

'I didn't realise you two were in touch,' Nina said. She wanted to say, *I didn't realise you even liked each other.* She knew they had seen each other briefly when they were away travelling, but no more than that. It was something she'd observed when she'd been around them and their school friends. The casual mention of bumping into someone on the Cook Islands, or a week spent on the same dive boat off the coast of Thailand. She used to marvel at these coincidences until she realised the people in Alice and Teddy's social circle travelled to the same countries, stayed at the same places, did the same things and congratulated themselves on how worldly they were because of it.

'It's Erasmus,' Alice shrugged. 'There's a group of us and we take it in turns to visit each other. Although we always seem to end up in Aix.' She smiled, shaking her head.

*Teddy's never mentioned that*, thought Nina. He'd said sometimes friends were coming down to visit at the weekend, but had never mentioned Alice's name among them. But who cared? *He was coming to see her!* Perhaps she wouldn't tell Alice just yet, perhaps she would wait until Teddy arrived. They could tell Alice and Jules together. Lemon basil ice cream had never tasted so good.

Jules arrived late to the bar that night, a cavernous brick room with low arched ceilings and cheap beer, enthralled by her new life in the City. Nina had never met anyone before who loved their job – or working – so much. It was like her first love; she wanted to speak of nothing else: how amazing the client lunches were, how swanky the offices were, how good the subsidised canteen was. It was like she'd joined a cult. Nina tried to look interested while she gulped down beer, feeling like a child playing at being a grown-up. The first time she'd met Jules and Alice, she'd felt like her life was finally beginning; she'd been swept up in that night, in a friendship with the only two women who could understand what that first trip to Paris was like for her: meeting, and quickly being rejected by, Samir. But lately it felt like their lives were marching on and hers was at a standstill. She was *so close* to things changing for the better and yet it felt so far.

She was quite merrily drunk and wending her way back

across the dance floor when she saw Teddy, for the first time in six months. He looked tanned and relaxed, life in Aix clearly suiting him; his smile was broader, easier. He was leaning in to speak to Alice, and Nina felt a clutch of nausea as the feelings she had tried to downplay all these years crashed in her heart. The loud dance music flooded her ears as she walked towards them, bubbles of love rising up to the surface of her skin. She felt soapy and liquid. He looked up and caught her eye, as though he could sense her watching him, and his smile matched her own. Her heart hammered in her chest.

'What are you doing here?' she asked wondrously, as though she hadn't known he was coming at all. When she knew. Deep down she knew. He had come for her.

'I came to see you,' he said, his words mirroring her thoughts. He reached down and squeezed her into a hug, lifting her in the air as Jules laughed and Nina squealed and Alice shouted 'Shots! Shots! Shots!' before exploding into her favourite dance move: Le Tour Eiffel. Teddy set her down and Nina doubled over laughing, her arms finding her friends in a loose embrace.

The rest of the night passed in a blur. Nina tried to find a moment to be alone with Teddy, needing to just stand beside him, feel the electricity of their connection buzzing between them, but she was always being thwarted, by him dancing with someone else, or Jules telling her the difference between a stock and a bond. Nina looked over her head for Teddy, or Alice, and seeing neither instead grabbed a random passer-by to yell, 'I fucking love this song! Do you?' And the night sped up and the fractions of time became harder to grasp as her head started to swell with the heat from sweet, sickly shots, washed down with lukewarm beer. She could taste salt, her lips dry. There was a stranger's hand around her waist. This was usually the feeling she craved, her brain growing fuzzy, like being wrapped in cotton wool, pushing out her conscious thoughts, the hard edges of disappointment – a stumble into a table, a skid across the wet floor – softened. She'd discovered in London that it was easier this way. Easier to exist when for a few hours there was no Teddy and no Samir Laurent and no broken dreams. *But Teddy's here tonight*, she remembered, looking around, but again she couldn't find him. A rough palm slid under the back of her knickers, squeezed her bum.

Teddy. Teddy. Teddy. Alice. Jules. *Where was everyone?*

She wanted to find them but the music was too good, the drinks kept coming, and just around the corner lay the promise of fun. Fun, fun, fun. It was hot and then it was cool, her sweat chilling on her skin, and then it was quiet and then it was dark.

She woke, as she often did, with her stomach retching, pulling her from sleep. She rolled on to her side, her arms up covering her face, while she tried to get her bearings and remember where she was. The pillow smelt sweet, the linen clean. She opened one eye and took in a bedside table with an empty floral teacup, a photo of a horse and a book of Mary Oliver poems, translated into French. Alice's room. Gingerly, she flopped on to her back and propped herself on her elbows. She reached for the bottle of water beside her bed and pressed the tiniest sips of liquid to her mouth, careful after each to check she wasn't going to be sick. She willed her stomach to settle as she shifted higher up in bed, her head eventually resting on the wall. She wondered where Alice had ended up and smiled – the hangover was always worth the debrief the next day as they blew half-moons on scalding hot coffee, laughing at what they'd got up to the night before.

She lay still for a while, shame creeping over her skin. *What had happened with Teddy?* She remembered approaching him, remembered slipping her sweaty hand into his own and trying to pull him towards her, she remembered his eyes, so clear and blue, falling towards him as she'd done the night they met, but this time his head jerked backwards and away from her. *Had he rejected her? But he'd come to see her.* Her heart rate quickened and climbed. *What happened next?* She frowned, clutching at shards of time and fragments of information she couldn't piece together. There was another man – the barman? – with a rough kiss and a hand grabbing at her bum. And then what? Jules. Jules took her home. Jules took her home and put her to bed. *Phew.* Her pulse abated. She was sure that was all that had happened, yet she still felt uneasy. Should she talk to Teddy? Make sure he understood how she felt? But it would shift the dynamic between them, the friendship she'd come to rely on as an interlude from the monotony she'd fallen into at home. Sometimes an email from Teddy was the only high point of her day. And what would Alice and Jules think? Would it disrupt things between them too? Alice had never been Teddy's biggest fan. But increasingly Nina sensed the feelings she was running from to be true: she loved Teddy. Was it time to swallow her pride and do something about it?

She shifted her legs to the side of the bed shakily. Alice must be in her flatmate's bed, who was away for the weekend. That's where Nina was supposed to have slept. She stood slowly, to gather the girls, or at the very least climb into the sofa bed with Jules to begin the debrief. Even though her head was thrashing, she was already on the brink of laughter. *The barman! What was she thinking!*

She was standing in the long white hallway, in a T-shirt and knickers, when she saw them together on the sofa bed in the living area, sleeping bodies entwined, sheets twisted and turned over in their slumber. Alice looked thinner, Nina noticed for the first time. Alice. Alice and Teddy.

She pulled on baggy jeans and some clompy platform espadrilles of Alice's – the first things she could find – and stumbled out of the flat and along the road, her hangover crashing and banging around in her skull, rooting in her bag for a cigarette as loose change, a ticket from last night and a piece of paper with a phone number on it all fell from her bag. She sighed and stopped to scoop it all up, and she was still crunched over on the floor when she looked up and saw the newspaper headline, pinned to a display stand, stacks of the same edition below: *LAURENT DOMMAGE.* There was a photo of her father looking particularly shady, staring malevolently at the pert derrière of a co-star on the red carpet. She stayed crouched on the floor, sweating, her eyes closed. *No wonder she picked the wrong men*, she thought.

It was cold as the three of them sat in enormous sunglasses at a rickety table in Le Marais. Her feet, still in espadrilles, were freezing. Nina's eyes swam at the variations of *oeufs* available; she pushed the menu away. It was lucky nothing appealed; she could barely afford this trip. She shouldn't have come.

'Good night then?' Jules said to Alice, grinning.

'Oh my goodness!' Alice squealed, concealing her face with her hands while Jules grinned at Nina and she tried to return it. 'Is it bad that I'm shagging Teddy? It's bad, isn't it?' She prised her fingers apart. 'But...' – she bit her lip and widened her eyes cheekily, almost in danger of winking like a pervert, observed Nina – 'it's so... *surprisingly*... good!'

'Oh my God!' breathed Jules, quickly asking for details while also exchanging that she too had recently experienced surprising – but ultimately brilliant – sex with an old course mate, Lev, who was working at a neighbouring bank.

'Sorry, Neen, I should've mentioned it yesterday, but I was embarrassed and Teddy and I hadn't discussed "going public" yet, but I suppose it's too late now!' Alice made a squealing 'eek' sound, clapping her hands on her cheeks. It felt so good to finally share what had been going on with her friends. She hadn't been sure what it meant, if it meant anything at all, the first time she and Teddy slept together. They were drunk. If you'd suggested she might fancy Teddy, she'd have laughed. Said she knew him *too well* to find him attractive. Now she wondered whether that was a story she'd told herself because she'd thought then that someone like Teddy Astor, someone who other women clocked and surveyed appreciatively with alarming frequency, would never fancy someone like her. Someone ordinary. Someone *chunky*. Before Australia, she couldn't imagine seeing anything redeeming in him at all. But travelling with Lulu was less fun than she'd expected, and it had been a relief to cross paths with Teddy and his friend Dickie at the hostel in Sydney. The four of them had travelled for a few weeks together, and she and Teddy had bonded over the lack of home comforts, sleeping in bunk beds and listening to Dickie's terrible guitar-playing. Then

they were thrown together again with Erasmus, each seeming
to the other a more pleasant prospect than the other students
they didn't know as well. They were homesick at first and
felt connected. Then there was the night he slipped an arm
around her and she immediately backed off, reminded him of
the unkind things he used to say about her, and that's when
he began to open up.

'Shagging?' Nina asked now. Shagg-*ing*. Not a one-off
'shagged'? Nina leaned back in her chair. 'I thought you
hated him,' she said, in that flat, blunt way of hers as she lit a
cigarette. She was so hungover her face was grey, Alice noted,
thinking of Turner's *Snow Storm* and unrelenting, unbidden
clouds.

'Hated Teddy?' Alice said, as though surprised, and for
the first time she thought, *Is this weird for Nina? Should I
have mentioned it to her first?* The truth was, Alice had been
walking on sunshine since she and Teddy had got together,
elevated by being loved by someone like him. Someone who
could have any woman he wanted, even Nina, and had chosen
*her*, Alice Digby. She knew that Nina and Teddy had kissed
after *le Bal*, but that was four years ago, and Teddy had said
nothing had happened since, it just fizzled out. *Might Nina
be jealous now?* It didn't seem possible. Not beautiful Nina
with the world at her feet? With her close-knit family, and her
movie-star father and a recording contract on the horizon?
But hadn't Jules mentioned Nina seeming off-kilter lately?
Drinking a lot. Making questionable choices with men. A
little lonely, perhaps, living in a new town? But things always
worked out, didn't they? Those things were just a blip, until
her music career got going? 'No, maybe initially, you know
the chunky thing…' She trailed off, with no hint of sadness.

'But I can see now that was less about me and more about trying to fit in with my brothers. He's never had that, has he? Family?'

Nina's face stayed impassive as she realised she wasn't the only person Teddy confided in any more. How had she not seen this coming?

Jules watched Nina from across the table. She was being especially prickly today, not surprising given her hangover. Jules shuddered at the thought, grateful that thanks to the medication for her skin she drank little, but slightly aggrieved at the role she'd assumed lately as Nina's chief picker-upper from whatever sticky floor she'd ended up on. It had been like this the last time Jules had seen her in London. She'd begun the evening excited, talking about how she'd reconnected with Samir, and how enthusiastic he was about her music, before growing quieter and quieter, and then suddenly loud again as she chatted someone up, or, at drinks in the City once, jumping on the table and air-guitaring along to a song. Jules had stopped inviting her to work drinks after that. 'Where's your crazy friend?' the other graduates asked her sometimes.

'Are you humming?' Nina asked, raising her head and frowning.

'Sorry,' Jules said, trying not to be too upbeat. 'I've got a song stuck in my head. Are you okay? You're shivering. Here, take my blazer. My dress has long sleeves, I'll be fine.'

Nina accepted it gratefully and surveyed Jules through squinted eyes as she shrugged it on. 'You've got so perky since you started at that bank. Aren't all bankers supposed to be miserable?'

'I'm sure my time will come,' Jules grinned, but she wasn't sure she believed it. In a similar way to how she had been outnumbered by boys during her maths degree, she was revelling in being the only tall, slim, blonde analyst now at the bank. Her skin was yet to transform as she'd hoped – the House of Vesuvius, the angry red lumps, marched ever onwards – but her dermatologist, paid for with her first pay cheque, had told her to give it time and she was so good at her job, had been so good at her degree, that her skin was no longer the first thing people noticed about her. In fact, she realised, people had begun to know *of* her, eliciting an '*Oh*, you're *Julia Frey, I heard about your work on Project Hummingbird*' when they met. It reminded her of a line from Roald Dahl – something about being nice and it shining out of your face like sunbeams. That's what excelling at work, at finally being taken seriously, was doing for her.

'It's in my blood anyway,' she beamed. 'My father's always loved working. You know what he's like.' The girls had met Jules's father, Douglas, at her twenty-first birthday earlier that year, a large catered marquee affair in her parents' garden, Douglas holding court affably at the centre of it all. A few years ago, her father had received a lucrative offer to sell his accountancy firm and retired early.

She reached for her new work BlackBerry to check progress on Project Iguazu and gasped at the headline of a News Update email. She clicked on the link.

'Have you seen this?' Jules asked grimly, waving the screen of her BlackBerry in Nina's direction, where a page from the *Daily Mail* was struggling to load… *Samir Laurent Sex Pest Shame*. Nina nodded, lips pursed. *So that's what's up*, Jules thought.

'*Samir Laurent has been accused of harassment by his co-star Mariella Ping. In a sign that executives are taking the matter seriously, he has been removed from the franchise and will be replaced in the current and all future films,*' she read. 'My God, what did he do?'

Nina shrugged, the effort exhausting. Jules continued her commentary: 'Nina, there's a photo of you! With him at the Savoy... Oh, and another story underneath: "*Samir Laurent reunites with long-lost daughter.*"' Nina knew instantly what that would be: a rival piece planted by her father's PR in an attempt to neutralise the sting of the exposé. Suddenly, it made sense: Samir coming back into her life without warning, their infrequent meetings at high-profile places where they were *always* papped. She was nothing more than a back-up PR plan.

'Oh my goodness!' Alice exclaimed as Jules continued to read the article, a palm across her mouth. Her perfect mouth, which had spent the night with Teddy, Nina thought. Alice reached over the table and touched her cheek. Nina rested her face against Alice's soft palm, felt the hard sun on her skin, closed her eyes to stop the tears that were building. She needed Alice and Jules more than she needed Teddy, she told herself. She loved them more than she loved him. *Didn't she?*

'That's it then, isn't it,' she said flatly. 'It's all over, isn't it? There's no way any music executives will listen to him now. And he told me to give up my course! Told me it was a waste of time and money when he had so many connections.' She swallowed. It was a relief to close her eyes and allow her head to collapse into her arms, the image of Teddy and Alice wrapped up in bed together lining her eyelids like a projector screen.

'Can you go back and finish it?' Jules asked.

Nina shook her head. 'I couldn't take out another student loan. It's hard enough paying off the amount I had for the first year.' She couldn't help the loaded emphasis to her words, knowing concerns about fees and money were something her friends had no experience of. She felt angry, bitter. Life was easy for some and it wasn't fair. She couldn't ask Sylvie for the money, couldn't admit how wrong she'd been.

'So, you and Teddy then?' Jules said amiably to Alice, directing the focus away from Nina but still stealing glances in her direction to check she was okay.

'There you are! We were just talking about you!' Despite the circumstances, Alice's face split into a grin as Teddy appeared.

*Great*, thought Nina. *Just great.*


Nina couldn't tell if she was imagining it or if Teddy was avoiding her gaze, as he sat beside Alice, his lean body angled forward, his hair tipped over his face, his hands clasped between his knees, saying 'I need water' as Alice reached over and squeezed his knee. The vision seared against her eyeballs. They were acting like a couple. They were even dressed similarly, both in loose grey hoodies, but for Alice's pink pashmina scarf, worn loosely round her neck.

'I saw the headlines about your father,' Teddy said, looking at her now. 'Are you okay?'

Nina nodded, her sunglasses still fixed firmly on her face, a welcome barrier. *Did she come on to Teddy last night?* She wished she could remember.

They walked back to Alice's flat after lunch, Nina and

Teddy drifting behind Alice and Jules. Nina was going to pick up her stuff and head over to see Sylvie again before she left. She supposed she'd have to break the news about Samir, but didn't expect it to come as a big surprise.

Her grandmother was the only person who knew about her true feelings for Teddy. She looked forward to curling up on her chaise longue under a blanket and telling her everything. She hoped Sylvie had picked up some cakes on her morning constitutional to La Grande Épicerie, ideally a large *tarte aux pommes*. Only apples cooked in butter and brown sugar could help right now.

'It's been so good to see you.' Teddy smiled slowly, sunlight fanning through his hair, highlighting the lightened tips. The Aix effect, she thought. 'In person. Not just over email.'

She had half expected him to avoid or deny their correspondence, it seemed so incongruous to the situation, but now she wanted to ask, *What's going on?* A jangling sense of shame was building, embarrassment that she had got things *so wrong*. She had been at home, or trimming stems in Joanie's floristry, *pining* for him. Pining for a man who was now shagging one of her closest friends. She may have loved him first, but he was Alice's now. And they could never be. Not now. Not ever. The finality of it was gutting.

'You too,' was all she said.

He glanced at her as they walked home. 'I wanted to see you,' he said. 'To tell you in person about Alice and me.'

She nodded, afraid if she spoke her voice would squeak or tears would cascade down her cheeks. 'It was unexpected,' he said, as if by way of explanation, his tone awkward. 'I'm so sorry about your father, Neen,' he added, as though that were the cause of her sadness. Maybe he genuinely thought it was?

Nina nodded again, her eyes fixed ahead. Suddenly, Teddy stopped and reached for her. A gasp caught in her throat as he pulled her against his chest. She could feel the drum of his heart against her cheek, could smell his scent, which she thought she had forgotten but was as real and familiar to her as the night they had met and sat wrapped around each other outside Le Sacré Coeur. He gripped her a little too tight, his groin pressed a little too closely. The air around them felt charged, like someone turning on the power in a nightclub. She wished she'd told him how she felt. She would never be able to tell him now.

'I've never had a friend like you before, Nina. Someone who's understood me...'

Nina had a swift and startling vision of him in the bar after *le Bal*, the blue of his eyes as their faces drew nearer. She wanted to wind her hands around his neck, pull his lips to her own.

'It works. When I'm with her family, with her brothers. I kind of fit, you know?' Nina bit her lip. How many conversations had they had about feeling like they didn't fit anywhere, the subtext that they fitted together, fused along the phone line, but he'd somehow found a *better* fit? Had she read it wrong all along? Was she just not enough? Had she imagined the pulse of connection between them?

Her hands were around Teddy's waist now, wanting to push him away and hold him close all at once.

She turned her face away from his chest and realised that up ahead Alice had gone into the apartment building but Jules had stopped and was watching them. A frown passed over her face, the curves and contours forming a question mark.

Nina jerked away from Teddy, turned and ran a little way

along the street, where she was sick in a bin. Wearing the T-shirt she'd slept in, baggy jeans, platform espadrilles and Jules's blazer.

'*Les Anglais,*' an elderly woman muttered as she passed, and Nina had never felt less connected to her roots, to her blood, to her friends, to her favourite city. A part of her floated away.

# 4

## Friday p.m.

*Alice*

*Ah, Paris*, thought Alice, as she almost tripped over a bijou-looking little dog on rue de Sèvres. She could have happily spent the afternoon taking in the view from Nina's balcony, which overlooked Le Bon Marché department store on the corner and, beyond, the Eiffel Tower and the domed church of Les Invalides, and eating the remaining pastries from the train, but Nina had insisted they go out – '*We need to feel Paris in our bones!*' – so they'd dropped their stuff off and were almost immediately outside, ogling, as they had always done, the bags and accessories on display in the windows of Le Bon Marché.

'Which one are you going for?' Nina asked Jules, and Alice was surprised to see a flash of irritation pass over Jules's face. If they weren't even on safe ground with accessories, they were in for a rougher ride this weekend than Alice had anticipated.

'I'm cutting back,' Jules said. 'Just in case...' and her eyes wandered to the sky. Nina had them moving quickly onwards, in the direction of the river.

Nina had become one of those active, busy people, Alice realised. A grab-life-by-its-horns person. The thought of it made her feel dizzy and exhausted. *What sort of person have I become?* she wondered, but she didn't really want an answer, her brain moving automatically to the messages to Mr Hough she'd been composing in her head all morning. He had finally messaged her back, just as they'd arrived at Nina's apartment, and she'd squirrelled herself away in the bathroom to read it. Lucky she had, as it made her gasp:

You look beautiful Alice. Have fun in Paris x

Her whole body contracted and her heart beat faster in response, as though trying to free itself. *It crossed a line, didn't it?* He'd crossed a line. *Well, she crossed it first,* but now he'd stepped over and joined her. What did it mean? *Oh Alice,* she chided herself, it doesn't *mean* anything. *He's five years younger than you and entirely out of your league, even if you weren't married with three children. He's being nice. He feels sorry for you, Alice.* At this realisation, all energy slumped out of her body; she pictured it pooling on the floor, like puddles of dark rainwater, as Nina called that they should go.

Jules looked up from her phone to navigate around a chalkboard outside a restaurant by the river with a red-and-gold striped awning and said, 'Ooh, look! Oysters. And wine! Late lunch?' Alice vaguely remembered having eaten here once, with Ted. She couldn't remember what they ate but she remembered them holding hands as they gazed over the river, the light gilding its surface, as it was doing now.

A look of horror crossed Nina's face as Alice and Jules stopped walking and she put a hand on the small of each of their backs and tried to steer them away, as if the very idea of sitting still and relaxing was abhorrent to her. *Not appreciating*, Alice thought, *that they were at very different stages in their lives.* Alice had got up so early that morning. Her legs were weary and her heart was heavy. She needed to regroup. If she had the choice, she'd have spent the weekend lolling around, in silence, eating as much nice food as possible and moving as little as possible. That's how you avoided burn-out, not being marched around a city.

'*No!*' Nina said. 'Plenty of time for that later. We're in Paris, together, for the first time in three years. Let's explore! I've brought the rest of the mini baguettes from the café.' She gestured to the paper bag in her hand. 'We can walk and talk and eat...?'

Alice hadn't realised it had been three years. It was Jules who would insist she was too busy on a transaction, or in the lead-up to an IVF cycle, to make a trip to Paris, but Alice was always secretly relieved, the thought of leaving her children, and Charlotte especially, too stressful. It explained Nina's frenetic energy, Alice supposed, her desperation to recapture the magic of Paris while they were here, to make the most of it, but she didn't need to do that. It was *Paris*. As low as she'd been feeling lately, there was still something about it; it got under your skin, it wasn't easily shaken off. She took a deep breath, the air that skipped across the Seine catching in her nostrils, the waning light from the afternoon sun warming her face as Jules continued to implore Nina: '*But coquilles Saint-Jacques, Nina!* Your favourite!' And Alice thought,

*Lordy, when did Jules last eat shellfish? Throw her a bone, Nina, for goodness' sake.'*

'It's a bit early to get started, isn't it?' Nina asked, but it was 4 p.m. and in previous times 4 p.m. would have been a bit *late* to get started.

Jules sighed, taking this hesitation as an enquiry as to whether *she* would like to be drinking, or not, so early in the day. 'I'm totally happy to sit with a glass of wine,' she said. 'In fact, I'd like nothing more.'

Alarm persisted across Nina's face. 'I just think if we stop now, we won't get any further than the end of rue du Bac.'

'It is a very long road,' Alice interjected.

'But we're only here a few days. Can't we at least walk up to the fountains? Take a quick turn around the Jardin des Tuileries? And then we could swing by the Ladurée near the Louvre for macarons...' she wheedled. 'Didn't you want to pick some up for Luca?'

Alice and Jules exchanged shrugs, although they each longed to sit, the sounds and smells of Paris washing over them, losing themselves in the activity of a busy city, albeit for different reasons.

'Okay,' Alice acquiesced, 'but let's go to the one on Bonaparte? It's so opulent, I love it.' She smiled, feeling cheered. At least if she were on the move, she wouldn't have her phone out, re-reading the message from Mr Hough every few minutes, although that didn't seem to stop Jules, who possessed a sixth sense for avoiding collisions with other passers-by, her eyes down, glued to her phone. Even Ted was on his phone less than Jules, and that was saying something. Surely she was allowed one day off work?

'Shall we go to the cinema tonight?' Nina asked as

they reached the Pont Royal bridge and crossed over the Seine.

'The cinema?' Jules asked, aghast. 'In Paris?'

'We used to love going to the cinema!' Nina's eyes were wide, defensive. And it was true, they did, to the little cinema in a bright red pagoda with a beautiful Japanese garden, not far from Nina's apartment.

'When we had plenty of time to ourselves,' Jules said. 'I didn't come to Paris to go to the cinema,' she scoffed, and to Alice's surprise Nina, *easy-going-c'est-la-vie-Nina*, seemed affronted.

'You'd have to turn your phone off too,' Nina said pointedly, and Jules rolled her eyes and shook her head in a typical *you don't understand* kind of way.

Alice felt uneasy; it was tension like this she had come away to avoid. She felt obligated to defuse it, just like she did at home.

'Sorry, Neen,' she said, in her calmest smoothing-things-over voice, 'but I actually made us a dinner reservation for tonight. I felt bad about you organising everything and I wanted to do something helpful...' This wasn't strictly true, it was more Nina's insistence that they *didn't* book anything, and they just *see where Paris takes them* that had compelled her to book dinner. She didn't want to risk wandering around at 10 p.m. trying to find somewhere on a Friday night in Paris with space for them. She wasn't sure she could last past 10 p.m. without falling asleep. 'At Georges?' she added in a hopeful tone. It was selfish too; Alice couldn't come to Paris and *not* go to the restaurant at the top of the Georges Pompidou centre.

'*Nice*,' Jules said approvingly and Nina muttered a muted,

'Okay, thanks.' The tension stilled and cooled and Nina shot a conciliatory smile in Jules's direction, who, to Alice's surprise, granted one back.

'I'm sorry,' Jules said, acknowledging the phone in her hands. 'I... I can't seem to help it.'

They all stopped then, in the Jardin des Tuileries, where groups of people sat on the chairs around the lake, sunglasses on, chatter rising like the warmth of the sun on the water's surface. The gardens were coming into bloom, bursts of colour contrasting with the lush green grass.

'It's a distraction,' she said softly, and Alice and Nina nodded, understanding, their arms around her. They knew that was a lot for Jules to say. 'But I should take a break.' She slipped her phone into her leather tote. 'My battery's about to die anyway.'

They continued to walk on, in step with each other, commenting on shops and things that had changed since they'd been here last: *There's more dogs, right? – Oh, I used to love that restaurant! Remember the maggot in your oyster? And how annoyed the waiter was when you complained!*

The whole time Alice was participating, but her own thoughts ran in tandem: Should she reply to Mr Hough? It felt so loaded. Or did it, was she reading too much into it? She should say thank you, shouldn't she, at least? She couldn't decide and her thoughts see-sawed as they walked until they reached the spot they knew so well. The two huge fountains at Place de la Concorde, the grandeur of Hôtel de Crillon behind them. Standing before the beautiful hotel where they'd met, in the city that made them, Alice felt for the first time that her extensive preparations to ensure she could come – including the negotiations with Dimples the

Unicorn – seemed worth it. Jules's phone stayed in her bag, and the nervous look on Nina's face shifted properly for the first time since they'd arrived. They linked arms, like a chain, and smiled.

*Jules*

They passed a pleasant hour in Ladureé, plates of rose pink and cream, lilac and mint macarons, washed down with tea. Jules discreetly tapped away at her phone, the background noise melting away as her senses sharpened and honed in. A steep rise. An unexpected fall. A netting effect. Her brain ticked over quickly, wondering what to do next. She could feel the girls politely ignoring that she was working, no doubt thanks in part to her admission outside Le Crillon, their conversation continuing with occasional glances in her direction.

'I've just realised,' Nina was saying, 'how similar it is in here to your drawing room, Alice.'

'I may have taken a little inspiration,' Alice was grinning. 'If anyone can make teal walls, blush-pink ceilings and a leopard-print carpet work, it's Ladurée.'

'And you!' Nina chuckled. 'I love your carpet.'

Jules was sitting opposite them both so they couldn't see her phone, which was fortunate. They'd never understand the sums involved. The high stakes. They'd think she was mad. It might *look like* she was consumed by it, but it was good for her, this sort of mental workout. *Pity the man with nothing to keep his brain occupied*, her father used to say. Paul didn't understand it, he wanted her to go back to being carefree, as she had behaved in the early days of their relationship, but what he didn't realise was how hard Jules had had to work to appear that way. To appear like she could be chilled out and relaxed, seizing the day. It was exhausting. Jules loved the deal. Always had, always would.

She didn't realise how quickly phone batteries drained until a 'low power warning' flashed up; ordinarily she would have it plugged in most of the day, either at work or at home. She gasped in alarm and quickly tried to save and close down all her accounts so nothing would be lost. '*Fuck's sake,*' she muttered under her breath, drawing an 'is everything okay?' from her friends. She nodded quickly, not having the time – or the words – to explain.

'Well, that was fun,' she said breezily, moments later, sliding her phone into her bag. 'Shall we get the bill?'

'Sure, we can get the rest to take away, or...'

'Brilliant idea!' Jules said, waving the waitress over and standing and stretching her legs as they waited for the bill. Nina and Alice were still finishing their tea when Jules was outside and beginning to walk back to the apartment.

'What's the rush?' Alice asked, catching her up.

'No rush,' Jules said simply, but her long legs continued to stride ahead, Alice and Nina having to work hard to keep pace with her along the bustling streets.

'Shall we stop at Sephora?' Alice enthused. 'You two can tell me what products I need to buy!' But Jules visibly recoiled at the suggestion and Alice's stomach clenched with embarrassment.

'Can we head straight back?' Jules asked. 'I really need the loo. I forgot to go at Ladurée. And to be honest, I'm feeling quite tired. Why don't you and Nina hit Sephora? I'll go back to the apartment and chill out for a bit.'

'No, we won't leave you on your own,' Alice said, but she could feel Jules bristling.

'We don't have to be stuck together all weekend, do we? We're all adults.' She said it lightly, but her expression changed to one of shock, as if she couldn't believe she'd let that slip out herself.

Alice's face burned. 'No. We don't. I just thought...'

'I'm sorry,' Jules said quickly. 'I didn't mean it like that.' She sighed; she felt like she spent her whole life apologising these days. To Paul, to her boss, now to her final refuge, her friends. In truth, she wasn't used to being around people this much. At work, everyone kept largely to themselves. At home, she and Paul dealt with things in different ways: him in the gym and, having given up trying to speak to Jules, speaking to friends; her at home, with her own company, how she liked it.

'Of course you didn't,' Nina said, wrapping an arm around her. 'We want to be here for you but if you need time to yourself, that's cool too. Just let us know.' Jules saw Nina looking at Alice sympathetically with a half-smile, a *just let it go* expression, and Alice biting on her lip and looking away. Jules felt terrible now. Absolutely terrible. When had she become so critical? No wonder her marriage was in such a mess.

'I thought you'd want to take in an art gallery?' Jules asked Alice, trying to smooth over the fissures she'd created.

'Yeah, maybe,' Alice said. 'We're not here very long though, are we?' She shrugged, still looking hurt, her eyes on the pavement as they walked back to the apartment awkwardly, Alice no longer pointing out shops or making suggestions of things they could do tomorrow, and Jules felt on the one hand awful and on the other hand relieved. She needed to refine her strategy.

Nina assumed the role of peacemaker, initiating a conversation with Alice about the mums at school, a topic that always provided much material. 'Any recent dietary advice from Chernoble?' she asked.

'Chernoble?' enquired Jules politely.

'Chernoble and the Glossy Mums. They're her sidekicks. I always like to envisage them as a band, Chernoble on the mic, the others with guitars and saxophones.' She air-guitared a riff as they walked down the street. Jules always thought it a shame that Nina had stopped playing the guitar, after that business with Samir.

'Victoria Noble,' Alice supplied, 'my school nemesis. She's a nutritionist and is constantly suggesting things I should cut out for Charlotte *"that might be a contributing factor"*.' She put on a snippy, pious tone. 'It's broccoli at the moment,' she added to Nina. '*"Lots of links to behavioural problems"*.' She did the voice again, which made Nina chuckle. 'Last week it was oranges. *"Orange oil is in everything, Alice! You need to be so careful."*'

'God, I couldn't bear all that school gates stuff,' Nina said in a faraway voice, stopping short in case she'd offended Jules, but Jules was pulling a face too and agreeing.

'That would be one silver lining at least,' she said, attempting a joke. She was feeling a bit better about things by the time they got to the apartment, until it transpired there was only one phone charger between them. Jules tried to keep a smile on her face but *my God*. It had been so long since she'd been to Paris, or travelled at all, she hadn't thought to

bring an adaptor. And neither had Alice. So that left the one –
one! – that Nina had in the apartment.

'I used to have more,' Nina said apologetically, 'but the
Airbnb-ers kept taking them so I stopped replacing them.' She
shrugged, like it wasn't a big deal. All the appliances in the
apartment had continental plugs so it was only their phones
they needed to charge.

'I need my phone for work,' Jules said, in a way she felt
precluded the other women from using the charger first. What
could she do? She was desperate. She'd been offline for almost
an hour. She had catching up to do.

'I need mine to call home,' Alice said in a measured tone.
'In case there's an emergency.' And Jules bit the inside of her
cheek; she couldn't argue with that.

Nina stayed silent, humming as she busied herself around
the apartment, opening windows and rearranging cushions
and objects. There was something off with Nina, Jules thought
fleetingly. She was still her usual self – calm, considerate,
content – but like she'd been speeded up a bit. Jules closed her
eyes. It was her, wasn't it? Nina was on edge because of her?
Trying her best to make sure Jules was okay. Worried about
her, perhaps, not just because of the IVF but because of Paul.
She'd heard their conversation on the train, she wasn't asleep:
she was buying herself some time to figure out a plan. She
felt a curl of shame as she recalled it. Their concerns around
Paul. They had no idea. Sometimes she wondered whether
she should tell them everything but as soon as she considered
it, it was like her brain shut down. No. She couldn't do it.
She hadn't been raised that way, she didn't work that way.
And this was way beyond a boozy confessional with your

girlfriends. This was on another scale. She wasn't even sure they would believe her. There wasn't a single person who she thought might understand.

'Is it okay if I just plug it in for ten minutes?' Jules asked. Somewhere along the Left Bank her phone had run out of battery and turned off completely. 'To check nothing urgent has come in? And then it's all yours.' She smiled through gritted teeth as she connected her phone and waited for the battery sign to illuminate. It did and her phone came to life, vibrating gently with new messages.

There was a text from Paul, visible on the lock screen:

You can't just ignore this Jules.

She angled her phone away from her friends as a cold, tight feeling settled over her skin.

Usually by now Nina would have unlocked the antique display cupboard and retrieved her grandmother's crystal coupes, and they'd be drinking Kir royales. It grated on Jules, this booze-free regime, which she was sure was for her benefit.

Another text:

Come home.

She took a deep breath to still her shaking hands.

He often asked what drove her to do this sort of thing and it angered her, that he pretended not to get it. Not to understand how deep her grief ran, how she needed something – anything – to fill it. But it wouldn't always be this way. It wouldn't be like this, if she could only have a baby. A baby, a family, was all she truly needed.

'I don't want you to end up in prison!' he had said the last time it happened and she had promised him, sworn on her future cytoblasts, that she would never do it again. But she couldn't resist.

Another text:

Jules this is serious. You could be sacked for this.

But she doubted that. There were men in her team who had done the same with far larger sums of money. It just depended on how much you were still bringing in as to how valuable you were. Her thoughts got stuck there, as if hooked on a rusty nail, because she'd made a number of mistakes at work lately and she had the distinct impression that Ralph, her boss, was counting.

Her hands still shaking, she replied:

'I'm sorry. I'm fixing it. I promise.

How many times had she said sorry? For this, for her body, for her defunct womb. How many times had she failed him? She didn't even cry any more. She didn't really feel anything most of the time.

She turned her phone off, slipped it into her case and took out a second, fully charged phone. *Time to up my game*, she thought.

★ ★ ★

*Nina*

*My God, pretending you're not pregnant is difficult*, thought Nina, as their taxi moved slowly, roads and pavements full of people heading out for drinks and dinner. Like *really* difficult. Who knew there were so many things to avoid? Shellfish and cheese and partially cooked eggs and juicy, raw steaks. She'd never wanted to eat a juicy, raw steak with a glass of Pinot Noir so much in her life. What do French women *eat* when they're pregnant? Where were all the healthy juice bars hiding? She'd been *dying* to eat coquilles Saint-Jacques washed down with a crisp, peachy Sancerre by the Seine earlier. She was *in Paris*!

They alighted from the taxi and made their way across a cobbled street towards Le Centre Pompidou, a vast contemporary art space with a rooftop bar and restaurant. They had been here countless times and it never lost its charm. Things had been harder than she was expecting. Not just with Jules – which she expected to be a little strained – but with Alice too. Nina felt on edge, like she was annoying Alice somehow, although she wouldn't have been able to put her finger on why. And similarly, she felt like all day she'd been biting down on her own irritation. Like why was it less important she had *her phone* fully charged, since she had a business to run, after all? Jules and Alice acted like they had *more* responsibility because they had a boss and a family, respectively, but didn't that mean they had more support? And therefore *less* responsibility? The success of La City Pâtisserie rested squarely on Nina's shoulders, and hers alone.

As the escalator ascended the side of the building, its transparent structure affording the best views as it raised them above the rooftops, it felt good to be out in Paris at dusk wearing a dress, and heels, even if they did keep catching in the cobbles. She rarely dressed up any more. No one knows what it's like to walk in someone else's shoes, she reminded herself, not even if they're – she eyed Jules's pumps – Alexander McQueen. She thought uneasily of the message she'd seen from Paul on Jules's phone, before Jules had snatched it away: *You can't just ignore this Jules.* Ignore what? Did Jules suspect Nina was pregnant? She'd always been so good at observing people. Had she been venting to Paul and he was telling her to ask Nina? It would explain why she was being so snappy, although surely that was the pressure of her upcoming IVF? But then what was Paul referring to? Was he exerting some sort of pressure on her? And were her friends missing it, putting her behaviour down to stress, missing what was really going on?

'You don't wear brands any more, do you?' said Alice, a step below her on the escalator, her eyes travelling over Nina's dress. She sounded almost alarmed. 'You're one of those cool no-label people in classic cuts and muted tones. Oh Lordy. You *accept yourself*, don't you?' Her tone was theatrical, but she was only part joking.

Nina grinned. 'I don't make them myself. I buy them in shops.'

'Which shops? I need to know everything. I need to know how you look like this. Tell me your secrets!' And Nina laughed along, her smile masking the sick sense of fear in her stomach at the idea of something, at that very moment, growing inside her body, altering it. *It's natural though*, she reasoned to herself, and marvelled at that thought. She'd asked herself whether she wanted a baby hundreds, if not thousands, of times. How could she not, with the bombardment of pregnancy propaganda, launched like missiles as soon as a woman approached thirty, if not before? She'd wondered if something was wrong with her, that she didn't experience the broodiness she witnessed in her friends. She thought it had a practical explanation: she'd been a teenager when her little sister Carey was born, had seen at close range the demands of a child, was alive to the reality of having a baby in a way that her friends weren't. She expected that, when she was ready, maternal feelings would come. But her thirties were almost over and they simply hadn't. If anything, she felt squeamish at the idea of something growing inside her, couldn't help the horrible scene from *Alien*, a hand clawing its way out of Sigourney Weaver's tummy, flashing in her mind (how many women of her generation had been traumatised by that movie as a child?). Yet here she was, pregnant, the bubbling of anxiety subsiding, assuaged by her own calming thoughts. *It's natural.*

'Everything okay?' Nina asked, as Alice checked her phone and frowned.

Alice blushed red. 'Yeah, I was just waiting for an update from one of Charlotte's teachers. I thought he might send it by the end of the day.' She shoved her phone back in her bag.

A blast of cold air signalled they were almost at the top of the escalator. They were propelled upwards, closer towards a ceiling of stars. Nina couldn't help a silent, inner squeal. The beauty of Paris always got her.

Nina was careful to accept wine but to drink it very slowly, reminding her friends if questioned that it irritated her IBS. She made her meal choices with gusto – *Grilled chicken with rice! Delicious!* – although they were usually the very last thing she would have chosen to order. It felt like a punishment. A punishment for falling pregnant. *But we used a condom!* she wanted to scream at the sky as Jules knocked back another beading glass of champagne while she munched on a piece of asparagus, the hollandaise sauce discreetly scraped off. Old Nina, pre-therapy, would have believed this *were* a punishment, she thought, and she was grateful to have moved on, even if a tiny little voice was occasionally whispering, *maybe Old Nina was right.*

The night passed in a blaze of chatter:

'Neen, whatever happened to that fit Finnish guy you were seeing?'

'Yes! The Viking! I liked him!'

'So did I, but he totally ghosted me after, like, our fifth date.'

'What does ghosted mean?'

'He just cut off contact. Dead like a ghost. I never heard from him again.'

'That's a shame. Hey, did you hear about—'

'No! Really? Although, I did always think—'

'—*Before* they were married apparently. But why go through with it?'

They buried themselves willingly in their pasts: in shared jokes, and wardrobe malfunctions, and stupid things they wished they hadn't done at the time but now wished they could do all over again. As they did, memories of hot, sticky bars and heart-broken confessionals on dirty pavements weaved around them, as it had so many times. It was like wrapping their arms around each other as they braced themselves for a long walk home in heels. They were back in their Paris bubble. Nina felt the relief of it acutely.

'That woman on the bakery counter always hated you,' Jules was laughing.

'I know! And *every time* I asked her for a *demi-baguette classique*, she would reply in English.' Nina gritted her teeth in mock angst. 'I always wanted to say, *I'm French*! Half of me is, at least.'

'All you'd have got is a "*bof?*",' grinned Alice, and they did the thing they did when pretending to be a disinterested French person. *Bof*, she repeated, shrugging her shoulders, Nina and Jules laughing too and also shrugging.

Their waiter returned at that moment, clocking the *bof* and scanning them all for signs of whether he was the source of their mirth. '*Plus de vin?*' he asked suspiciously, the three of them roaring with laughter as he walked away to retrieve it.

Their eyes were shining, glossed with tears from laughing. They were connected by these cobbles, these balconies, and a language they all loved but despite their best efforts could never quite master.

After dinner they picked up their glasses and stood by the glass-edged terrace, Paris laid out before them: Sacré Coeur, Notre-Dame, the Eiffel Tower.

The city of love, Nina thought, her eyes alighting on Le Sacré Coeur. She felt a knuckle of pain in her chest. The contrast with the warm depths of her friendship with Alice and Jules and the weight of the decision she had to make. When had it become a decision, she wondered, and not a *fait accompli*? As she gazed over the city, studded with lights from towers and apartment blocks, feelings she had discussed in therapy, trauma she had processed and filed away, were resurfacing.

Guilt was hovering; in her thoughts, in her heart. *It was a long while ago*, she reminded herself. You were a different person then. You've worked through it, you've moved on, you're out the other side. Her therapist would almost certainly attribute this rush of feelings to the tiny cluster of cells in her uterus. *Could she make it work?* she wondered. *Could she have a baby and raise it alone?* She didn't feel compelled to; not in the way she felt compelled to bake and create and to drive her business forward. To travel, to spend time with her friends, to spend weekends exploring markets in foreign places. That to her was what life was about. Nights like this. And she couldn't have a baby unless she was totally committed to it, to giving it the best life possible. That's what every baby deserves, she thought, and her father, Samir, flickered in her mind. He hadn't wanted a baby, had he, and she'd spent her life rebounding from that? From his mistake. What was a blessing to Joanie had been a mistake to him. But she was here, wasn't she? She was here in Paris with her friends. She had a full life. She had a *good life*. Parents didn't need to be perfect. They just needed to show up. Surely she could do a better job than Samir? The conflict of her decision left her breathless.

It's not a baby yet, she reminded herself. It's a small cluster of cells. No point in attaching romantic notions to it. She wondered how many weeks pregnant she was. She had purposely not inputted the date of her last period into the calculator she'd seen on the NHS website. She had a vague idea – around a month – but she didn't want a precise number of weeks, to track against the links to detailed growth charts she'd seen online. She remembered a religious education lesson in her Catholic school, recalled being surprised at how early a foetus had a detectable heartbeat. There was no need to get caught up in detail like that until she'd decided what she was going to do.

'I always forget how beautiful Paris is,' said Jules, her eyes alive, rather than glazed, as she drank in the city. She hadn't taken her phone out of her bag all through dinner, which Nina took as a good sign. It was working, the magic of Paris was having an effect. Paul was right.

# 5

## Paris, 2008

*Part One: The Day Before the Wedding*

Jules stepped on to the concourse at the Gare du Nord, still
in her suit, and felt unexpected relief rush through her. She'd
told herself she didn't want to come, felt guilty to be away
from home for the weekend, but as she clipped through the
station, absorbing things she had forgotten but that were as
familiar as an old friend – like the jingle that preceded an
announcement over the tannoy, the rush of people, snatches
of French words and conversation – she felt herself breathe
properly for the first time in months. *She was in Paris!* She
spent all her weekends at her parents' these days. They'd
downsized, fortuitously shortly before her father had had his
stroke, moving from their large house outside Guildford to a
smaller house further south. Whereas once her mother had
taken great pride in her interiors, the new house was shabby,
the effort of taking care of her father clearly sapping all her
mother's energy.

Jules tried to make herself useful when she was there, but

she felt like an intruder in her mother's kitchen – *It doesn't go there, Julia! No, not like that! Use this!* – so mainly she sat with her father, reading out who was racing that day and taking the merest grunt or flicker from him to be an intention that she should place a bet on his behalf. He'd always liked a flutter on the horses – *just a little one* – and it seemed so cruel to Jules that he had been robbed of this last pleasure. They'd watch the race together, her cheering on whichever horse she thought her father would have picked to avoid the tears pricking her eyes, the memory of being a small girl watching the races with her father neck and neck beside her. Occasionally, her mother would enter the room, tut and leave, but Jules was sure she was doing some good when Jabbers Gut won a race and her father very slowly and deliberately moved his hand on to her knee. She felt the faintest pressure as he tried to give her knee a squeeze, before promptly falling asleep. She sat there with him for hours, not wanting to move, conscious of the passing of time, that the window of opportunity for moments together was getting smaller and smaller, the shutters coming down on her father's life. He'd always seemed so vibrant, it didn't seem possible.

She would have stayed, missed the wedding, but her mother insisted she go. *Insisted* was a polite way to put it: she reminded Jules that her brother, William, was coming home that weekend with his tedious alpha-mum wife, Gilly, and son Jasper, and there wouldn't be room for her anyway. *Will and Gill and Jasper*, she grimaced, recalling their home answering machine. Her mother would be in her element, doting on the three of them in a way she never had with Jules.

Now she was here, though, she was relieved. She hadn't realised how much she needed a break. Although whether it would be a break was debatable. She was under strict instructions from Alice's mother, Clemency, to go straight to the hotel to help with the wedding preparations.

She hoped there wouldn't be too much to do as she was desperate to spend some time with Nina. Alongside her work and her father's health, she had this consistent worry about Nina, nudging away at her. Should she be doing more to help Nina? The death of her grandmother, Sylvie, had hit her hard, and her career in music was faltering. She had built up a big following on Myspace, but promoting herself as a serious musician proved impossible while her father, Samir, kept becoming embroiled in tabloid scandals – and eventually *Life in general and love in particular*, her album, the thing she seemed to have all her hopes and dreams pinned on, had flopped.

Each time Jules had seen her in London recently, she seemed to have deteriorated further, and at Alice's hen do she'd been in a terrible state, drinking at least three bottles of Prosecco at the spa and passing out before dinner. At least there weren't any men there.

For Nina, the Samir debacle had become a sort of repertoire, a verbal vomit she expelled whenever she met someone new. Especially if it was a man she liked: 'Well, my dad's pretty famous, you might have heard of him, Samir Laurent? Yes, that's the one. Well. He pissed off when he heard my mum was pregnant, then he sent me a beautiful note when I was sixteen, apologised for everything and invited me to a fancy ball to show me off. And then he told me he'd help me become a star – *ha!* – but turns out he just needed some PR points because he was sleazing on his co-star and then, when that didn't work – oh yeah? You saw it in the papers?

Me too! – he pissed off again. *It's a really lovely story!*' she would usually end it, downing whatever drink she had in her hand just to punctuate how jolly she found the whole thing! It was like she had to lay bare her whole family history in a take-me-or-leave-me fashion, the very antithesis to how Jules preferred to operate. Jules would try to take her politely to one side as she shrieked: 'It's. So. Fucking. Funny! Isn't it?! *Isn't it????*'

God knew what would happen at the wedding.


Nina had managed to delicately swerve being at the beck and call of Alice's mother today by reminding her that she needed to undertake her own preparations: sorting out, and deciding what to do about, her grandmother's apartment. It had been a huge shock, her grandmother leaving her the apartment, not just for her but for Samir too, who was furious. She hadn't heard from him since. The loose plan was she would declutter it and let it out while she decided what to do. Jules had suggested listing it on a new website she'd heard about where you rent out your own place for short breaks. It would give Nina the flexibility to stay there when she visited Paris and she'd still earn some money from it.

She'd intended to spend the morning carefully packing away her grandmother's things but had been surprised by how little she wanted to part with. Her grandmother's aesthetic felt grown-up minimal and she liked the elegance of her surroundings, knowing that each piece of art would have been carefully chosen and curated by Sylvie. She'd expected the apartment to feel like a mausoleum, but instead it felt like an oasis of calm. When the buzzer rang mid-afternoon, she expected it was Susu, her grandmother's upstairs neighbour who often forgot her front door key, so she buzzed her in unthinkingly and jumped when there was a knock at her door seconds later.

It was Teddy. Or Ted, rather – he'd decided to rebrand when he began working in the City. She hated how her heart still stuttered when she saw him; how her breath caught in her throat. He looked wedding-ready, his hair tidy and swept to one side, his skin clear and bright, suggesting he had stuck to the pre-wedding routine mapped out for him by Alice and Clemency (no late nights or booze, less caffeine, eight hours' sleep). 'Good practice for when we start trying straight after the wedding!' Alice had said on her hen do, a spa weekend, and on this one ground Nina felt that history was working out as it should: both Alice and Ted were desperate for a family, while Nina found it hard enough to look after herself; she couldn't imagine ever wanting to do the same for a child.

'Walk with me?' was all he said. It was a month or so since she'd last seen him, when they spent an evening drinking and compiling questions and answers for a Mr & Mrs game for Alice's hen do.

Nina looked down at her clothes. She was wearing an oversized white shirt and skinny jeans, with a floral scarf fashioned into a headband and knotted at the top. 'Sure,' she said. Her head was pounding with a red-wine hangover and she thought some air might do her good. Somehow, once Ted and Alice were in a proper relationship, first moving in together then getting engaged, it made things easier between her and Ted: their friendship walked in the sunshine now, it wasn't hidden away in emails and long correspondence, though they did still email, rambling missives about what they were watching at the moment or what music they were listening to. Ted had even joked about making her his best man, but Alice chidingly reminded him that she'd got there first.

'So this is yours?' Ted said, standing near the doorway as she skittered around looking for a cardigan and her keys. He wore his usual Ted uniform: a casual shirt and chinos with deck shoes. She noted the tone of approval in his voice and saw him again in her family's little terraced house, so incongruous to the scene.

'Yeah,' she said. 'Mad, isn't it? I miss her,' she added.

It was a sunny day, the air box-fresh, with white brushstrokes layering the sky. Nina already knew where they would go, but it didn't matter really: it mattered only that they were together. She felt this sense, and she was sure Ted felt it too – they were on the edge of something, a precipice, between him being her friend and him being her best friend's husband. However much Alice accepted their friendship now, things would be different when they were married, but neither of them knew in what way. What mattered was now.

It didn't take long to reach Le Sacré Coeur.

'For old times' sake?' Ted asked, inclining his head to the magnificent cathedral, glowing pale against the sea-blue sky.

Inside it was hushed and quiet as they walked slowly to the votive lights. 'I've been thinking about them a lot,' Ted said as they watched the small bulbs of flames flickering, tiny fluting twirls of black smoke, like ink from a quill, weaving upwards to the dome. Nina lit a candle and thought of Sylvie. She crossed herself and looked up, sending a silent prayer.

Ted was staring straight ahead, swallowing, eyes blinking,

as though he were fighting back tears. She slipped her hand in his and squeezed. He closed his eyes and she saw tears flush silently down his cheeks. Nina knew that they would never mention this moment again. Ted's pain was too acute, his efforts to hide it too encompassing. She understood how it felt to have missing pieces. She was fortunate, in comparison to Ted; her pain at not having a father in her life had been abated by her mother, Joanie. Granted, Joanie was almost always working when she was younger, but they needed the money and she made sure Nina was safe and well looked after by Niamh and Seamus. She had one parent. Ted had none.

They stayed there together a while, Nina listening to the layers of hushed prayers filling the space around her: French, English, Italian, Spanish. Even though Nina wasn't sure she believed in God any more, the hairs on her arms stood on end.

Outside they sauntered around, entertained by the street artists, and as the light began to dim, they bought a small bag of salted pretzels and two ice-cold beers from a street vendor, sat on steps warmed by the fine weather and watched the sun set over Paris.

'You're getting married,' Nina marvelled. She'd never really believed it would happen. What had she expected? Behind them, a woman began playing the harp, the melody as enchanting as the balmy air and coral-streaked sky. It was so beautiful, it seemed other-worldly.

He didn't reply, looking at her and away at the view. Once, then twice. He seemed agitated. Nervy. Pre-wedding jitters, no doubt. He placed his bottle on the step and stared again at the horizon, his countenance grave.

'Do you ever wonder...' he started. He jammed his hands into his pockets as if at war with them. 'Do you ever wonder if things might have been different?' He turned his head to look at her then. Properly. He didn't need to say anything else. And nor did she. They locked eyes and it was how it had always been. Since the very first time they'd met at *le Bal*. Questions between them but answers too. An understanding. A connection so deep it made her legs buckle and her heart ache. A connection second only to her love for Alice and Jules.

'No,' she said crossly. '*No*.' She stood abruptly, tearing her eyes away from his. 'No,' she said again, standing. Fury in her veins now. He couldn't do this. It wasn't fair.

'Nina,' he said, scrambling to his feet and reaching for her, but she shook him away. Angry with him. She had been in love with Ted for so long she had worn those feelings like a second skin. She had accepted it, grown a third skin that buttoned her feelings down. He couldn't strip that away.

And yet a tiny part of her was saying, *you've always loved Ted, Nina. Maybe this is your shot at happiness? Your only shot.*

No. No, no, no. *When will you accept it?* she thought to herself bitterly. *When they're at the altar?*

It was a fairy tale, her and Ted. It was never meant to be, because if it were, it would have happened, wouldn't it? If she had a big family like Alice, and *money*, and *connections*, then perhaps things could be different. She thought of the way he had appraised Sylvie's apartment earlier, contrasted it to his awkwardness in her house in Mile End after *le Bal*. Things she had always tried to deny bubbled to the surface. 'It could never have been me. I've never belonged to the right club or holidayed in the right places, have I?'

'What are you talking about?' he said, aghast. 'That was never… It was *you*. From the moment we met. The digs about me, the teasing. You always made it clear—'

'*I wasn't good enough for you.*' They said the words in unison, holding their anger in clenched jaws and tight lips, arms rigid by their sides, their indignation matched.

'What—?'

'But you always said—'

'—It was just a casual thing—'

They were each betrayed by their mouths smirking.

The tension broke, their repetition at once amusing and a sign of what they'd both missed out on. They had each made the same assumption about the other. They'd both let the other slip from their grasp.

'You said that day on the bench, you said it had to just be casual because you were going away travelling.'

'*You* said it was just a casual thing,' Ted said, 'you were always so aloof. I never knew what you were thinking…' Ted trailed off as they came to the same realisation: it didn't matter, because he was marrying Alice tomorrow.

Nina knew it was done but she needed to know more. She needed to understand so she could get closure. 'How were you not good enough for me?' she asked quietly.

'Too arrogant. Too entitled. Too—'

'I didn't say those things.'

'I think you say them sometimes without even realising it. The sneers about my *gap yah*. The eye-rolling whenever I mentioned Exeter. *Full of posh pricks*, you said once. I thought

I wasn't cool enough for you. Not edgy enough.' He grinned tentatively and reached out to touch her hand.

'Well, that's probably true.' She smiled, allowing him to clasp her hand in his, the touch as sweet and sharp as rhubarb, but she felt guarded. Why had he never tried to kiss her since that last time in London? Never told her how he felt?

'It doesn't make sense,' was all she said. 'You never...'

He frowned and the way his face moved made her bite her lip. How had they got here, on the eve of his wedding to Alice?

'Why didn't you say anything sooner?' she asked.

'I don't know,' he said. 'I suppose I just never saw it working. It felt like too big a risk. You're the only person that's ever really understood me. With my parents and things...' He shrugged, still finding it difficult to discuss. 'Why didn't you?'

'I was going to,' she said. 'But then you and Alice got together... and, you know... that was it...' The stakes had always felt too high. Soulmates. Better to have him in her life than not, she had reasoned. They stared at each other sadly, knowing this was the end of the line.

'You're going to make a good husband,' Nina said. She pressed a hand against his chest, the longing they shared now so intense she could feel it, a pressure between them like an unwelcome guest at a party.

He put his hand over hers, still staring into her eyes. His palm was warm and soft. He moved her hand to his cheek. She closed the gap between them, pressing pause on this moment mentally in her mind. Wanting to feel it, to capture it somehow, knowing she would return to it, time and time again. She wanted to stay suspended in this pinch of pleasure and pain for as long as she could. Her hand on Ted's cheek and his eyes on hers – because once they moved, even an inch, they would each return to reality, to Ted marrying her best friend, and they would never have a moment like this again.

Would Nina *ever* feel this way again, with anyone? Was she destined to spend the rest of her life reliving these precious minutes on the steps of Le Sacré Coeur, this connection between the two of them, always seeking but never finding the same thing? It seemed as predestined as them meeting in the first place. That's why she stood so still. That's why she didn't move. That's why when Ted finally, painfully and slowly, so carefully it made her heart burst and her body throb and the rest of her feel like she was floating, dipped his face to hers and kissed her lips, she kissed him back. That's why when he picked her up, she didn't resist. Why she wrapped her legs around him, why she ignored the whistles – and some tuts – of passers-by, why she eventually pulled back, caught her breath, hailed a cab and took Ted back to her apartment.

# 6

## Saturday a.m.

*Alice*

*I blame Paris*, thought Alice as she stared at a topless photo of Mr Hough, drops of water and streaks of early morning sun slanting over his skin. She rolled on to her side and pulled the pillow over her head and groaned. Was she having an affair? Was this an emotional affair?

She removed the pillow and looked back over their messages. They were innocent enough, on the surface:

Thank you. I hope you're having a good weekend? xxx

She'd replied last night, around 11 p.m., when she was drunk on the sights of Paris and friendship; they'd shared two bottles of wine, Nina attentively topping up their glasses, but Alice felt as though she'd drunk two bottles herself.

*Three kisses!* And it wasn't even the weekend yet when she'd sent it. *Lordy, you sound so desperate*, she thought. But then she'd woken to this photo. Mr Hough on the beach, his wetsuit peeled down to his waistline. She gulped, following the lines of muscle definition downwards to a smattering of hair. Briefly, she imagined licking the salty sea water from his skin, the coolness of the droplets and the heat of her tongue… He hadn't mentioned going to Cornwall this weekend. In fact, he'd said he didn't have much on. An impulse decision. Imagine living like that, so freely. She thought of Nina. She thought of Paris. She thought of how trapped she had become in her own life, entwined in PTA meetings and fundraising initiatives and sports kits. She wasn't free. And she wasn't happy. *Had she been unhappy for a long time?* It had worsened as Charlotte's problems had, but was it there before that? This creeping realisation that the life she had dreamed of didn't feel the way she expected it to?

She tried to call Ted to check in on the children but he didn't answer and instead sent her a text message as soon as she hung up: 'All okay here. Hope you're having fun X.' Saturday mornings were hectic. Football, cricket, gymnastics. She almost texted him back reminding him to take snacks but stopped herself.

She hadn't always been this way. She used to be spontaneous and ambitious like her friends. Ted spoke of Nina in a tone of almost awe these days at what she was achieving with La City Pâtisserie. The expansion plans and expected return of investment to his firm. It irked her. For one, it had been her idea for him to invest and for another, what did he think Alice was doing all day? She was CEO of her own family office, which Ted was willingly blind to: the hours she invested in food procurement and preparation for five (all with differing catering requirements), the constant churn of forms for school, sports clubs, Brownies, Beavers, the paediatrician (whole days lost to admin and forms), the logistics of moving three small humans with their own (strong) wills and desires around in circles, at slightly different times. Drop-offs, pickups, play dates. The £1s that had to be remembered and collected: Wear Something Purple Day, Endangered Animals Day, International Day. Being there for them. Listening to their concerns about where Bluey, the half-dead fledgling they'd found in the garden, was now, consoling them he was probably with his mummy and daddy and not in the shallow grave she'd dug.

There was the volume of messages in the class WhatsApp groups. Forget the workplace, this is where the real battle for feminism was lost. Ted outright refused to join them. *I don't have time for 60 messages on whether it's PE today or not*, he would say, eyes to the heavens, and Alice would snap, *Neither do I, but one of us has to be on there.* This passive-aggressive snip-snap had become the background patter to their relationship. Alice hated it. Wished she could return to the days when they would swoop around Paris together, making plans for their future. For travel and good food and long sunny days. It was like she'd been sold a luxury villa holiday via a glossy brochure but when she'd arrived she was on the ground floor of a grotty block of apartments, cockroaches for company and a view of a construction site.

And then there was the time dedicated to the puzzle of Charlotte: parent Facebook support groups, online articles, podcasts, books, meetings with the headmaster who, like Alice, was at the end of his tether. *It can't go on like this* had recently changed to *If this happens again it will be a fixed-term exclusion.* The pain Alice felt at those words. At the judgement of her sweet little girl, who'd spent the first few days of her life asleep on Alice's chest, who'd followed her around with big smiling eyes every morning asking, 'What be doing today?' and who now, more often than not, shouted *Shut up!* at her, while slamming doors. Her little girl who, in Alice's better moments she understood was scared, afraid, lost, and in her weaker moments wanted to be far away from, she wanted to prise those sticky fingers, which gripped her so tight at the end of the day, away from her. That little girl who she sometimes looked at and thought she'd been mis-sold a dream. And then she hated herself some more.

She could never explain it to Jules, who was desperate for her own children, or Nina, who wasn't interested in them. *They're all hard work, aren't they?* Nina would say, but the truth is they weren't. Wilf and Phoebe were sailing through life. The contrast between them and their older sister was palpable: a gulf of experiences. One marked from her first day at school as naughty, difficult, volatile, the others praised for their conformity, their adherence to the rules: *A pleasure to have in the class! A delight to teach!* Charlotte heard all this and she knew she was different, however hard Alice tried to protect her. Mr Hough as her form tutor this year had been a blessing; he had quickly recognised her neurodiversity and engaged the school's SENCO, liaising with her to ensure Charlotte got some support, but the damage had been wrought in the intervening years. Charlotte was anxious in school, traumatised by her experiences, prone to explosive tantrums when she felt overwhelmed. Alice wondered sometimes how much more it would take to break her, the fruitless pursuit to make her square peg of a daughter fit into the round hole of school.

And *on top of all that* she had been trying to launch her own business enterprise. Although she conceded that had been a disaster.

She looked again at the photo of Mr Hough. Felt a heat rising up through her body. *Enough,* she told herself. *This has already gone too far.* But she craved his attention. Craved the way he spoke to her like she mattered, like she wasn't mad, or neurotic, when she advocated for Charlotte. She couldn't remember the last time someone had told her she looked nice, or pretty, even, let alone *beautiful.*

She scrambled out of bed and pulled on a blue-and-white striped shirt dress, tying it at the waist. She needed to move, to shift her thoughts. In the main living area the shutters were open, framing a beautiful day. Pastries and fresh bread were arranged on the table with small pots of jam and butter. She walked into the kitchen, where Nina was brewing coffee in loose cropped jeans and a simple vest top, frowning. Alice could feel Paris calling, longed to lose herself in the Louvre or the Museé d'Orsay, but feared the reflection it could bring; the mirror it might hold up to the younger her, who trawled art galleries and worked at Sotheby's and had *dreams.* Things she wanted to do. She felt a pang as she thought of her business, failing before it had even begun.

'Let's do something touristy!' Alice said by way of greeting, suddenly nostalgic. 'A boat trip along the Seine! Or the Eiffel Tower!' She immediately cringed. *There she goes, being all basic again.* No doubt Nina and Jules would want to take in some sort of chic flea market, or a sample sale of a brand she'd never heard of on the outskirts of the city. But instead, Nina rearranged her frown into a smile and said, 'Great idea!' and when Jules emerged from her room half an hour later, she was enthusiastic too. 'A boat trip would be perfect!' she said.

Jules's eyes were red and bloodshot, as though she hadn't slept well, and Alice felt a pang for all Jules had ahead of her in the coming weeks. The hormones, the anxiety, the unknown. She tried to think of something she could do or say to help but reminded herself, *that's why I'm in Paris. What we're all here for*. To take Jules's mind off things, to give her a chance to relax. A sojourn from her concerns and, hopefully, her phone. She pushed her own worries aside. She would do whatever it took to make sure Jules had a fun, relaxing day.

*Nina*

Nina had woken early – had she ever slept? – and made her way down to La Grande Épicerie, the food hall at Le Bon Marché. Because it had been her grandmother's nearest place to buy food – and, as far as Nina could tell, the only place she would buy food from – it had been some time before Nina realised that 'popping to the shop for a baguette' and going to La Grande Épicerie was akin to popping into the Selfridges food hall for a loaf of bread.

She had always sought solace here, the rows of gleaming products offering respite, for a moment or two, from whatever was going on in her world, but this morning she found herself staring longingly, realising so many delicacies were off limits, imprisoned behind their shiny glass counters, while she was pregnant. It was strange, really, since she was certain she wouldn't be pregnant for too long, that she nevertheless felt a deep sense that it wouldn't be right to eat those things while she carried a tiny human in her body. As much as she kept reminding herself the baby existed only on a microscopic cellular level, her brain had begun attributing characteristics to it. *There's a baby in your uterus*, it whispered. *You're growing a tiny human.* Hormones, she reasoned. Worst of all was her mother's voice, even louder than last time, saying *It's a blessing.* Of all people, Nina's mother knew how this felt, didn't she? She'd fallen pregnant by accident and, luckily for Nina, she'd kept her baby. *You were a blessing to me*, her mother had often said. But Nina didn't feel blessed. Nina felt conflicted.

She glided along the aisles, looking up foods and recipes, picking up items and putting them back. No pâté, no prosciutto, no shellfish, no Camembert or Roquefort. Some foods were on a maybe list but came with warnings, like sushi, rendering them banned. No wonder, she thought idly, as she replaced some rich dark chocolate (*Don't forget that chocolate counts as caffeine too! No more than 200mg of caffeine a day is probably safe*), that women lost themselves in motherhood when this kind of conditioning and restricting oneself from pleasure began in pregnancy.

She couldn't identify anything troubling in croissants and pastries and she also bought a small jar of okay-looking decaf coffee, which she'd try to make when Jules wasn't looking. She hated lying to Jules – and Alice – but how could she break Jules's heart? How could she tell her that she'd fallen pregnant by accident? While using a condom? She didn't understand how that had happened herself. She knew how much Jules had scaled back her life since her fertility problems. The careful trimming of her female friends from university and work and her West London set. It wasn't because she was jealous, it was simply too painful. And Nina couldn't bear to bring her friend more pain, especially when she was unlikely to keep the baby.

*Unlikely* to keep the baby... it was strange how something that seemed so certain on Thursday evening was now admitting another possibility. Her work was flexible and she made enough money for childcare. One child wouldn't scupper all her travel plans, surely. In fact, in some ways, it might be... fun? She rubbed her eyes with her thumb and index finger, trying to conjure a vision of herself with a child. A little boy perhaps, with long hair like Flynn, or a girl, with his big brown eyes and...

She turned sharply towards the checkouts, a queasy feeling bubbling at the base of her throat. It was too early for morning sickness, wasn't it? This was fear. This was how she used to feel, in her drinking days, certainly through most of her car-crash twenties. She should tell Flynn, but she couldn't see him enthusing about the insertion of a baby into his life, which was spent working in La City Pâtisserie by day and performing spoken-word poetry by night. He was just starting to gain traction as an artist. But he had a right to know, to make the decision for himself.

On a whim, she called him, stepping out on to the muted street, bathed in early morning light.

'Hi,' she breathed. 'I wasn't expecting you to answer.'

'You okay?' he asked.

'Hm,' she said. She bypassed the huge wooden door of her building and kept walking, turning right at Hôtel Lutetia, where Alice had once charmed the night porter into letting them in to the hotel bar by performing a cabaret skit involving a lamp post. She smiled, and chatted to Flynn about how his gig had gone last night and about her weekend.

'Is there anything else?' he asked, sensing her reticence.

She sighed, reaching the park. She'd never had to say this to anyone before. It wasn't like in the movies. There was no sweet partner desperate for the news, no dick on-off boyfriend who would flee at the first hint of a baby. This wasn't a test, there was no arc, no moment of redemption ahead for them both. There was her friend and co-worker Flynn and somewhere in the past there had been a faulty condom. Perhaps he *would* flee but she wasn't emotionally entwined with him; she knew she could survive it if he did.

'I'm pregnant,' she said. And the news flew from the Jardin du Luxembourg all the way to a small B&B in Edinburgh.

'Oh. Okay. Wow,' he said. 'How are you feeling?'

'I don't know,' she said. 'Okay, I think… I guess… I'll have a… termination. I hate that word.'

'They should come up with something better,' he agreed. She heard a kettle in the background, pictured early morning light streaming in through the B&B's windows. He liked to meditate in the morning.

'I don't want children,' she said, swallowing.

'I know,' he said. 'And that's okay.' His voice was soft and gentle, like a balm. She imagined incense wafting around his room. She suspected he travelled with incense.

'But,' she continued, 'this could be my last shot. If I change my mind, will I always regret it? Do *you* want children?'

'I think so. I hadn't planned to just yet, but one day…'

She stopped walking and closed her eyes. Felt sunbeams lie flat on her eyelids. There was a cool breeze and children shrieking in delight as they pushed toy sailboats into the lake.

'Or maybe *this day*, if that's what you want? It's your decision, Nina, but if you want to keep the baby, I'm here. I'm in. I'll support you, whatever you decide. You know that, right?'

She nodded, tears beginning to stream down her cheeks. She hadn't realised how much she needed to hear him say it.

'Nina?'

'I'm nodding,' she said and emitted a short, strained laugh. 'Thank you.'

'I'm glad you're with your friends.'

'I haven't told them. It's complicated. Jules has been trying for so long and I've not had the chance to tell Alice and… I don't know. It might be weird to. Or to tell her and not tell Jules.' She was talking herself into knots. How could she explain it all to Flynn?

She thanked him again, clicked off the call and held her phone to her chest.

*You have options*, she thought. They'd only recently started sleeping together but she'd known Flynn for three years. They were friends. She knew his sister, Luna, a photographer who took photos of La City Pâtisserie for her sometimes; she respected – and mostly agreed with – his political views. He was reliable and trustworthy and kind. He would make a good parent. One day. Or today?

She hadn't long been back at the apartment when Alice awoke, bouncing into the kitchen suggesting they do something touristy. Alice seemed revitalised after just one night away from the kids. Nina hoped her enthusiasm might be infectious and was happy to be swept along as a tourist for the day. At least it would give her some time to think and they were unlikely to encounter shellfish and champagne at the usual tourist hotspots.

'I'm in,' she said. And she thought of Flynn and smiled.

## Jules

Earlier that morning, Jules had heard Nina and Alice in the kitchen and wondered how long she had until she had to go out and speak to them. She didn't like to think or feel this way about her friends; she knew the whole purpose of this weekend was for her benefit, but what she would really like to do is remain alone in her room, time stretched as her focus intensified. The thing you had to understand was: she was desperate.

She hadn't slept. With Paul and her friends asleep, she had had full control of the charger and both her phones. She was £47,000 up after a night of online poker on her 'extra' phone (with no chance of Paul seeing her online and trying to call again), and betting on football matches across the world with her 'work' phone. It was carefully orchestrated; she'd set alarms to remind her which games were about to start, and she couldn't afford to stop. She was doing it. She was winning it all back.

She took breaks, of course, just like if she were in the office. That's what often lets people down, not taking a break, not seeing the bigger picture. She thought again of Paul: this was all part of the bigger picture. Their future together. If she could make enough to clear her debts – £80,000 spread across multiple credit cards and accounts – and recoup the bonus she'd lost on Thursday, another £70,000, she'd be squared up before she got back to London tomorrow. She'd tell Paul everything, even about the debt, and they could start again.

Paul had forgiven her before. He'd forgive her again, surely? This time she wasn't asking him for anything. This time she'd fix it herself and they had the IVF coming up and hopefully, hopefully, they could move on from all this.

The first time was awful. Paul and Jules had separate bank accounts, which their salaries went into, and a joint account they each put a set amount in to cover their bills and expenses. Once Jules had maxed out her own account, she began dipping into the joint account. At first Paul hadn't noticed the small amounts disappearing from the joint account, but £500, withdrawn to cover her stake in a poker game she'd lost, drew his attention. 'New shoes,' she smiled. 'Sorry, I must have used the joint account card by mistake. I'll transfer it over.' That's when she started using credit and it was amazing, with her salary, how many cards she was allowed to take out, how many accounts she could open with gambling companies. Once she maxed out one, she simply opened another. And another. But then her bank cards started being declined. Warnings, sent by credit card companies because there were insufficient funds for her direct debits, arrived. Paul picked one up from the mat once, frowned at the bright red 'WARNING! ACTION REQUIRED!' on the envelope. Jules took it casually. 'Junk mail,' she shrugged, and then she changed all her statements to online. It didn't feel like lying. She couldn't explain why. It felt like she was protecting herself. This was her way of coping with the relentlessness of her losses, emotional rather than financial. And already then, after two rounds of IVF and two miscarriages, the impact of the financial loss paled into insignificance compared to the emotional loss. The horror of knowing there was a baby growing in your body and then, suddenly, not. Her thinking became disjointed. She moved from moment to moment, finding different ways to cope. To keep going into the office, and pretending she was the same. Julia Frey-Jackson, on the fast-track programme to becoming a director, with no interest in starting a family any time soon. She was discovered, quite horrifyingly, when two bailiffs turned up at the house and tried to seize her car.

'Julia?' Paul had called frantically from outside. 'There's two guys here and they say you owe a lot of money. There must be some mistake?' But she could hear the uncertainty in his voice as she came downstairs, pale, shaking, and she could almost hear him thinking: *oh right*, as he pieced things together: her failure to put petrol in the car for weeks on end, how she pretended to forget his birthday last month but the following week lavished him with gifts. She'd never seen a look in his eyes like that before. And she couldn't bear to see it again.

He'd paid off her debts that first time. It was £200,000, draining his own savings, an act of love, protecting her from something he couldn't begin to understand. Unwittingly, he'd given her a clean sheet, to begin again. She hadn't intended to. She really hadn't. She made it through another round of IVF, another miscarriage, but the fourth proved too painful, the 'free' deposits the online casinos were offering her – even though she'd closed her accounts – too difficult to resist. One had given her £10,000. Available with a single click to reactivate her account. With the stress of work and the IVF and their relationship – the way he'd begun regarding her, looking at her differently – she did. She clicked. It happened again. She became used to the feeling of shame flooding through her. Waited for it, welcomed it. Anything to mask the pain of her true loss. The one that couldn't be won back. *Why do you do it?* he'd asked her the first time, and she couldn't translate her feelings into words.

This time, the bonus had gone into her account on Thursday: £70,000. In the days leading up to it, she promised herself she'd put it towards her credit card debt. Close some of her accounts. But the temptation to use it as capital, to invest it and earn enough to pay off *all* her debt, was too much. After all, that's what she did for her day job. It was the same, wasn't it? The money was gone in a couple of hours.

Beyond the shutters of her bedroom, she could hear Paris yawning awake below; the white lorries arriving with deliveries at Le Bon Marché, shutters clattering at the local shops. A city readying itself for a new day. She buried her head in her hands, rubbing her fingers up and down her smooth forehead. It was the last time. She just needed to recoup her losses and that was it. She'd quit for good this time. She needed £150,000 by the time she returned home tomorrow and it was totally doable. That's what she kept telling herself. You've got this, Jules. She'd once made £500,000 in a day for the Mantel fund, famously holding her ground shorting Santosa Banking Corp stock before the market knew that it would tumble. She could *easily* make £150,000 over the weekend to save her own skin.


'Hey, remember Valentin? I wonder whatever happened to him?' Alice asked a few hours later, as they walked towards the boat terminal by Îl de la Cité. At Alice's insistence they'd strolled up through the Latin Quarter, stopping for coffee at Café Mabillon – a favoured haunt of theirs historically, as it was always open super late – and along boulevard Saint-Germain, the scene of many a shopping spree, and had a brief browse at the bookshop they all loved, Shakespeare and Company.

Jules shrugged disinterestedly. Alice was in a strange mood, regaling them with reminders of previous nights out and things they'd got up to when they were younger, and Jules was trying to concentrate. It was busy around the boat terminal, with flocks of tourists figuring out where to go. A few knocked into Jules as she steadfastly stared at her phone.

'... Remember when you bumped into that guy you were seeing from your course, Neen, on your way home, and you were wearing the same clothes from the night before?' Alice laughed, as they settled on the boat's orange-red plastic chairs.

Jules felt her eyelids flicker, weighted by the rocking of the boat. The adrenaline that had kept her up all night was abating, the waves lulling her towards sleep. The light was almost blindingly bright so close to the water, sun streaks obscuring her vision as she squinted. She was finding it really hard to keep her eyes open. She had some study drugs one of the interns had given her in her desk at work. She wished now she'd had the foresight to bring them. Actually... didn't she plan to bring them home to dispose of them? She rooted around in her bag and found a pack in the secret pocket. It was like an epiphany. *Yes!* she thought to herself. *Yes!* She knocked two back with some water.

Her brain felt sharp again. Focused. She drew herself back

in, her phone out of the other women's sight line, and set up a couple of accumulator bets, placing large sums of money on each. Then she hit the online slots, hitting the same button again and again and again. She didn't like to bet this way, leaving everything to chance, she was more at home with poker and sports betting – she liked to think they had more cachet, being skills-based – but time wasn't on her side and, overall, her numbers were edging up and up. Her heart was really pumping now, sweat gathering on her brow. She didn't notice Notre-Dame or the little kid kicking her seat behind her or the concerned looks passing between Nina and Alice, who were by now quite bewildered.

'Jules, is something going on?' Nina asked eventually. 'Is there a problem at work?'

'Or... with Paul?' Alice added tentatively.

Jules ignored them, silently calculating her total amount of winnings over multiple accounts and apps.

*£82,000. Over halfway!*

*£83,000.*

She was almost awed by herself; the average person couldn't gamble like this. It was because she was clever and focused and had the requisite risk appetite.

'Jules?' Nina placed a hand over Jules's phone screen and Jules jumped, snatching it away. Her eyes wide, she glared back down at the screen, checking Nina hadn't inadvertently made a loss. Jules was gambling with large sums of money now and the slightest error could cost her dearly. She breathed out slowly as the roulette wheel once again fell in her favour. *£84,000.*

But it wasn't enough. She only had so many hours left and even she knew that she would have to sleep during some of them. She couldn't start making mistakes. And she couldn't tell her friends what was really going on. They'd never understand.

'Sorry,' she said. 'Just work.'

*£86,000.*

Time for a break. She clicked out of her accounts and apps and slid her phone into her bag. She closed her eyes and felt the spray of water and the sting of sunshine on her face. Was it morning or afternoon? Was she in Paris or someplace else? Behind her eyelids her vision swam with swirls of purple and jolts of white lights as her brain recalibrated.

'Hey,' she said, opening her eyes. 'I thought of something fun – and a bit different – we could do tonight… Who fancies a trip to a casino?'

# 7

## Paris, 2008

*Part Two: The Wedding*

Nina had been surprised to wake in her apartment without Ted there, but she wasn't alarmed. It had been decided before they eventually drifted off to sleep, strips of stardust and palms of heat still pressed against her skin. He would tell Alice first thing. Not about Nina, because it wasn't fair to hit her with being jilted and the betrayal of her best friend all at once. Ted would tell her he had had a change of heart about the wedding, they would send everyone home, and when the dust had settled, Nina and Ted would explain to Alice together what had happened.

It was strange, the feeling she woke with. On the one hand her gut twisted with the horror of knowing how hurt Alice would be, on the other a strange calm had descended on her, like things had finally slid into place since the moment she first laid eyes on Ted at Le Crillon. It wasn't great – in fact, it was a disaster – but nonetheless, it was how things were meant to be.

She paced the apartment in a T-shirt and knickers, drinking black coffee and smoking on the balcony, her eyes staring blankly over the rooftop of Le Bon Marché. *What was happening,* she wondered around 10 a.m. She hadn't heard from Ted or Alice, but he must have told her by now. She picked up and put down her mobile phone repeatedly, exhaling, her heart pounding with relief, or fear, she wasn't sure, when JULES eventually flashed up on the screen.

'Where are you?' Jules asked impatiently. 'The hairdresser's waiting for you.' Nina remembered Jules had been running errands for Alice's mother, Clemency, for twenty-four hours now. 'Did you go out last night? You'd better not be hung-over, Neen, for God's sake—'

'I didn't go out,' Nina cut in. 'The hairdresser's there?'

'Yes. You know this. The hair slots were from 9.30. You were 10.15.' Since becoming an investment banker, Jules increasingly spoke to Nina, and maybe everybody, like she was a child.

'I know. I just thought…'

Jules breathed heavily down the line and Nina tried not to let her irritability shine through. She knew how hard it was for her to be away from home, when her father was unwell.

'I'm not being difficult, I… Is Alice there? Is she okay?'

'Of course she's here!' She lowered her voice. '*Of course she's not okay*. It's her wedding day. One of her bridesmaids has gone awol and she's annoyed with Ted. Apparently he went out last night and got in really late, even though he promised he wouldn't drink before the wedding. Although he seemed fine to me,' she added as an afterthought.

'You've seen him?'

'Ted? Of course. I saw him down at breakfast. Why?'

'Did he seem okay?'

'He was eating. Chatting with Dickie and Lulu. Are you sure you didn't go out last night? You don't sound yourself.'

'I think maybe I ate something...' Nina trailed off, her speech faint, feeling then as though the life was drifting out of her body, twisting out of the windows and on to the streets of Paris. He hadn't told her yet. When was he planning to?

'You'll be fine, get over here. They're swapping you and Lulu around, so there's still time. Listen, Nina, I don't want to be unkind but... today's about Alice, yes? Don't make it about you.'

Nina winced. Most of the time she appreciated Jules's directness but today it stung, whipped over her skin like an icy wind.

'I would never do that.' She knew that she already had.

She hung up and called Ted immediately. He didn't answer. She kept calling, over and over until it went dead. He'd switched off his phone. She felt frantic then, because what did that mean? Had he changed his mind?

And then an unsettling thought struck her: he hadn't told her he loved her. The hours they'd spent in bed together, and he hadn't told her he'd loved her. But then nor had she told him. Did she need to have done? Wasn't it writ large? Why then was he at the hotel, eating breakfast with Dickie and Lulu as though nothing had happened? As if she didn't matter?

She would *never* have done that. She would never have betrayed Alice, or betrayed *herself* by doing that, unless she thought it was worth it. Unless she thought that she and Ted had a real chance at something.

She was crying before she realised she was, crying until she was struggling to catch her breath, crying until everything hurt. Her head and her heart. Panic seared through her, blistering and raw. She turned off her phone, threw it against the wall and briefly felt better. She threw other things then – cushions, books, throws – stopping only when her movement emitted a nauseating flush of Ted's aftershave from her T-shirt, which she'd slipped on after they'd slept together and he'd lain against as they spoke in quiet voices about what to do.

She could still smell him on her skin, her fingertips, could still feel his hands gripping her thighs. She got into the shower, scrubbing at her scalp, scrubbing at every part of her skin that he'd touched. She banged her head against the shower tiles in frustration. *She would never have done that.*

She was a different person now. Changed. She was a person who would sleep with her best friend's fiancé.

*It didn't matter that she'd loved him first!* she thought angrily as she drove a fist into the tiles, the grouting scratching over her knuckles. *It didn't matter!*

*She would never have done that to Alice.*

She sobbed until her throat was sore and dry, until the water in the shower ran cold, until there was nothing left. Then she sat shivering, on the empty floor of the tub, her hands wrapped round her shaking legs, and cried some more.

Sometime later she heard a fist pounding on her door and to her shame she thought: *Ted.* She wrapped a towel around her and ran, wrenching the door open to a furious-looking Jules, who had her hair pinned up and was wearing a mac.


'Jesus, Nina. I've been banging on the door for twenty minutes. Do you want us both to be late for this wedding?'

She took her in, her bloodshot eyes, her red, scalded skin, and put her hands on her wet shoulders. 'What's happened?' As she moved her hands her mac fell open, revealing a button-front slip dress. 'Alice has everyone wearing these while their hair and make-up's being done,' she explained, looking down at herself and rolling her eyes.

'I was being sick,' Nina said in a small voice. 'I told you. I think I ate something.' It was like she had shrunk, halved in size or more. She looked like she barely had the energy to stand.

Jules sat her down on her bed, made her some toast and dried her hair for her while she ate it, Nina flinching as the hot air blew over her inflamed scalp.

Jules said nothing, watching her carefully in the mirror, bewildered about what was going on. Secretly, she assumed Nina had been drinking last night, alone, had fallen over at least once, judging by the state of her knuckles, the disarray of the room. It wasn't good for Nina being in this apartment alone, not when she was still grieving Sylvie and with her issues around her father. Jules swallowed at the reminder of being so close to losing her own. She'd paid up front for her room at Le Crillon but she'd stay here tonight with Nina.

She moved around and knelt in front of her. 'I'm sorry you're not feeling great, but we have to be there for Alice today. She's in a bit of a flap already and Lulu's not helping.' She grimaced. 'We'll get you fixed up, you just need to be there. No one will notice if you're not on form. Get through the service and once they've done the photos you can sneak off to have a lie-down in my room. Take it a few hours at a time, okay? I'll be there with you.' She reached down and hugged her, holding her tight, realising as she did that she needed this hug as much as Nina did. She and Lev were still on-off dating, had been for the last six years, but he seemed disinterested in Jules's sadness over her father's decline and in any event wasn't much of a hugger. Jules needed someone to speak to but, as ever, she felt incapable of finding the right words.

Nina felt like she was in shock. Despite the ringing in her ears she knew Jules was right. She couldn't ruin Alice's day by not turning up. Hadn't she done enough? She could get through a few hours at a time – minute by minute if necessary. Alice would be busy. She wouldn't notice Nina's demeanour, wouldn't sense her broken heart, or the depth of her shame. But what would she do when she saw Ted? She'd have to avoid him. It was the only option.

In the taxi she turned her phone back on. Four text messages flooded through at once. Three from Jules:

WHERE ARE YOU?

ALICE IS FREAKING OUT.

I'M ON MY WAY OVER IN A TAXI.

And then a single text from Ted:

I'M SORRY.

★ ★ ★

Alice couldn't put her finger on it, but something wasn't right. The flowers had finally come together; the place settings were immaculate; the chandeliers gleamed; the ballroom felt laden with anticipation, a heady mix of polish, vanilla and rose; but she felt a sense of unease she couldn't place. She'd felt sick all morning, her empty stomach swirling with acid, but was unable to eat anything.

'I felt terrible on my wedding day too,' the make-up artist chipped in.

'Maybe you've caught Nina's bug,' her mother said. 'Terribly unlucky.'

Alice glanced at Nina. She was staring out of the window, across Place de la Concorde.

She'd looked terrible when she arrived but fortunately the make-up artist had returned her to her natural pallor. She looked beautiful, of course, she always did, and Alice felt a frisson of pride at having Nina, Jules and Lulu by her side today, in deep-emerald asymmetrical gowns with a gold piping trim. Jules looked stunning; she'd had her eyes lasered recently and no longer wore glasses and the medication for her skin was working wonders. It looked so clear and fresh, almost flawless. Alice gazed down at the black-and-white tiles of Le Crillon and felt thankful. Grateful to this building for bringing Jules and Nina into her life.

Time passed at a dizzying pace: hair, make-up, photographs. Soon she was back in the ballroom of Le Crillon, facing Ted. *This was it.*

Ted was ashen grey. She smiled at him meaningfully, a sign of forgiveness for his going out last night. He was nervous about his speech, she knew, but he needn't be; he was a natural orator.

'I do,' she said, but it was just a formality: no one else knew that Alice and Ted had legally married last week in London (which saved a whole lot of bother in legal requirements) except for her parents, who had acted as witnesses. They'd all agreed to keep it quiet to preserve the sense of romance for the occasion. And then, *voilà*, it was done.

The dance floor throbbed with life as Nina wound her way through it. She had grown angrier – and increasingly intoxicated – as the day wore on, vexed and coarse, swearing and muttering to herself as she fake-smiled at the photos (*for fuck's sake*), at the little pageboy in tails who asked her to dance with him to the string quartet while they milled around before dinner (*little prick*), and after Ted's speech (*cunt, cunt, cunt*). She wasn't sure whether they were audible or not, but as the champagne flowed she cared less and less. The only thing that was making her smile genuinely was the tiny nervous glances Ted would shoot in her direction.

She was drunk enough to convince herself that what she'd done wasn't that bad.

*I fucked Ted because I am a woman and I am a sexual being and I have needs*, she thought to herself in the restroom's gilded mirror. *I needed him and he needed me and* – Wow. Even the walls are marble in this place... She ran a finger along the surface, simultaneously thinking *you are really drunk*.

Her mind slipped and rewound as she sashayed on the dance floor: *But what about Alice? Alice, Alice. Your* best friend *Alice—*

*No. No. No.* Nina wrestled the thought away as she knocked back the rest of her drink and threw her empty champagne flute behind her. 'Hey!' someone shouted, but she shrugged and carried on dancing.

She felt betrayed by Alice even though she knew Alice had done nothing wrong. Thoughts she had never before formulated came to her now, fully articulated. *I saw him first. He was mine.*

*But that's okay*, she thought, in a whiplash reversal, feeling truly magnanimous, dancing with her head tipped back and her hands stretched either side of her. *I've let him go because I love them both.*

She took a deep breath. *I love them both but I deserved that one night. I deserved the universe giving us one hot, perfect night because we needed to get it out of our systems. So the universe could reroute and take its expected course. So we could both go back to loving* Alice *because – Alice, Alice, Alice...*

She held her fingers to her temples, allowing the deep feelings of spirituality she was experiencing to wash over her, like the beats on the dance floor. And then she heard it. Like a calling card. That song she hadn't realised she liked so much, about wishing your girlfriend was hot like... *OMG she loved that song!*

It felt so right, in that moment, to embrace her womanhood and her sexuality and to unapologetically *give it* to the dance floor.

The dance floor heaved with hundreds of girls called Catherine and Sophie bumping and grinding to the music, singing at the top of their voices. The bounce from the parquet trembled from Nina's feet to her thighs, vibrated in her groin. She flicked her hair up and felt it settle back round her shoulders. *Sexy!*

She swung her body left to right, grinding her hips down towards the floor, curving her body like a wave as she moved back upwards. Her hands were grasping her own breasts when she spotted Ted across the room and bored her eyes into his in as sultry a way as possible: *'Don't cha?'* she crooned, thrusting her hips energetically. *'Don't cha?'*

She just about stopped herself from switching girlfriend to wife, feeling a deep and solemn loyalty towards Alice, and spun her head away from Ted's.

The more she jerked and twisted on the dance floor, the more the space seemed to open up and it spurred her on: the crowd parting, pulling back, to observe this woman in all her glory: this sexy, alluring *beast*. She started to crook her legs open further, her labia practically sweeping the floor as she rolled her hips, fingers in her mouth seductively. *'Don't cha?'* she sang, head bopping and wiggling from side to side. *'Don't cha?'*

She looked for Ted again but couldn't see him. Instead, there was a row of people standing, staring, open-mouthed – Ted's Uncle St. John, whom Nina had met earlier and whose name she couldn't pronounce, Dickie, Lulu, the little prick pageboy – *okay, maybe he's just a kid, not a prick,* she acquiesced – and Jules. Her beloved Jules. She looked cross about something. Something must be going on. Why is everyone looking?

Nina wondered whether she should go and try to help but she couldn't quite tear herself off the dance floor, the stirring, sultry beat slipping through her veins, her body moving now of its own volition. She was gripped by a sudden inspiration!

*I should do our dance!* The one we made up when we met! That will distract everyone!

Jules must've had the same idea because she was approaching the dance floor at speed. 'Jules! Jules!' Nina shouted, jumping up and down. 'Let's do the lift! Let's do the lift! No, you go back!' She gestured, shooing her away as she giddily hopped backwards to give herself a good run-up. She adopted an athlete-on-the-starting-line pose, her dress riding up further to reveal her knickers, and began to run, the dance floor seeming to elongate as she did. The more she pumped her arms, the further away Jules seemed, but soon Nina was upon her and Nina was so happy! So happy in that moment, to be there at Ted and Alice's wedding! So fucking happy!

She felt herself lift into the air as she vaulted towards Jules, heard the slit of her dress finally ripping as a rush of cool air met her knicker-line, and saw a look of sheer panic on Jules's face. Then it was over.


Alice felt as though she was in a dream. It had happened. She was married. Officially and now romantically. She shrugged off her feelings earlier as pre-wedding nerves, giggled with Ted about Nina's antics on the dance floor as they walked together to their suite. 'Shhhhhhhhhh,' he said, putting his finger to her lips and sweeping her up to carry her over the threshold of their room. Ted had seemed happier and happier as the day wore on, relief wreathed around his eyes after the ceremony, after the speeches, after the numbers on the dance floor had dwindled, and he had ended up in the hotel bar with Alice's father and brothers, where they'd spent the last few hours.

He carried her into their suite but tripped, and she fell, and they landed on the carpet in a heap together. Fat tears gathered in Alice's eyes as she laughed and they wriggled to face each other. Her tears quickly misted to drunk lust as Ted put both hands on her cheeks and kissed her, his kiss laced with whisky and salt. She tried to extract herself from her dress, winding her arms round to undo the bodice.

'Allow me,' said Ted, kissing her neck and flipping her over on to her front. They both chuckled, surprised by the smoothness of the move.

'Mrs Astor,' he murmured, kissing her shoulders, and Alice thought it was the sexiest thing she'd ever heard.

'I like it,' she said.

Ted took one look at the intricate lacing and decided to leave the dress on.

Ten minutes later it was done.

*Welcome to the rest of your life*, Alice thought happily as she fell asleep face down on the carpet of Le Crillon, Ted tangled beside her.


Four hours later and one floor below them, Nina gingerly opened her eyes, without a clue as to where she was. Her eyes felt glued together and she remembered her contact lenses, and her fake eyelashes and the layers of primer and shadow and highlighter caked over her eyelids by the make-up artist yesterday. *Why was she at the hotel?* She rolled over. Jules was next to her, her lip cut, one eye dark and swollen. *Wow, she must've had a skinful*, Nina thought.

She made it to the bathroom, her legs shaking as she did a wee. The longer her eyes were open, the worse she felt. She checked the time: just after 6 a.m. She performed her usual early morning routine – a large glass of water and painkillers – and climbed back into bed, falling straight to sleep.

A few hours later she heard something clunking near her head and opened her eyes to see Jules setting down a cup of coffee – black, as Nina liked it – her face set in a frown. This time when Nina saw Jules's black eye, she remembered. *Oh shit*. She groaned and covered her face with her hands.

Jules sat on the edge of the bed.

'Do you want to tell me what's going on?' is all she said.

The day and the night – and the previous night – came back to Nina in crashing waves of mortification. She curled up into herself, pulled the duvet over her head and from beneath it told Jules everything.

'How could you?' Jules asked, in a bewildered tone so foreign she didn't sound like Jules at all.

'I love him,' Nina repeated, over and over. 'I've always loved him.'

Jules sat beside her as her tears fell, not condoning her behaviour but not condemning it either. A gesture Nina would never forget. 'I know,' she said simply. 'I know.'

They sat together for some time, Nina in a white waffle bathrobe with her knees pulled up and her arms locked round her legs. Jules, dressed already in jeans, a shirt and a blazer, stared at the wall and every now and then delicately touched the swollen area around her eye with her fingertips. *She needed to get back to London, she was hoping to see her father this afternoon, but how could she leave Nina like this?*

'I'm going to tell Alice,' Nina resolved. 'I don't want to ruin their marriage, but she deserves more. More than both of us...' Her voice grew watery and thin. 'I know I don't deserve her friendship any more.'

The thing about not drinking, the thing about spending a lifetime observing people to try to fit in, as Jules had done, is you notice stuff. Like a bride raising a champagne flute to her lips and setting it back down without taking a sip, swapping it with her new husband's less full glass. Like a bride surreptitiously avoiding all the blue cheese in her salad course. Like a bride whose breasts are just slightly fuller, her corset requiring the tiniest fraction less tightening, the distance between the ribbons imperceptibly wider.

'Nina,' Jules said, 'Alice is pregnant.'

# 8

## Saturday p.m.

*Nina*

'What the fuck is going on with Jules?' Nina whispered to Alice back at the apartment. She had put a shirt on, open over her vest top, and it billowed theatrically as she gesticulated. Alice was looking equally aghast, both by Jules's behaviour and Nina's current outburst. She'd grown used to Nina's calm and centred demeanour and wasn't prepared for this change. 'She fell *asleep* on the boat! *What the fuck?* We're in Paris!' she said, as if it were a very affront to Paris. 'Motherhood, or the *pursuit* of motherhood rather,' she blustered, gesturing at Alice as if to say 'I don't mean you', but Alice took it that way anyway, 'makes women *crazy*!' Which was ironic, Alice thought, since she was the only one of them who was a mother and she was acting the least crazy right now.

'I know, right?' she said awkwardly. The weekend wasn't working out how she'd envisaged and she pondered why she wasn't wandering around an art gallery right now, finding some peace in this busy city and thinking about her own life and what she was going to do. She glanced towards the bedroom door, where Jules had crashed out a while ago. She'd slid between being asleep and awake on the boat, as if she'd been drugged, and when the trip finished they'd had to help her off and into a taxi and take her back to the apartment. She was fully clothed, in an oyster cashmere sweater, black cigarette pants and her Chanel ballet flats, lying on her back and snoring.

'Do you think she has a secret drinking problem?' Nina asked. '*Something's* going on, that's for sure. I didn't want to say anything, but I saw a weird text from Paul on her phone yesterday. Something about not being able to ignore something. She snatched her phone up so I couldn't see it properly.'

'Maybe you're right,' Alice gulped. 'When would she have been drinking this morning, though? Hang on a minute...' She crept into Jules's room, returning with her bag, withdrew a bottle of water and sniffed it. 'Definitely water,' she said. 'But this is odd...' she added, putting the bottle back and extricating two phones from Jules's bag. 'Do you think she's having an affair?' she asked.

'No way,' Nina said. 'She'd never do that.' But then the thought flashed in her head: sometimes good people do bad things. Hadn't she herself done the same? 'I'm sure I've heard her mention having a different phone for work. To keep things separate,' she mused.

Alice replaced Jules's bag, careful not to wake her. As she returned Nina's phone flashed with a message and both women started at the sight of the sender: Paul.

'Dammit,' muttered Nina, opening the message and reading aloud. '"Hey Nina, just checking in, I've not been able to get hold of Jules. Is everything okay?" That's strange, isn't it? She's only been away since yesterday.'

'Maybe you're right about Paul? Maybe he's controlling her and being away from him has turned her a bit bonkers?' Alice asked.

'But why would he book a weekend away if he was controlling? None of it adds up.' Nina frowned, tapping out a message back: '"Hey Paul, all good, we're chilling at the apartment." That's okay, isn't it? Do I need to say anything else? Oh! "We only have one charger between us so maybe that's why you can't get in touch with Jules."' She pressed send.

'She's under a lot of pressure. Who knows how the next month is going to go?' Alice said, twisting her wedding ring around her finger.

'Hm,' Nina agreed, but she was seething. She had so much on her mind she could hardly think straight. They were all here for Jules. And Jules was... she didn't know where she was, but not here in Paris, that was for sure. Nina's phone began to ring, and she groaned. *Paul.*

'Oh God, I have to answer, don't I? I've only just messaged him back.' She took a deep breath and smoothed down her hair, as if that might help. 'Hi, Paul!' she said, answering enthusiastically. There was something comforting about Paul's voice, it drew you in, warm and deep, and she felt inexplicably guilty when he asked to speak to Jules and she had to explain she was asleep. It was the middle of a sunny Saturday afternoon in Paris, after all. If Paul thought she was lying, he didn't show it. 'No problem, Nina,' he said, 'I'll check in with her later.'

Nina clicked off and Alice, who had been able to hear the conversation, shook her head in bewilderment. She looked through the door to Jules's sleeping figure. She looked peaceful and calm.

'Neither of us know what it's like, do we, to go through something like this?' Alice said, and Nina, whose heart had been pounding while she spoke to Paul, began taking big calming breaths. Alice was right. There's no correct way to behave when you're processing trauma – or preparing for more – in the way Jules was and they were her closest friends. Whatever was going on, they had to be here for her, however difficult or uncomfortable it might be.

At 7 p.m. they woke her. She opened her eyes, groggily at first, before they sprang wide open and she reached into her bag for her phone. Nina got there first.

'I don't know what's going on,' she said, placing a hand over the screen, 'but I do know a night out with your girlfriends – and not being attached to this – will help.'

Jules nodded meekly but Nina had the sense she was just doing it to acquiesce until Nina had left the room.

'Are you okay?' Nina asked. 'You know you can tell me anything?' and the secret flashed between them. Nina looked at Jules meaningfully; she would treat any confidence Jules shared with the same respect as Jules had done all those years ago for her. And Jules couldn't have done anything worse than that, she thought. But there was a misconnection between them, Nina's imploring energy finding nowhere to go and faltering. Jules wouldn't meet her gaze, her eyes downcast, as Nina left the room.

Jules took a long time showering, but still hadn't found time to wash her hair, Nina noticed, and a long time in her room getting ready, emerging in a sleek black silk dress, her hair piled on her head. She seemed happier, more like her usual self, as she strutted ahead to flag a taxi to Oberkampf, Nina and Alice close behind in a denim jumpsuit and floral cocktail dress respectively.

'Oh, Paul called,' Nina said, remembering in the taxi, as the city flashed past them, black and gold, their legs squashed side by side. 'He said he'd been trying you, but I explained the charger situ.'

'Oh yes, he said,' Jules answered, not meeting Nina's eye. 'I called him while I was getting ready.'

Nina glanced at Alice and she shrugged and pulled a quick *well, there you go* expression.

They sat at the countertop at the restaurant, over the open kitchen. It was industrial-chic, wood and steel, the food French-Korean. Nina watched the chefs carefully as they prepared the surprise tasting menu (the only dining option), hoping there wasn't any raw fish. Jules was on form, slipping away for long stretches to use the bathroom but returning happy, almost giddy. *Was she on drugs?* Nina wondered. But that wasn't the Jules she knew. So strait-laced in that respect, almost prim. She'd baulked when an intern gave her some study drugs and only pretended to take them at work to fit in.

'You're not drinking,' Jules said suddenly to Nina, her eyes flitting rapidly between the bottle and Nina's glass. 'Have you had a drink this weekend?' It was like Jules had been living in a fog but the fog had cleared.

'What? Of course I am,' Nina said in a strangled voice, taking a gulp of her wine and holding it in her mouth. She swallowed it under Jules's intense gaze and noticed Alice staring at her with a strange look on her face too, as though trying to work something out.

'We shared two bottles of wine last night,' Alice said, but her voice wavered, as though it was a question rather than a fact.

'I'm not drinking *as much*,' Nina said, waving her glass around. 'I told you, with the stress of the new launch my IBS has flared up and you know how red wine gives me the shits.' She smiled broadly, not letting the tiniest chink of doubt in. If her friends looked too closely, they would see. 'So what's the deal with the casino?' she asked, to change the subject, and because she thought at least an activity would get Jules off her phone. Nina had been to a casino once before and it had been fun. She'd won fifty quid.

'Tarv from work told me about it. He said it would be right up our street. Very glam,' Jules added, her eyes alight with enthusiasm. 'There's a nightclub on the floor above. An Oskia.'

'Isn't that the one with booths that cost a thousand pounds, and sparklers streaming from bottles of champagne and vodka are paraded through the crowds?' Alice asked. There was a branch in London that Ted frequented on work nights out.

Jules winced. 'Afraid so, but we don't have to get a booth. Anyone can go to the bar and Tarv said the music's great. I fancy a dance!' she added, unconvincingly: she looked exhausted.

'It's not very *When in Paris* though, is it?' Alice said, but she looked at Nina and had the same thought: at least it's something constructive to do and might take Jules's mind off work or whatever was going on. 'Fine. Let's give it a go.'

★ ★ ★

*Jules*

She was doing it, she was really doing it. She was up another £20,000, juggling apps while she stood beside the shower and in her room while the others were getting ready and setting up an accumulator on international sports while they were at dinner tonight. She'd crested over £100,000. She was on the home stretch.

The study drugs were a welcome addition, sharpening her brain like a pin. God, she'd be even better at her job if she took those regularly. Her performance at work had been questioned recently. There were concerns about her reliability, forgotten when she delivered extraordinary results, as she did every now and then. But that wasn't new. She'd always been like that, even at school; she was just better then at covering up her weaknesses. She wasn't always on the ball these days. Her mind had been elsewhere, in fertility clinics or gambling apps. But all that was about to change.

The casino was a master stroke. It meant she could be gambling physically and digitally simultaneously. She watched Alice nervously place a €5 bet on the roulette table. €5 and you could get the same buzz as €500. Maybe a better buzz even, she mused, watching Alice's face twist in excitement as the croupier spun the wheel. Alice won! She squealed as the croupier handed over her chips.

'See?' Jules said. 'It's fun.' But watching Alice's glee, she felt something buckle inside her. Momentarily blindsided by the simple pleasure Alice gained from winning a €5 bet – €180 in total – compared to the stomach-knotting mess she'd found herself in.

She gravitated over to the poker table and waited quietly for a space to become available. When she played online her username was CityGirl1199, her avatar a cartoonish figure with long blonde hair, a cinched-in waist and a swag bag with dollar signs swung over her shoulder. That's who she was when she came to the table. She didn't often visit casinos, but when she did, she loved this bit. When she would slide on to a chair and the other occupants – men usually – would give her a cursory glance and maybe a smirk. *You have no idea*, she would think to herself before slowly commandeering the table, taking them out one by one.

Tonight was different. There was another woman, older than Jules, early fifties she would guess. She looked sensational, in a clinging red dress that accentuated her still high breasts – implants? – and blonde hair in a sharp, angled bob. A thick black stole adorned her shoulders.

'Celeste,' she said. She eyed Jules as you might a steak: hungrily, greedily. Jules was shocked to meet her eyes and see a jolt of recognition. They were the same. And in that moment, to Jules, that didn't seem like such a bad thing. She looked great, she was obviously doing well for herself and she was having a good time. Jules wondered what pain she was burying beneath the stacks of chips and then wondered if it mattered.

Celeste wasn't a bad player but Jules had her tells mastered quickly: her bob tucked behind her left ear, a twist of the hoop in her right. Jules knew her own tells and worked hard to override them.

'*Pfft!*' Celeste would exclaim when she lost a hand, often followed by an '*Alors…*' with a shrug. It was usually at this point that a woman would make her way over to Celeste and they would speak rapidly in hushed tones. Jules couldn't tell whether it was friendly or not.

'They always want me to stay! They love me here!' Celeste said melodramatically, and Jules swallowed uncomfortably, her eyes raking over the room. Noticing the small interactions between clients and croupiers and the casino management for the first time. Drinks being brought over, small gifts, extensions of credit. Jules was here of her own free will, as she was when she gambled online. How many of the others here were? There was a grubbiness to the scene she wanted to distance herself from.

Nina and Alice crashed over then, giddy. Alice up a couple of hundred euro and Nina down. 'Come on,' Alice was saying, 'champagne on me.' Jules saw Celeste smirk and felt a wash of embarrassment. They didn't see how things worked here, even though it was right in front of them.

'You guys go ahead, I'll catch you up,' Jules said, but to her irritation her friends stuck around, curious. She felt unmoored, exposed, her two lives intersecting.

'Where did you learn to play?' Nina asked in between hands.

'I'm no expert. We've had a few work things at casinos.'

'So you start with two cards, and if they're good you put in money to stay in the game, and if they're bad, you fold and leave the game?'

'Right,' said Jules, but she sounded distracted.

'And then three cards are laid in the middle, which anyone can use?' Nina continued. She'd spent a lot of time in pubs with her Uncle Seamus growing up.

'*The flop*,' Alice giggled. She knew that bit.

'Then you can put more money in and play on for another card...'

'*The turn*...'

'Right, *the turn*, and then if you're still going, and you put in even more money, there's one final card, *the river*?'

'Yep, you've got it,' Jules said quickly, then indicated it was time to be quiet as a new hand was dealt.

Jules looked at her cards and instantly stiffened, every hair on her body standing on end. She had a good hand. A damn good hand. She found the strip of white light in her head, the beam of calm. Focused on it, thinking ahead, through plays and possibilities. She surveyed the stacks of chips before her. She took a deep, steadying breath and pushed the whole lot over the betting line. €3,000. Behind her, she heard Alice gasp and she wondered what Nina was thinking. When it came to her friends, was this her biggest tell of all?

A squat, sweaty man folded, crossing his arms and glaring at Jules from beneath big bushy brows. She continued to glance at the other players. No hair tuck or earring twist from Celeste. Jules could hear the clatter of chips at other tables, the hiss of ice as glasses were set down. Her success was swift.

She played on. Winning more pots. Accumulating more chips. She was hitting the cards. There was a crowd building around their table now. Alice and Nina had moved to get a better position and on a rare occasion when Jules looked up, her attention briefly stolen from the game, she saw Nina and Alice were staring at her, beaming. Looking confused, but proud. She allowed herself a small, tight smile back.

'You only started with €50!' Nina whispered in a break and Jules didn't correct her. When her friends were busy playing roulette earlier, she'd slipped off and drawn a €35,000 cash advance from the new credit card she'd taken out last week, exchanging the cash for chips. Most of the €1,000 chips remained in the square gold handbag resting on her lap. She didn't know how she could get them in play without her friends noticing. Would she need to wait until they got bored and went off to the bar? That could take hours.

'Keep this up and you could quit the fund,' Nina quipped.

'Tarv said Oskia can get pretty busy.' She slid a €1,000 chip over to Nina and winked. 'Get the drinks in, yeah?'

Nina tsked and pushed the chip away with her hand. 'I'm not spending that on a night out. You should save it.'

Jules pushed it back towards her. 'Honestly, Neen, I want to. How often do we get to have a night out together? Let's do it properly. We'll get a booth.'

'It's €1,000,' Nina said.

'But I just won it. It's like... free money,' Jules said, although she hated saying it. She'd earned this money through skill and hard work. 'Seriously. Let's have some fun. I'll finish this hand and come join you. Why not? *When in Paris...*' she wheedled.

'If you're sure,' Alice said. She was quite drunk already and buoyed by her own win, forgetting her earlier reservations.

'Sure I'm sure,' Jules said, and she shooed them away good-naturedly. 'Go get some sparklers,' she smirked.


Once they had safely gone, she unclipped her bag. She checked her phone; her accumulators were coming in. Another £5,000 up. She removed the rest of her chips: €28,000. With her winnings at the table, she had €52,000 in chips in total, but that included the cash advance she'd withdrawn. Celeste watched her appraisingly, nodding her approval. 'You play,' she said, in a tone that suggested *You play properly, like me.*

Jules signalled to the dealer and kept her breathing steady as she lifted her new hand. She kept her face as neutral as possible. Her two cards were playable. An ace and a nine, suited: both hearts. Not the worst she'd had at this table, but not the best either. Luckily, nobody else knew that. The sensible thing, with the stakes they'd been playing, would be to call, but she had the crowd – and the table – in her palm. That counted for something. So rather than call, she raised, pushing in €10,000, upping the stakes. She resisted closing her eyes. Instead, she followed the game around the table, daring the other players to call her. Half the table folded, fearful of Jules's form and swagger, and she was confident her game plan was a success until it came to Celeste. She whispered to her casino contact, signed something, and raised Jules's hand: €20,000. *Was she calling her bluff?* Jules wondered. Without showing any hesitation, she called the extra €10,000. She had €20,000 on the table now and she fought to keep her breath calm and steady.

The dealer dealt the flop: five of clubs, six of diamonds, eight of diamonds.

A crack of a smile flashed over Celeste's face before it became impassive once more.

*Fuck*, thought Jules, *fuck*. There was nothing she could pair, not even any cards of the same suit! There was nothing she could do. Celeste pushed in another €20,000. If she called Celeste now she'd be betting with nothing, just to see another card. But she had over €20,000 on the table already. Too much to walk away from.

*You should fold*, she thought. *Fold*.

Celeste twisted her earring hoop and Jules tried to ignore the beads of sweat creeping into her hairline, the sudden fierce itch around her knicker elastic, the satin-like fire against her skin.

*You should fold...* an inner voice urged. But she didn't. She couldn't. *It wasn't in her DNA.* Instead, she leaned on one hand, curled her lips into a bored-looking gesture, and let her gaze rest on Celeste. Then she called.

In the seconds that the dealer turned over the next card, *the turn*, Jules's heart pounded. Sweat gathered under her arms and behind her knees.

He placed the card on its back: nine of spades.

*Fuck, fuck, fuck.* Her response was part jubilation, part trepidation. She paired her nine, but could Celeste have something? The possibilities ricocheted through her head. A straight? A flush draw? Perhaps even a higher pair in her pocket cards? And then Jules's pair of nines would lose. *Fuck*, she thought again.

Jules was still considering this when Celeste doubled the stakes, raising an eyebrow at Jules as she did. Jules breathed through her nose rather than swallowing, even though her throat was constricting. She couldn't lose €30,000, the money she'd put on the table. And she couldn't walk away from the total pot, nearing €100,000. Enough to bring her to her goal. But she didn't think she could win, either.

Her gaze was locked down now. All the other players had folded. Celeste was unlikely to have another nine, *but she could have...*

*Fold, Jules, fold.* Jules switched off her rational voice as quickly as it had come. Inside her shoes she curled her toes, flexing them backwards and forwards against the leather.

Celeste untucked and re-tucked her hair behind her ear, thin strands of blonde hooked between her fingertips.

*Play to win. Play to win*, she repeated to herself, her father's mantra. She pushed the rest of her chips in, sliding them across the table, Celeste's eyes alive, a vivid sage, matching the green baize surface.

'*Retournez vos cartes*,' the dealer said, and Jules noticed he had ceased being bored, his eyes darting between them as he – and the rest of the table and crowd – waited for them both to reveal what they held.

Jules turned over her cards and Celeste followed: a five and a four of diamonds.

Celeste was betting on a pair of fives and hoping for a miracle, or rather a seven, to win. Playing loose to get Jules to fold. Jules was doing the same, on a pair of nines. She would win unless Celeste got the straight.

Jules dared not breathe as the dealer turned the final card. The river.

*Not a seven*, she thought, *please not a seven*.

It was a king. The king of clubs.

Jules's hand flew to the bridge of her nose and she closed her eyes. She had won. It was over.

'*Pfft. Alors*,' said Celeste, pulling her stole tighter around her shoulders.

The dealer gathered the chips from the middle of the table and pushed them over to Jules. A fruit cocktail of chips. She touched them with her fingertips, hardly believing it was true.


As they left the table, Celeste sidled up to her. During the course of the game, her make-up had smudged, one shoulder of her dress had fallen down. Up close, she looked older, the glamorous sheen rubbed off. She put her red lips close to Jules's face and spoke slowly, every word carefully enunciated and laced with gin. 'Put... it... all... on... red,' she said, winking.

Jules walked shakily to the toilets, found an empty cubicle, mercifully cool, and sat on the closed ceramic seat, taking deep breaths, the heat and tension in her body beginning to evaporate. She'd done it. She'd really done it. She popped out her shoulder, clicking her fingers, the way Paul did sometimes when he listened to jazz in the kitchen while he seasoned steak and chopped vegetables.

She'd made around £165,000 in twenty-four hours, more than she'd intended to, successfully avoiding her husband and evading the attention of her friends. The additional £15,000 could even cover the cost of their IVF cycle next week. She couldn't resist relishing in the pride that consumed her. She wished she could tell someone. She felt bad keeping this all from her friends, but it was so close to being over now. She was so close to her next cycle of IVF, and they were sure they had the mix right this time, to stop her body attacking its own embryo... She was so close to her dreams coming true.

Fear tapped away at the edges of her subconscious. What if it didn't work? What if... she needed another cycle, and then another? What if they realised there was something else they could try, a different procedure or cocktail of drugs? Could she persuade Paul, to try again? It would be easier if she had the funds ready. Soon she was back inside one of her gambling apps, at a virtual poker table this time, but as real as the one she had just left. *I'll only gamble £5,000,* she promised herself. *I can make that back easily tomorrow morning. £5,000 and if I win, wonderful, and if I lose, I'll walk away.*

An hour later and she was another £30,000 up. Enough for two more cycles. She'd done it. *She'd really fucking done it!* She abruptly dropped her phones in her bag. She wished, fleetingly, that she could chop her hands off to stop her going back in for more. Chopping her hands off right then seemed a more realistic prospect than closing down all her apps and leaving them alone. She retrieved her phones again and turned them off. She considered flushing them down the toilet – her money was safe in her account until she transferred it – but it would be such a pain having to remember her passwords and set them up again. She drummed her fingers against the silk of her dress, then scooped the fabric into her palms, squeezing it as she fought the urge to succumb. Thoughts whizzed through her head. She needed to find her friends. She needed to celebrate. *Why do we celebrate so little these days?* she wondered. *You become an adult and what do you get to celebrate? When did life get less* fun?

She rubbed under her eyes in the mirror. Reapplied her lipstick. There was something else. There was something about Nina, tugging at her subconscious. Nina, Nina... what was she trying to remember about Nina? She pushed it aside. Her stock was up, her account was full, she had done the impossible. This was how she knew she wasn't an addict. She'd made back her losses, she'd pay off her debts and she'd be free. Free to start again.

She stretched her arms out and flexed her knuckles. The feeling coursing through her veins acutely pleasant, a divine high. She pulled her square gold bag over her shoulder and went to find her friends. Right then, it was the only thing that mattered.

*Alice*

The club was busy. Nina was chatting to a man when Alice returned. He was tall and well dressed in what seemed to Alice a very French way: blazer, T-shirt, casually tailored trousers, with a short dark beard and piercing eyes.

'Ah, here she is!' Nina exclaimed, gently signalling to the man she wasn't interested.

'He's hot,' Alice noted, as he retreated and Nina shrugged.

'I'm not looking for love,' she said, and Alice wondered how that could be true. Wasn't *everyone* looking for love?

'Did you speak to the children?' Nina asked.

'Hm,' Alice said, twisting her wedding ring.

'Everything okay?'

'I think so but, I don't know, you know when you get a vibe?' Alice huffed, puffing out her cheeks. '*Getting a vibe,*' she repeated, eye-rolling, scolding herself. *Why can't she speak normally?* 'Oh, I don't know. Ted said everything was fine, but he seemed a bit uptight and when I spoke to Charlotte – who should be in bed – she seemed a bit off. Speaking very fast, something about BTS, and not making much sense. Talking about a game with her friends.'

Charlotte had matured later than her peers, so Alice had been initially delighted when she became interested in the Korean boy band BTS, and it was a welcome break from Pokémon, her previous special interest, but six months of non-stop trivia and their insanely catchy songs was wearing thin.

'That's good, isn't it? She's playing with other children?'

'Yeah, *online*, but you have to be careful how long she's on there for. It scrambles her head a bit. And I don't know, sometimes the other children can get a bit mean. You have to keep an eye on it. I do tell Ted all this stuff, but he only ever seems to be half listening. He'll just be pleased she's on the computer, keeping quiet.'

Nina listened to all this anxiously; she'd been copied in to a number of work-related emails from Ted this afternoon. She felt somehow responsible, and she didn't want Alice to know his attention was being split between the children and work. She reached over and gave her a squeeze. 'Listen, I know it's difficult being away from them, but I'm sure Ted's got it under control. And even if he's finding it difficult, they're at home, their dad's there, they're safe,' she said firmly. 'Try not to worry. It's our last night in Paris, let's have some fun!'

Nina ordered champagne. '*No sparklers!*' she emphasised, but the weight on both their shoulders wouldn't shift so easily. Alice was worrying about Charlotte, Ted and the embarrassing messages to Mr Hough. Nina was worrying about the baby, *her* baby, and although she had only been taking tiny sips of any alcohol when she had to over the weekend, she was starting to feel uncomfortable about that too. As much as she had been trying to ignore it, or to tell herself she didn't want it, there was a baby inside her and that meant something, didn't it? What it meant, she wasn't sure. Both women looked down at the table, lost in their own thoughts, the liquid in their champagne glasses – Alice's half empty, Nina's barely touched – vibrating with the bass.

'Jules is right. You're not drinking, are you?' Alice said and Nina wondered whether she should seize the moment. Tell Alice about the baby. But her thoughts were too jumbled, tied up in what had happened before. She didn't know where to begin.

'I don't drink as much these days,' she said, which was true, but she knew that ordinarily she would still have drunk *something*. 'And it aggravates my IBS,' she added, but it sounded feeble, like she was clutching at straws.

Suddenly Jules appeared. She seemed longer limbed, her dress catching more light, her hair more lustrous and full. She was electric. Gliding, euphoric, on a high. She slid on to the circular leather couch and reached for the champagne bottle and a glass.

It was unspoken between Alice and Nina that they would drop their conversation now Jules was here.

'Did you win?' Nina asked.

'Oh, *I won*,' she said, beaming. 'When in Paris!' The champagne bubbled and fizzed in her glass. 'What's happening?' she added quickly with a frown, as she clocked the downcast mood.

'It's nothing,' Alice said quickly. 'Just me moaning about motherhood. I'm sorry. I know I shouldn't moan.' She stopped. She'd had enough of pretending her life didn't have its own challenges and they were of equal weight to Jules's. Maybe it was the champagne talking but everything felt overwhelming, and she needed to offload to her closest friends. 'But...' She took a deep breath. 'I'm finding everything so hard at the moment.' Her voice was low, catching on her words as though she were struggling to maintain control. Her friends only just heard her over the thrumming bass in the club.

*There it is*, she thought. *I've done it*. And in the same way as when she asked Ted a question about the kids or spoke to the headmaster at Charlotte's school, she braced. Because her problems weren't as deep as Jules's. She had a family, children, the one thing that Jules wanted and couldn't have; and complaining about it, when they were here to support Jules before her IVF, wasn't on. She took a deep breath, her teeth digging into the flesh of her cheek, in anticipation of the fallout. But she needn't have. Jules, imbued with a bonhomie Alice couldn't recall seeing in her since their early twenties, angled herself towards Alice and swung an arm around her, squeezing tightly.

'You can say whatever you like, Alice. Don't ever apologise,' she said, almost fiercely, because Jules could see it too. The delicate erosion of Alice over the last few years, the absence of Ted to support her. Jules realised she'd been watching her friend, in water up to her chin, drowning, not waving. The messages about her forgetting a school appointment, or another catty comment from a parent in the playground. All prefaced now, Jules realised, with a laughing or crying face emoji, to soften any irritation Jules might feel. And she had felt it on occasion; she'd wanted to be there in the water with Alice, managing the juggle of family life, the maelstrom of those busy days. That was why she didn't know all the names of the mums at school, like Nina. She'd done what she could – like the ASD auction – but from a safe distance, paralysed on the shore.

'The truth is,' said Alice, 'I feel like I've lost something. I've been cheated. Being a mother... it's not... it isn't...'

Rather than Nina looking awkward, as she was sometimes

wont to do, her eyebrows moved together, like a bridge, perfectly symmetrical, her eyes full of understanding. Jules wore a similar look of compassion; of something clicking into place. It emboldened Alice to continue.

'I know I'm so lucky to have them, all of them, but I feel like I'm letting each of them down in different ways. Charlotte's a puzzle I keep trying to *fix* but I can't... Phoebe and Wilf miss out because I'm so preoccupied with Charlotte and it's frustrating – we're all frustrated – because when I do get to spend time with the twins it's so *straightforward*. And imagine having three like that! Three straightforward children. Yes, there's scuffed knees and moaning about all the usual things, but it's so *easy*. And there's so much fun stuff we could do together. But *nothing* is easy, and *everything* is difficult and being a parent to an autistic child is *much, much* harder than I could ever have anticipated and I'm messing it up. I'm constantly messing it up.' Tears rolled down her cheeks and on to the velvet top of the table. 'I could've been a really good mum to a neurotypical child – or two or three of them.' She sniffed. 'Imagine the craft projects!' she said, attempting a smile.

Jules leaned forward. 'Well, maybe you could be a really fucking excellent one to an autistic kid,' she said, squeezing Alice's knee.

'With two really excellent aunties,' Nina added.

The women wrapped themselves around each other as Alice shuddered and rubbed under her eyes.

'It'll make them cooler people, you know,' Nina said. 'The twins. I know it's tough for them, but they're also learning. They love Charlotte, right? They're going to be kind and compassionate.' She smiled, then joked, 'Once they've got all their angst out in therapy.' And Alice laughed. 'Oh Lordy,' she said, head in her hands. 'The therapy bills!'

'Look, my mum was great, she worked hard and made sure I grew up in a house full of love, and there were no meltdowns or things like you have to deal with, but I still found it hard when she had Carey. I still felt pushed out. Even though I love Carey, and I would never change things. Families are complicated.' A look crossed her face which Alice couldn't read.

'You were like an extra parent to Carey,' Alice said, recalling Nina's weekend trips to the park with her little sister when Joanie and Liam were working. Alice had joined them once and it was clear Carey adored Nina, always side by side with a gappy-toothed smile.

'You know she's going off to uni soon?' Nina said, shaking her head. 'It'll be challenging for Phoebe and Wilf, of course it will, but it'll be so much more than that, Alice. Their lives will be full and rich and it will be because of you.' Nina's eyes were shining now and she sniffed. Alice felt her own eyes fill.

'Thank you. Both of you. I mean it. I really needed this weekend.' Her friends, and Mr Hough, were right. And something else was emerging. Something she wasn't ready to confront and name. 'Come on,' Alice said, standing up. 'Let's do this. Who are we if we don't embarrass ourselves on a dance floor?'

'I spot a raised platform!' bellowed Jules, wiping tears away from her own eyes as she led the charge.

They bopped with gusto, an enthusiastic trio, retriangulated on the dance floor. As they raised their hands to the sky, heads tipped back, Alice, not used to wearing heels, realised she couldn't feel her feet any more, but she didn't care. She felt so *happy*, so completely and utterly happy to be there, dancing in Paris, with her two best friends in the world. Her body felt like her own again, not the decaying temple of her younger self it had become since she'd had children.

*This is how we do it...*

For the first time in ages, she didn't care if she was doing something ironically or unironically, she was just enjoying it. She felt a hand around her waist and swung her hips backwards, laughing, expecting it to be one of the girls, but then she spun around and the hot guy Nina had been chatting to earlier unwrapped her from his embrace. She shook her head shyly and pointed at her ring finger. He shrugged, a slow, lazy smile. Alice locked eyes with Nina, who shook her head at her and waggled her eyebrows, in a *dirty dog* kind of way.

'Still got it,' Alice said, sashaying over, wondering briefly whether that was true. Deciding she didn't give a fuck. Beside her, Jules was dancing with an energy not witnessed since their uni years, both hands in the air, her hair flicking from side to side with abandon. The She-Ra.

'You're nuts but I love you!' Alice shouted.

'What?' Jules shouted back.

'I said... Oh, forget it.' Alice turned around and ground against her while Jules twerked and Nina clapped and laughed.

*Who could blame her?* Alice pondered later, luxuriating in the oozing softness in her brain, the velvet edges of her thoughts, as she stared at the photo of Mr Hough and tapped out a message to him.

*I have a crush on my teacher*, she wrote.

Hm. Too creepy?

She deleted 'on my teacher'.

Stared at the words until they swam hypnotically.

*I have a crush...*

She looked again at the photo, at the drops of sea water on his skin that she was desperate to lick off. The months of tension, of daydreaming, and now him, in message form, seemingly wanting the same. How could she resist?

*I have a crush on you*, she added.

Satisfied, she clicked 'send' and flopped on her back. She giggled to herself as she messaged the girls next door, then placed her phone on the nightstand beside her. She smiled in the darkness. Things were going to get better. She was fast asleep in minutes.

In the room next door, Jules had turned on her phone and a number of missed calls from Paul flooded the screen. She felt a tug of sentimentality. Her husband. Despite it all, her husband still loved her. She was loved. She called him back. She was ready to explain, to reassure him she'd fixed things. The phone rang out. Something was amiss but she couldn't place it. She clicked off sleepily. *I'll try again in the morning*, she thought. Like Alice, her hangover was already rattling in her skull, but her heart was full. She hadn't noticed the international ringtone.

In her bedroom, Nina was already asleep, her body curled on its side, less a question mark and more a haven, her hand on her stomach.

Alice, Nina and Jules slept deeply, happy in their Paris

bubble, content to know the other two women were near, their friendship as strong as it had ever been.

Each of them unaware that it would be a long time until they slept that way – or saw each other – again.

# 9

## Paris, 2015

Jules wandered around the Marché Raspail in a chic pale-blue linen dress with thin straps and a tie front, immersed in the scent of seaweed and brine as her head dipped to peruse the wares at a seafood stall. She and the girls were preparing dinner together later, one course each, and in a step change for Jules she had come without a list, ready to be inspired, and settled on oysters, shallots and Tabasco sauce.

Jules had always been a perfunctory eater; it brought her little pleasure. She understood the satisfaction in slicing through a steak as cleanly as butter, or the comfort of roasted garlic chicken with mash, but she wouldn't go out of her way to eat those things. A sandwich from Pret at her desk suited her fine, sushi if she had some extra time, but since meeting Paul she was enjoying food in a way she hadn't done previously. She was enjoying *life* in a way she hadn't done previously.

Jules had never believed she could be so happy. It was the sort of happiness she would have thought felt frightening, but it felt the opposite: safe, warm, content. Paul was the opposite to Lev: proud when she succeeded, supportive when she failed. He was secure in himself, which was the difference, and he felt fully evolved in a way that none of her previous partners or dates had been. He gave her space when she needed it, and she gave it back in return, not having to hide underlying feelings of clinginess, of wanting to grab on tight to him and not let go. Somehow, instinctively, she knew that she was his and he hers. *She knew*. And he knew too.

'This is Julia Frey, from the London office,' Hank had said when she arrived in New York for her secondment. The office was in the financial district, the sidewalks below as busy and bustling as Jules could have imagined, but up here, in the clouds, there was only the quiet buzz of industry. She loved it already. 'Julia, Paul. He's your competition over here.' Hank had winked, but when Jules looked at Paul – and saw him good-naturedly rolling his eyes and shaking his head at Hank – she didn't see competition at all. She saw confidence, sure, but no arrogance. His behaviour wasn't spiked with the desperation to prove himself of other bankers she'd worked alongside. His limbs were long and languid, his expression relaxed.

'So you're here to make sure we're not getting up to no good?' he enquired. The regulatory climate was intense at that time, compliance and anti-money laundering high on Austen Miller's agenda.

'Not quite. The opposite, actually. You've got more comprehensive AML processes over here – I've got to feed back on how you do it so much better.' She hadn't meant to sound flirtatious, didn't know why it came out the way it did.

'Really?' he said. 'How about that...' as she blushed.

'How *the New York office* is doing it better,' she corrected, adding *sexy* to her list of Paul's attributes. 'But I'm primarily transactional. Like you.'

'Well, I look forward to working with you, Julia Frey.' There was something about the way he said her name, a rough glint of cheekiness beneath his smooth tone.

She moved along to her own desk and sat down, blinking at the range of screens. *What had just happened?* It felt like someone had taken her to the top of the Rockefeller Center and pressed the button for the ground floor. Her stomach rose, her heart flew to her head.

'Drink later?' was all he said over the partition, and as she looked up and caught his smile she realised with relief that whatever she was feeling, he was feeling it too.

She nodded, surprised at herself. *What is wrong with me?* she remembered thinking. One of her personal rules was no dates with co-workers, and here she was five minutes in the New York office and finding it hard to concentrate. She tried to focus on the screens, on getting her bearings with the US systems, but the songs that so frequently got stuck in her head had changed their soundtrack. Snatches of love songs went in a loop around her brain. As soon as she managed to banish one, a different one would emerge. She was in trouble.

Eighteen months later and Jules and Paul were living together in London. It had been strange, actually, to leave him for the weekend, although now she was here, she was relishing the time with her oldest friends. She continued around the market, purchasing a sourdough loaf, some Mediterranean salted butter and a bottle of organic red wine.

She had a new job too: her boss, Ralph, had recently moved

to a hedge fund, and Jules had moved with him. Her first bonus was double what she'd have earned at the bank but instead of treating herself to a new pair of shoes and putting the rest into savings, as she ordinarily would, she had been dreaming of a trip to California with Paul, wine-tasting in Napa Valley, driving along the coast with the wind in her hair.

She joined a long queue at the end of the market and smiled to herself: she didn't even know what she was queuing for, but it smelt amazing. Ten minutes later she was eating a freshly made potato and onion *galette*, a warm pancake with Gruyère cheese oozing from its middle. She *mm*-ed with pleasure and licked her fingers as she strolled through the market. Strange it was a fellow investment banker who'd taught her to enjoy life, she thought, but Paul was very clear on his mandate: he did this job to enjoy nice things. 'I had to work twice as hard to get here,' he often said, and she didn't doubt it; she could count on one hand the number of black investment bankers she'd met at his level. 'I'm going to enjoy it twice as much.'

*What's the point in working these hours unless you're going to do this?* he'd said to her from a rooftop hot tub in Miami, an icy lime and soda in his hand, a month or two after they began dating and at the end of a particularly fraught transaction – her first in New York. For Jules, it had always been about the work. She hadn't considered what happened after the work, or outside of the work. She just wanted to be the best at her job.

*What drives you, Julia Frey?* Paul had asked, and she found she couldn't answer the question. *To do my best, to be my best*, which was true, but sounded too immature, too schoolgirl-like.

*To make my father proud* died on her lips, because although that was also true, her father wasn't here any more and she was still too close to her grief to articulate the way his death had left her unmoored. She worked because there was safety in it. She knew if she stopped, if she took time out, allowed her mind to wander, the strong current of her loss could quickly pull her under, the waves closing over her head. Work kept her focused.

The next morning Paul was up early, towel slung over his shoulder, his perfectly neat six-pack gleaming. 'Look at it out there!' he'd said. 'Let's go for a swim.'

Jules frowned. She'd had a number of emails come in overnight. Post-completion matters. She glanced at her laptop and he followed her gaze.

'It can wait,' he said. He was copied into the same emails. He held out a hand, drawing her up out of bed, kissing her neck as she stood. 'This can't.' He scooped her legs up and carried her, naked, over to the balcony where the sun was rising lazily, hazily, over the ocean.

'Come on. You've got to greet the day. Start it right!' His enthusiasm was contagious.

She slipped on her black bikini and a green silk kimono and they made their way to the beach.

'Come on, put your hands up! Come and greet this beautiful day!' he said, walking into the sea. Jules laughed, shaking her head, but followed him in, the water cool as it rose from her ankles to her calves. She put her hands up. With Paul by her side, she had begun walking into the sea with her arms open wide.

★ ★ ★

Her friends, of course, had noted the difference.

'I've never seen you like this,' enthused Alice, in an orange and blue maxi dress with a kente print and a navy chunky cardigan, sleeves pushed up as she laid the long dining table at Nina's apartment for dinner, candlesticks, fine china and all. She felt a tug of longing for the first flush of love. She was in the midst of married-with-three-children-and-no-sleep love. The kind of love that brought you coffee in bed in the morning and closed the door so you could drink it in peace, rather than whisking you off to Miami for the weekend.

'It suits you,' agreed Nina, appraising the activity in the kitchen in wide-legged jeans, a cropped olive-green jumper and one of Sylvie's silk scarves, a vivid tangerine, which she'd tied over her head, securing it with a knot. Still deeply committed to therapy, she had already probed Jules for details of Paul's background to check for any red flags and had come up with none. Earlier, she'd bought a loin of lamb from the butcher, cubed it and marinated it in a za'atar rub with a twist: cinnamon. She'd been steaming it for hours, a technique she'd found in one of Sylvie's old cookbooks. The aroma was wafting from the hob. Her favourite of Sylvie's cookbooks was well thumbed, splashed with tiny sprays of oil and small smears of herbs. Some of the dishes she recognised Sylvie having made for her and she was working her way through it, as a labour of love. The Middle Eastern twists had begun to seep into the menu at La City Pâtisserie too and had been a big hit with customers. There was talk of Nina bringing out her own cookbook, a fusion of Middle Eastern flavours and patisserie, but she felt that would be quite a leap.

She'd volunteered to cook the main course; since Alice prepared meals for five people three times a day, it seemed fair that she be the one to pick out a cake from the pristine counters at Le Bon Marché and she'd chosen well; a *gâteau Saint-Honoré*, circles of puff pastry and cream, decadently surrounded by small baked profiteroles dipped in caramelised sugar.

'We wondered how you were fixed for September?' Jules asked casually. She had changed out of her linen dress and into grey cashmere sweats to cook, finely chopping shallots into a yellow ceramic bowl with a Moroccan *safi* design she'd fished out of a cupboard.

'September?' Alice smiled, pausing from decorating the table, a glass of blush-pink wine condensing on the tablecloth.

Nina's thoughts (could she use coconut cream and caramelised honey with a sprinkling of toasted almonds for a City Pâtisserie take on the *gâteau Saint-Honoré*?) were interrupted and her eyes popped open wide. 'Is this for…?'

Jules nodded, her face the happiest her friends had ever seen it. She was radiant, resplendent with love.

'Yes,' she nodded. 'We're getting married.'

'Did he—' Alice stopped herself, feeling clunky and old-fashioned sometimes around her friends. 'Did you – did either of you – propose?'

'No. We had a conversation about it. Agreed we both wanted to get married. Decided September seemed like a good time.'

'Nice,' said Nina. She was liking the sound of Paul more and more by the minute.

'We wondered if you would do our cake? We'll pay you, of course,' Jules said. 'And Alice, if Charlotte and Phoebe could be bridesmaids and Wilf a pageboy? It'll be small. Just our families and close friends. In London.'

'I'd love that,' Alice said, but she felt a crackling of anxiety. The idea of getting Charlotte into a dress with her hair styled brought her out in a cold sweat. Charlotte had recently begun refusing to wear a school uniform, or to have her hair tied up per the school rules. 'But getting Charlotte dressed up might be tricky,' she said diplomatically, already wondering what she could effectively bribe her with.

'She can choose her own dress,' Jules said.

'Can she choose her own shorts and T-shirt?' Alice grimaced.

Jules laughed and both Nina and Alice were wowed again by this new, relaxed version of their friend. 'Sure she can. The important thing is she's there. That you guys are all there.'

'I would *love* to make the cake,' Nina said, already picturing layers of delicate sponge spiked with orange blossom and pistachios atop swirls of honey and cream. La City Pâtisserie was doing so well that she had been approached by investors, keen to help her expand with additional premises across the City. Nina couldn't believe her luck. A job she loved, that she was good at, and it was actually going well. But best of all was the deep pleasure she gained from her work. She found calm in the clean precision of patisserie, safety in the row upon row of identical items, light in the bright colours, delight in the names and the juxtaposition of textures and the histories behind each delicate morsel. She didn't need to do the baking any more, she had a small team she oversaw, but most days she made something, unable to resist the call of flour, sugar and butter; simple ingredients transformed into something spectacular.

She even felt better about what had happened with Ted. It was her rock bottom, her reckoning. She had accepted it; had forgiven herself for the mistake she made seven years ago. She knew she would have to tell Alice one day, but not yet. Not when things were going so well. Why would she undo that, and to what end? She snubbed the question out as quickly as it had appeared. Ted's firm had relocated and now occupied a floor of a shiny City tower close to the patisserie. He and one of his business partners, David, were keen patrons and one of the firms who had approached her regarding an investment. Alice, who had got wind of this plan, or was maybe even behind it, was keen. Nina thought she could work with Ted and David and it made sense with them being so nearby and her knowing Ted. She could ask him stupid questions and not feel embarrassed, as she might with someone she didn't know. She was considering it, fortunate to have options.

The women sat by candlelight in Nina's apartment, the Eiffel Tower flickering in the distance, making plans for the wedding and agreeing Jules didn't have to have a hen (Alice tried not to take offence at her friends' careful sidestepping of her own traditional nuptials, with – *gasp!* – a proposal and hen and stag dos), and yes, La City Pâtisserie would make an excellent venue for a reception dinner, and for the first time in a long while, things felt exactly as they should.

The next morning they'd sat on Nina's long balcony, eating croissants and reading magazines. Jules leaned her head on Alice's shoulder contentedly. 'Virginia Hoof at 3 p.m.,' she pondered aloud, looking up from her phone. 'In form, stays the distance, will be suited by the firm ground.'

'What are you talking about?' Alice giggled, a fizzing sound like soda hitting ice, and Nina felt so light and happy inside.

Jules smiled. 'It's my little thing. For my father. I put a bet on the horses once a week. Like we used to do together...' Her voice drifted but she wasn't adrift. She had come out the other side of her grief. She was grateful to her work – the long nights and fast pace having helped her weather the storm at its fullest. At her hardest moments – crying in the toilets, or unable to sleep after multiple Diet Cokes – she knew her father would have been proud. Of the way she kept going. Of the way she continued to excel. *Play to win*, he'd always said. And that's what she was doing; what she'd always done.

She placed the bet and looked up to the sky.

# 10

## Sunday a.m.

*Jules*

It was 7.30 a.m. Jules stared at a message from Paul in confusion. It said: 'I'm outside.'

Her eyes narrowed as she rubbed them, trying to clear the fog from her head. She wasn't used to drinking so much. *He's outside where?*

The doorbell rang. Suddenly, she was out of bed, pulling on her green silk kimono, the one that, many years ago, she had worn to stride into the sea with Paul but was now wearing to stride towards the front door, her heart hammering in her chest, like a horse on the final furlong. The apartment was silent, no sound coming from Nina or Alice's rooms.

'We need to talk,' was all Paul said when she opened the door, the middle of her dressing gown clutched in one hand.

'Hey,' she said quietly, shyly, as she stood back to let him in. 'What are you doing here?' she whispered, leading him into her room. He stared at her disbelievingly.

'I've been trying to get in touch with you all weekend,' he said.

She felt nervous then and opened the blinds and the window, suddenly self-conscious that her room might reek after her boozy evening with the girls. As light flooded in, she saw Paul surveying the scene, her laptop on the dressing table, the two phones strewn on the bedside table. They met each other's eyes and a wave of cold fear rushed through her, like being submerged in icy water.

Paul shook his head and she saw sadness rocking his eyes, like waves through a porthole. She stepped towards him but he moved back, swallowing, clearing his throat as if trying to avoid a rush of tears. His eyes kept falling to the two phones. She had promised him she had only one. For a time that had been true.

'I'm sorry,' she said, but it sounded too small against the weight of emotion in the room. She had been sure she could fix things with Paul when he was in London and she was here in Paris, the idea of it seemed possible, but now he was before her she wasn't sure. 'I… I need to explain. I'm going to tell you everything. And…' She stopped, trying to make eye contact with him, but his face, his beautiful face, was drooped towards the floor. She placed her hands on his jawline, flecked with stubble, and gently lifted his face to hers. He was crying. He flinched at her touch and she dropped her hands, his eyes remaining on hers. 'I'm going to change,' she said. The 'change' was anguished, her voice stretching and rising as she struggled to contain her emotions. She'd kept them so tightly locked all weekend but with Paul in front of her they threatened to overspill. 'I mean it this time. *I promise*,' she said fiercely, a sense of self-preservation kicking in.

He opened his mouth to speak but words deserted him, buckling under the force of his distress, as though sadness was filling him up. He shook his head.

'Paul, *please*. I...'

He drew in a jagged breath. He was drowning in his sadness and it was because of her.

Eventually, he spoke. 'I came to tell you.' He swallowed. 'I can't do this any more, Jules.' His tone was flattened with grief. 'I can't go ahead with the IVF. I'm done.'

'That's okay,' she said quickly. She felt a stab of guilt then. She knew how much Paul had been struggling with the IVF, but she hadn't tried to help, had she? It was like with Alice, she'd seen her struggling, but she'd felt powerless to assist when her own pain was so raw. It was like she was in a glass box, watching her friends and family moving around her, but she was unable to break out, to live beyond the confines of her grief. Her husband had needed her, and she'd deserted him and he couldn't do it any more. It was her fault. 'We can delay it. Wait for a bit—'

'No,' he said, his eyelashes batting as he struggled to make himself clear. 'I'm done. I'm leaving.' He couldn't bear to append a 'you' to his sentence, but Jules understood. They both understood. It was over.

She was staring at him now, her eyes and mouth open wide. She'd never seen him like this. Never felt his easiness solidify into something more resolute. She felt the barrier between them as though it were a physical wall; he had created his own glass box.

'You can't,' she said, disbelieving. 'Please, Paul, let me explain.'

'No.' He was firm.

'You're right. I did do it again. But I won it all back! Everything. And more. Almost two hundred grand! Enough to pay off my debts and for two, maybe three, more cycles! I'll transfer it to you now. And then I'll close my accounts.'

'I can't, Jules. I can't live my life always waiting for the next time. How do you think this weekend has been for me? I've been frantic. Ever since you left. Trying to speak to you. Trying your friends. And when I spoke to Nina yesterday and she said you were asleep, I *knew*. I knew you'd been up all night. And they couldn't see it!' he said incredulously. 'Your friends couldn't even see it. Because you're *so good*. You've got so good at lying' – Jules flinched – 'that your oldest friends can't even tell. I hoped...' He faltered. 'I hoped you'd tell them. Or I hoped they'd *see*. Or I hoped...' He was waving his arms around as though conducting an orchestra, summoning a sweet melody that might save them. '...that being with them would help you see how far in you are. How far away you are from the Jules I know.' He had his hands on his chest now, as though his heart had arrested and needed kick-starting.

'It's not the gambling. It's the—' She gestured at her abdomen.

'I couldn't have a baby with you like this, Jules,' he said softly. 'Even if we were able to.'

His words hung in the air. Years of trying. Years of failure and disappointment and grief and he wouldn't have a baby with her even if he could. The rejection permeated every part of her, every muscle tightened. She felt light-headed and her teeth began to chatter. She tried to keep talking. While he was still here, there was still hope.

'When did you come to Paris?' she managed to ask, the chattering not abating.

'Last night,' he said. 'I booked the next Eurostar after I spoke to Nina and came straight here, but you were out. I stayed at the Lutetia, down the street. I couldn't tell you this by text and I wanted you to have your friends around you.'

Even as he was leaving her he was trying to protect her. What had she done? Why had she driven him away?

'Maybe stay on in Paris for a few days with them. I'm sorry. I thought I could give it one last shot, but I can't. Not now. Another £70,000, Jules. What were you thinking?'

'How did you know?' she asked.

He shrugged. A gesture so familiar it made her ache, as though he were already gone. 'It was how you were behaving on Friday morning. Jittery, jumpy, as if you couldn't wait to get away. I knew something was going on but I couldn't put my finger on it. And then I looked out to your car, realised I hadn't seen you driving it in months, like last time. It all clicked into place.'

'But I've got it all back! Look, I'll show you. I've got it all back so we can start again.'

'It's not the money you need, Jules. It's something else.'

'A baby! I need a baby!' she said, hysteria in her voice now as her heart beat faster.

'You know...' he said. 'I'm not sure that's it. I've got to go. I have an early Eurostar. I'm going back to London to pack up my things. I'll stay at a hotel until I find something more permanent.'

'But that's madness! *Why?* Paul. *Please.*'

She began pulling on yesterday's clothes: cigarette pants and a cashmere sweater. She bundled the rest of her things into her case, the capsule wardrobe her personal stylist compiled in disarray.

She was outside, running to keep pace with Paul along the street, her small suitcase clattering behind her. The harsh sunlight reminded her she had a strident headache. Her throat was dry, her skin hot. She longed for water. She strode alongside him, him wiping tears from his eyes, her imploring him, begging him, to reconsider.

Finally, he stopped. He placed his hands on her upper arms and she grabbed at them, trying to draw him closer to her, wanting nothing more than for him to wrap his arms around her and tell her everything would be okay as he had done countless times before. He was her person. And she was his. *Why was he doing this to her? Okay, she hadn't always supported him but why wasn't* he *supporting* her *now?* In spite of everything, a surge of indignant anger rose up and submerged her guilt. *He was no better than her, if he left her like this?*

'Can we sit?' she asked, gesturing to a bench. 'If we could just sit down to talk? Please?' Hysteria was driving her voice upwards and her overriding sense of shame and not wanting to cause a scene was battling to keep it down. Against the tidal wave of emotion – frustration, anger, fear, shame – Celeste's voice sliced through, clear and calm: *put it all on red.* She shook her head free of her thoughts. The streets were still quiet but she was dimly aware of the Parisians who passed them, heads tilted with interest. She sniffed and composed herself, her fingers knotted in her lap.

He sat angled away from her, his eyes raking over the cobbled street, the small fountain, towards the river.

'Do you still love me, Jules? Sometimes I wonder, if you loved me maybe you'd stop? Maybe I'm not enough?' He was crying again, like he had all the times they'd received bad news, like he had the first time she'd done this. 'Actually, you know what, forget it. Forget I said that.' He pulled his jumper sleeve over his knuckles and rubbed at his eyes. He rolled his shoulders back, squaring his posture. She could sense him mentally preparing to leave, could imagine him reminding himself of what his therapist would have told him. She knew he knew but she reminded him anyway. She owed him that at least.

'It's not about you,' she said softly. He nodded.

'I know,' he said, 'I know. I wish I could reach you,' he sighed, but she was already shutting down, shifting further along the bench away from him, her own self-preservation stepping up.

'Can I transfer you the money, anyway?' she asked.

He turned and stared at her for a long time. His eyebrows furrowed, his lips pursed. 'Huh,' was all he said. 'Huh.'

She rolled her lips inward as she watched his expression unfold, surveying her.

'You know you'll gamble it. Two hundred thousand bucks and you know you can't hold on to it,' he said. 'Huh.' It was as though he was seeing her afresh. Had he realised she was in a worse position than he thought or were his worst fears being confirmed?

'No, that's not it,' she said, but her eyes had flown back down to the pavement. 'I know you'll look after it, that's all. It's a lot of money. And I've got debts to repay. I've enough now to cover it all. To start again. *Please*,' she said. 'Please take it.'

'What is this, if not an addiction?' he asked, his brown eyes burning into hers.

'It's a coping mechanism,' she snapped defiantly, in an *obviously* tone.

'Same difference!' He threw his hands up, exasperated.

'It's not my *fault*. If we could have had a baby, then…'

'I lost the chance to have a baby too.' He stood, his hands in his pockets, as though he were bracing himself against the wind, but it was a mild, sunlit morning. 'I'll always be here for you, Jules, but if I don't step away, this will destroy us both. I can't keep bailing you out.'

'You don't *need to*!' she said, standing up and clutching the handle of her suitcase. '*I won back the money.*'

'This time. You're an addict, Jules, and you need to do something about that.'

She watched him walk away. His shoulders hunched, his head bowed. '*But I love you!*' she shouted down the street, horrified but desperate.

He turned, put both hands to his mouth and extended them towards her: a goodbye kiss. His eyes were brimming and overspilling with tears. He didn't need to say it. He loved her too. He always had. But he was still walking away. He turned and left, his footsteps quicker this time, his head still shaking.

She looked down at yesterday's clothes; at the suitcase beside her. Her forehead was slick with sweat and she could feel her clothes sticking to the damp patches under her arms. It wasn't just sweat she was coated with, it was shame. She hated herself, she realised. She hated her job; what had once felt fresh and exciting now felt relentless and stale. She hated her boring, staid clothes. She hated her boring, staid life. She hated that she'd driven away the man she loved. The man who made all those things tolerable. The man who brought colour and joy into her life when she was so used to living in black and white. She hated that her body had failed her. Denied her the thing she wanted most of all. Driven her to this, because if she'd had a baby, none of this would've happened, would it? She hated that she'd betrayed her friends, had lied to them, and because of that she couldn't go back to the apartment and be wrapped up in their embrace. Because how could they ever forgive her? How could they ever understand when not even Paul, her person, her husband, could? She hated that she was alone in Paris, with nowhere to go and no one to talk to, knowing when she arrived back in London there'd be no one there either. She'd cut everyone off. But what she hated the most was that despite all this, all she could think was, *I should've put it all on red.*

*Nina*

Nina had also woken abruptly that morning. In fact, when Jules had ushered Paul into the quiet apartment, she hadn't noticed that the bathroom door was closed. She didn't know that Nina was in there, staring in shock at her knickers. She didn't know that Nina's heart was also pounding, rivulets of sweat pouring down her face as she gulped and wiped, trying to stop the flow of bright red blood.

'*No,*' she whispered to herself quietly. '*Please, no.*' How had she found herself here again? The same bathroom, the same moment of fear, the same feeling of judgement, from a higher power that she knew did not exist. Except last time she was there, it was the shock of new life growing inside her; this was the shock of a death. Although she knew better, it still felt like a punishment for what she chose to do then and the position she found herself in now.

'*But I wanted to keep you,*' she whispered, only realising in that moment that it was true. She leaned forward and opened the bathroom cupboard below the sink, hoping to find a sanitary towel. She was in luck. She was about to go to her room to find a fresh pair of knickers when she heard Jules in the corridor outside, talking to what sounded like *a man*. Her hand froze on the door handle. *What the fuck?*

Her eyes darted around nervously. She couldn't see Jules *now*. She couldn't explain. How could she find the words? As much as she loved Jules, and wanted to protect her, she needed to look after herself. She didn't have the headspace for Jules's grief – or anger – on top of her own right now. She heard the voices retreating, disappearing as a door closed. *Did Jules have a man in her bedroom?* She pulled a face – *Had she gone back out again last night? Brought someone back? Could she behave so out of control? It didn't make sense* – but she didn't have time to dwell on it; she needed to get into her room, get dressed, and get back to London, to a hospital. Suddenly she didn't want to be here, in France.

She heard Jules's bedroom door close and bolted to her room, dressing quickly in jeans, boots and a pale grey sweater, and throwing things into her small case.

She deliberated outside Alice's door. Alice would help her, but she wouldn't understand the riot of Nina's emotions; the acute sense of reckoning throbbing in her ears, as though she'd brought this on herself.

It was a quick and easy decision she had made, in this apartment, thirteen years ago. After Alice and Ted's wedding she'd stayed on in Paris, to avoid her friends and to get the apartment ready to let so that once she left, she didn't have to return. She couldn't imagine ever wanting to be within its walls again. It reminded her of her betrayal of Alice, her night with Ted and the baby she didn't want. It reminded her of a pregnancy test, taken at the end of that month, delivering a devastating result. Nina had never wanted a baby. When she pictured her future, it simply didn't have a baby in it. She didn't know why, and perhaps there was no reason; perhaps, as she was beginning to suspect, there didn't need to be a reason. Maybe Samir felt the same. Maybe it was one of the few things that united them.

The problem, thirteen years ago, was she didn't see anything in her future at all. She was pregnant by her best friend's husband. And her best friend was pregnant too. While Alice was in London excitedly telling her parents, Nina was alone on this floor, laptop beside her, googling abortion clinics. She remembered the realisation dawning. She couldn't carry on living that way. Car-crashing through life. Making one bad mistake after another – wrecking her career, her friendships, her relationships.

That month changed her life. That day in particular. She had stepped out into the bright sun, dazed by her news, on autopilot to her refuge, the one place that filled her with a sense of calm: the patisserie section of La Grande Épicerie.

*Plus ça change*, she had thought as she entered, filled with self-loathing, her eyes gliding over the trays of their signature Opera cakes, the chocolate hard and shiny, wishing she were here to collect something to bring to Sylvie. Later, when she was back in London, recovering at home, fearful of Joanie discovering her secret, reliving those awful days, her mind kept settling on that moment and she wondered whether the answer had been in front of her all along.

She closed the door quietly behind her and descended the stairs. She placed her keys in the key lock downstairs and hoped Jules and Alice remembered to do the same later. She should text them but she didn't know what to say. Outside, the streets were quiet as she made a lonely pilgrimage to the metro. Twice she had found herself pregnant and in Paris. But things were different this time. She had been starting to think that perhaps she did want to keep this baby; perhaps she could see a future in which a part of her – and a part of Flynn – had been replicated in a child. It hadn't happened too often that she would see Charlotte and wonder how her own child with Ted would have been, growing alongside her, but it had happened. She had everything she needed to raise a child: she was independent, financially stable and the father was a good man. But now, as quickly as the idea had been planted, it was being taken away.

She swiped at tears in the empty metro carriage and booked herself a space on the first available Eurostar at the station. She didn't want to tell Flynn she was losing the baby; telling him would only make it more real. But he had a right to know, didn't he? She felt almost like she was making a point to herself; Ted hadn't deserved to know, and that's why Nina had never told him, but Flynn did and Nina responded accordingly.

She sat alone in the terminal, ever so slightly shaking. It was a Sunday morning, so she couldn't contact her GP. Who could tell her if her baby had died? The hospital? Would she need an ultrasound? Could it detect something so tiny? Would it matter to anyone else but her? Her face felt hot but her fingers were cold. She typed in the name of her local hospital and asked for the maternity department, which rang out and out, clicking and transferring to unknown departments and receptionists, until eventually someone answered and in an uncertain voice suggested she go to A & E.

She couldn't bear that. To wait in a busy A & E department for hours, only to be told that her baby had died. She'd read the statistics on early miscarriage, knew instinctively that the best thing to do was to go home, to have the miscarriage there, to process the happenings of the last forty-eight hours. She had transitioned from shock to blossoming acceptance and now it was gone. Sadness enveloped her as she waited for her train.

She texted Luca to let him know she was coming home early, and explained she wasn't feeling well. His cousin had been staying in Nina's room that weekend and she wanted to crawl straight into bed and cry unhindered.

*So this is what it feels like to lose a baby*, she thought. *So this is what it feels like to want a baby.*

Her phone beeped with a text from Flynn: 'Hey, just checking in, you okay? What time do you get back later? I can come over if you want to talk, or we can catch up in the week, whatever suits?'

Her heart sunk further in her chest, the weight of her sadness pulling her deep into her chair. How could she have been so foolish, just a few days ago, on Friday, to think that everything was a mess when really it was exactly as it should have been? When things were working out?

She held her hands flat against her abdomen, felt a need surge through her to protect the baby in her stomach for as long as it was there, whether it had died already or not.

She stared up at the huge black clock, beneath which passengers flurried, ticket inspectors gathered and disseminated, friends greeted each other and departed, and she waited.

## Alice

The apartment was silent when Alice woke, a door banging in the hallway waking her. There was a hazy memory, struggling to untangle itself from the others: winning at the casino, Jules doing the She-Ra, and the Firework, and the Wild Cat, *oh Lordy, the Wild Cat.* She grinned, remembering Jules on all fours on a leather banquette, flicking her glossy blonde hair, a gaggle of wide-eyed French men around her. There was flirting, she remembered, flirting with the man on the dance floor, and then more champagne – *with extra sparklers!* They'd screeched and then... *Oh no.* She groaned, the rest coming back in a rush: stumbling through Paris singing, collapsing into bed, the message to Mr Hough. She moved her head to the left, staring at her phone, as if it might spontaneously come to life and tap dance over to her. *The message.* She pulled the spare pillow over her face and groaned into it, fearful of waking her friends.

No. That's just what she needed. She needed to tell her friends what was going on. She needed to speak to them. Hadn't she felt better when she confided in them last night? Wincing, she picked up her phone. There were no new message notifications on the home screen. She wasn't sure if that was good or bad. Did she want Mr Hough to reply? And if she did, what did she want him to say? *I have a crush on you too Mrs Astor. Let's do this!* Or *Thanks but no thanks?* Maybe that's the sort of response she needed to shut this childish fantasy down. Because that's what it was, wasn't it? A fantasy? Or was it…

She tipped her head from side to side, as if she might slide the hangover out of her ears. It had been a long time since she'd felt this bad but Lordy, was it worth it, for a night like that. A night like that in *Paris*, with her best girlfriends. A melancholy had wrapped itself around her lately, as she moved towards forty, a feeling like her best days were behind her, but something else tugged at her today: she'd weathered the baby years, her children were all – at least for now – at school. She had friends, she and Ted were comfortable, and there were still nights like that. Was it possible she was at the beginning of something, rather than at the end?

Despite her throbbing head and the accompanying waves of nausea, she wanted to be with her friends; to regroup, laughing, over breakfast; to rehash the events of last night. And she wanted to tell them what had been going on with her, to expand on what she'd shared with them, her feelings of failure around motherhood. Her guts knotted at the memory of the confession, like she wasn't sure if she had done something wrong, but hadn't they embraced her wholeheartedly? Hadn't they told her they understood, even though it was removed from their own experience, their own struggles? Warmth surged through her, melting the anxiety, briefly downgrading her hangover.

*That's odd*, she thought when she emerged from her room. No Nina humming in the kitchen with freshly brewed coffee and pastries, no Jules tapping away next door, or on the L-shaped sofa in the lounge.

She glanced at the time: 8.30 a.m. Her phone was almost out of battery. She didn't want to creep into Jules's room for the charger and wake her. She tossed it on to the sofa and made herself a cup of tea. It steamed lazily as she stood by the shutters, the cool, crisp air medicinal. Her friends were asleep and a sun-dappled day in Paris was unfolding below. Suddenly, she didn't want to miss a single minute of it. She showered quickly, removing the traces of last night – cigarette smoke in her hair, stale sweet sweat from dancing on her skin – and threw on her favourite voluminous floral dress and her white canvas trainers. By the time she was ready her phone had died, but the thought of being without it for a few hours only made her more eager to get going.

She left a note for her friends: *Heading out for a walk, see you at brunch. Could you put my phone on charge please and bring it to Le Fumoir? Ax*

She stepped out on to the Paris streets with a grin. She smiled at everyone she passed and one or two smiled back. The years of walking around Paris with her friends ensured she didn't need a map, but she chose *rues* she couldn't remember walking down before, *places* she didn't usually cross: she wanted to get lost in Paris, to wrap herself up in the city and emerge feeling more like herself. Like Alice Digby. Lordy, she missed Alice Digby.

These thoughts floated around her as she entered the high vaulted ceilings of the Musée d'Orsay. She felt herself in the art as her eyes took in dropped-shouldered ballet dancers, a woman forlorn above her drink, nude bathers, bare-backed, exposed, the isolation in the *Little Dancer*. She felt the sadness in the pieces acutely, but she felt hope too. Hope in the *plein-air* paintings, in the work of the impressionists for so long denied success by Le Salon – Monet, Renoir, Pissarro – because they saw things differently: she thought of Charlotte, banging her own drum, and felt a clutch of pride. Perhaps it could be that way for Charlotte too? After two days apart, she felt affection even for Dimples the Unicorn.

She didn't realise she was crying until an older man clocked her tears. '*L'art c'est beau*,' he said. '*Trop profond*,' Alice nodded, '*trop profond.*' She sobbed, grateful he didn't know she was crying at the memory of Dimples being fitted for a new pair of school shoes – a prerequisite for Charlotte to get her own feet measured, even now at thirteen – by the frowning owner of the shoe shop in town.

She left the gallery and made her way over the Seine to Le Fumoir, one of their favourite spots for brunch. She was the first to arrive. She shrugged happily, her legs grateful for the break, casting her eyes over the menu hungrily. Light streamed in the tall windows as she ordered tea, smiling widely at the aloof waitress, humming softly to herself.

As she stirred her tea, the feelings she'd had last night in the club when she was ensconced in her friends' embrace emerged again. She was only just realising how unhappy she'd been. She couldn't carry on that way. She saw herself, the old Alice, young Alice, as she skipped through Paris: singing at Place de la Concorde, falling out of bars with her friends in Le Marais, walking around galleries and dreaming of art and ideas and her future ahead. And who was she now?

It wasn't Alice's fault, and it wasn't Ted's, but they needed to work on their family together. She needed to be able to dream again, they needed to dream *together*. What was this fascination with Mr Hough if not a fantasy? An escape from her unhappiness. She felt a sudden urge to return home. To remind Ted of them sneaking out of *le Bal* – would either of them do that now? To remind him of the hazy, sun-dappled weekends they'd spent in Aix, their wedding day in Paris. How come, she pondered, they could leave convention behind enough to ditch the biggest society event of the year – striking themselves and any future offspring off the debutantes' list – but were afraid to home-school Charlotte, because of what people might think? How had they moved so far from the people they were twenty years ago?

Perhaps they should have a weekend in Paris together? Although they would need to bring the children, there was no one they could leave Charlotte alone with for an afternoon, let alone overnight.

Time crept on and Alice felt a squirm of embarrassment. She kept the waitress at bay for as long as she could, insisted her friends would be there shortly and they would order together. Her French wavered with the combination of a hangover and mortification and the waitress mistook her linguistic abilities, slowly repeating her question in English as to whether it was just a table for one, and not three, as had been booked? The restaurant was busy and heads craned in her direction.

When the table became at risk – 'You must order or you must leave,' the waitress said bluntly – Alice ordered: *Eggs Benedict sur English muffin, sauce hollandaise*. It was a set menu: coffee, juice, an assortment of 'house breads'.

'*Les pains sont pour une ou trois personnes?*' the waitress enquired. One or three?

'*Trois*,' Alice responded firmly. They might be late but they would definitely come. They wouldn't leave her here alone at brunch, she thought irritably. She shot desperate glances at the door while trying to look aloof. She no longer felt free without her phone, she felt disorientated. No distractions were forthcoming, she had no book, no phone, no friends. Where *were* Alice and Jules?

By the time the breads arrived – cinnamon and cardamom rolls, scones, banana cake – she was starving. She scoffed her share, and then continued to eat. She felt guilty but they could hardly complain, could they? They were fifty minutes late. Surely one of them could have called the restaurant to let her know?

When her eggs followed, and there was still no sign of her friends, tears pricked her eyes, but she blinked them away. That would be the final indignity. She ate without tasting. After three people's worth of cake, she wanted only to finish so she could leave.

She signalled for the bill. When it arrived, she had been charged for '*trois personnes*'. A hundred euros for a humiliating brunch alone, she seethed, but then it hit her. Something bad must have happened.

'*Il y a eu un accident*,' she declared. *There has been an accident*. She gestured vaguely at her bag as though she had received a call. Perhaps it's true, she thought, hailing a taxi back to the apartment. She was an explosive mix of anxious, nauseous and angry, but as her taxi wound over the river and along boulevard Saint-Germain, angst took precedence. Would she find one of her friends unwell? Hurt? Sick? On fire? She almost hoped the apartment *were* on fire because it needed to be something good to have stood her up like that!

She slipped a key out of the key safe and took the stairs two at a time, charging into the apartment, calling their names. It was as silent as when she left it. Her phone and note were still on the table. *For goodness' sake*, she muttered, no one had even bothered to charge it. She marched into Jules's room. Empty. Nina's room. Empty. She checked the kitchen, the bathroom, the balcony. Empty, empty, empty. Her friends had gone. And they'd left her alone in Paris.

# 11

## Le Gare du Nord

*09.30 Eurostar Departure, Paris to London*

Nina boarded the train, checked how long until it would leave and bolted to the toilet. There was more blood on the sanitary towel. Some brown and some bright red. Alone in the cubicle, her feelings engulfed her. *No, no, no*, she kept thinking. *This is so unfair.* She hadn't known she had decided until that morning. Until it was too late.

She cried until she couldn't breathe, her head in her hands.

'*Excusez-moi, avez-vous besoin d'aide?*' came a voice, and a gentle knock on the door.

'*Non merci*,' she replied through sobs.

The knocking continued. Eventually, Nina wiped again, pulled up her knickers and jeans, blew her nose and washed her hands. In the small square mirror, she looked pale and drawn. *No wonder*, she thought. *Something is dying inside you.* She closed her eyes, prolonging the moment until she had to leave the toilet. Even though it was impossible, she yearned for Jules and Alice to be waiting on the other side of the door, as they were at *le Bal*. Instead, there was a young woman with long red braids in yellow corduroy dungarees, asking if she was okay?

Nina nodded, her shoulders curving in on herself, her head tilted down.

'*J'étais enceinte…*' she said, her voice quivering. *I was pregnant…* She wanted the train to start moving and this journey to be over.

The woman returned with her to her seat, asking if there was anyone she could call. Nina shook her head. She couldn't tell Jules and Alice what was happening; she was grateful for the radio silence in their WhatsApp group. They should both be waking up now, getting ready for brunch. She wondered idly what they'd make of her note. She had left a note, hadn't she? Scribbled on the back of that receipt, but where had she left it? She couldn't remember.

Finally, the train began to move, and she felt as though she was having an out-of-body experience, soaring above like a bird, watching herself, not only then, sitting with the woman in yellow, shaking her head at her various offers of help – tea? Something sweet to eat? *Non, non merci.* – but also herself fourteen years ago, leaving Paris alone to have an abortion in London.

She had spent the intervening years working on herself – countless therapy sessions, the patisserie and business courses, running and spinning and stretching herself into the woman she was now. A woman she was proud to be. And yet here she was again, alone.

*It doesn't have to be this way. You've got nothing to be ashamed of*, she reassured herself, but it didn't help.

As if to prove it, she picked up her phone and replied to Flynn: 'Something happened to the baby.'

*14.00 Eurostar Departure, Paris to London*

Alice fought to control her tears. She'd been feeling insecure all weekend, and she was right to be: her friends weren't interested in her. Just like Ted. Just like the Mantels. She was easily forgotten, dismissed. Not worthy of being loved, or paid, or told she was being stood up. She had stayed at the apartment long enough to charge up her phone to one bar: she had hoped for a flurry of messages and calls: from her friends, from Mr Hough. One message came through, enough to know it wasn't a problem with signal or her phone: a stilted update from Ted, saying everything was fine but asking for the party details, which she'd sent him last week.

Even if you're hurt, or in an accident, or something bad has happened, you can send a quick message, can't you? And they must be together? One of them could send a message? But Alice knew, they didn't think she was important. They hadn't meant to make her feel this way, they'd just forgotten to let her know what was going on. The fact was, she thought bitterly, her problems were not of significance to their own. And what problems did Nina have really – problems with her expanding entrepreneurial empire? No doubt she'd been called away to some business emergency or other. True, Jules had had more than her fair share of bad luck, but it would help if she wasn't working all the time, chained to her phone.

As the train pulled out of Gare du Nord, Alice began

composing a text message. An angry message, demanding to know where they were and why they hadn't thought it necessary to let her know. But she stopped herself. *Why should the onus be on her?* No. She'd wait. She'd wait to see how long it was until they got in touch with her.

She broke off, staring out of the window, moving closer back to her life in Oxfordshire. How had she felt so full of hope and promise this morning? She felt deflated, crushed by disappointment and the thought of returning home. She'd confronted her unhappiness, but what could she realistically do about it? Ask Ted not to work as much so they could spend more time as a family? Return to work herself, to carve out some independence? Neither was feasible when Charlotte needed so much support.

She returned to her phone and taking a deep, shuddering breath, wrote a message to Mr Hough:

Hey. I'm sorry about my messages this weekend. They were inappropriate. I'm working through some stuff and I shouldn't have dragged you into it. You've only ever been lovely and respectful towards me...

She trailed off, thinking of the photo of him on the beach, water glistening on his carved abs, and gulped.

I hope this doesn't affect anything between us and you can continue working with Charlotte as she really enjoys spending time with you.

She added 'She's got good taste! :-)' but immediately deleted it. *No*, she remonstrated with herself.

Instead, she put 'Alice x'. She paused and deleted the kiss. *No kisses.*

She looked sadly at the empty seats around her, where her friends should be, and felt a wave of humiliation. Although she was upset with them, she'd half hoped they'd materialise at the station with various apologies and excuses, and she could sulk for a bit but then they could finally catch up on last night and giggle and gossip and for another few hours things could have felt good.

The *When in Paris* WhatsApp group remained resolutely silent. Where *were* they? Had they left together on an earlier train? Why didn't she even warrant a goodbye?

*Whatever.* She was sick of everything being about them: the years spent worrying about Nina's drinking, the hours dedicated to Jules's infertility, all while she felt unable to express her own struggles and when she finally did, they disappeared the next day. *This friendship group is a crock of shit*, she thought, surprising herself with her language.

Resolving to enjoy the last few hours of peace alone, she turned her phone off to conserve her ailing battery, closed her eyes, and spent the rest of the journey wrapped up in a series of delicious daydreams concerning a half-naked Mr Hough. She luxuriated in it, sunlight warming her face through the window, promising herself this was the last time she would submit to this particular fantasy. As soon as she was home, she'd speak to Ted about home-schooling Charlotte, however radical it seemed. She thought back to the night they slipped away from *le Bal*, casting aside tradition and incurring the wrath of her mother, who had only truly forgiven her when they announced their engagement. 'So you *did find a husband at le Bal?'* she'd smirked. Alice and Ted could do radical, they'd done it once before.

## *15.30 Eurostar Departure, Paris to London*

*You have a chance to start again*, Jules reminded herself, squirming in her seat, as her train departed. Fearing she might bump into Nina or Alice she had walked all the way to Père Lachaise Cemetery, stopping only for a ham and cheese baguette and a deliciously cold can of Coke from a small *épicerie* to appease her hangover. She traversed the cobbled, tree-lined alleys of the cemetery, barely seeing the grand mausoleums sculpted from marble and stone, her suitcase bumping along behind her, until she knew the 14.00 Eurostar she, and the girls, had been booked on had left. *What was she going to do?*

*All is not lost*, she reminded herself. *You won back the money*. But she was struggling to hold on to that thought. It was being drowned out by the waves of fear washing over her, the almighty claps of spray and thunder that were jumbling in her ears and which, when they retreated, rhythmically, every minute or so, left behind the same words on the blank sand of her mind: *put it all on red*.

It was a cymbal in an orchestrated piece, an exclamation mark in a chorus, a green light in gridlocked traffic. It was a 'stop' and a 'go this way' all at once. It made no sense and it made everything clear at the same time. It was comfort, before it was pain. It was burying herself in the familiar, in the scent of her father's coat or his soft green scarf, rather than starting again, alone. How could she ever do that? How could she ever start again, alone? Without Paul, without her friends, without any hope or prospect of a baby? What would that life look like? She could think of nothing more frightening. Putting it all on red was an innately more comforting option; it was tangible, it was real, it made sense to Jules in a world that had, for her, long ago lost its sheen.

*No*, she told herself. *No*. Think of the stress you put yourself under this weekend. *You can't live that way any more.* This is a clean slate. A chance to start again. Alone. The thought was too fleeting for her to process, the tingling in her limbs too distracting. The cymbals started up again. The dizzying spray, the building chorus, the urge to scream into the void. *Alone, alone, alone.* Who would save her now? Who would want to? Would Alice ever forgive her? Would Nina, when she knew the extent of her problems?

She was grateful to be sitting down because her legs were wobbling. Her whole body seemed to be swept up in a sense of inevitability. It was like she didn't need to think through to the next step because the next step had already been decided for her, and that was a relief.

Her hands stopped shaking as she opened the app. As the roulette wheel pixilated on the screen. She put it all on red. And she lost.

# 12

## London, 2018

She stared at the date on her phone, still in her dark trouser suit from work. All day she'd been trying to avoid it. She knew she shouldn't work out her due dates, but each time she was unable to resist. Now they sat silently alongside the calendar year, unmarked but ever present, permanently filed away in the storage system of Jules's brain. How many hours left of today? Another four, still. Too many. She swiped away from her calendar and into her favourite gambling app. Her favourite not because she won with them more, but because they gave the best free stakes when she lost.

It had started with Jules's weekly homage to her father: a flutter on the horses. A flutter. A twist. A stick. Moved on to cards, like they used to play. It was something in common between them; they'd always played games together since she was young. Board games, then chess. She knew he admired her mental agility. He was proud of her and she basked in that glow, like a cat in a pool of sunshine, warmed through, skin to bone.

As she got older the subtext to it changed, so subtly that

only Jules could see the difference. He loved to see her *win*. Prizes, scholarships, trophies. And she loved to win for him. She loved to hold whatever accolade she was collecting and to look out across the hall or sports field and see the apples of her father's cheeks so hard and shiny from grinning she could imagine them slicing through his skin. It was in their DNA. They were the same, something her mother and brother could never understand. 'Maybe you're working too hard?' her mother would frown, and Jules and her father would catch each other's eyes, discreetly raising them in a look of recognition: she didn't understand. But Jules did. Jules got it. She wanted only to be like him. She wanted independence and freedom and money. She really wanted money. She wanted to fix her face and buy a nice house. She wanted all the things her father had. And she didn't see anything wrong with that.

It didn't become a problem until after her second miscarriage. Jules, who had always been *so good* at achieving, was no good at falling pregnant and no one was quite sure why. But they fixed that, they made it happen with IVF. And for a month, Jules felt on top of the world. She was a solution-driven person and the solution had been found. Until it hadn't. She miscarried a month later. And after another successful round of IVF, she miscarried again. Now they had a different problem. Jules could get pregnant, but she couldn't *keep* the baby. *None of the high-achieving years that preceded this prepared me for being such an abject failure as a woman*, she would think, tears streaming down her face. Her shame was so acute she couldn't even tell the girls. She couldn't tell a soul.

Paul wanted to talk, but she couldn't get the words out. She felt like a teenager again, on the sidelines, watching others and weighing up what to say but never quite getting it right. It was all too painful to explain, how incompetent she felt, how it didn't matter how many times Paul assured her that she wasn't, that he didn't blame her. The words couldn't penetrate her anguish, they provided no balm or salve. They were just words, meaningless words, which bounced off her and she remained feeling empty and alone.

She gambled to stop the thoughts. She gambled because it was fun. She gambled because it was easier than going on to social media, a horror story of birth announcements and pregnancy news, or going to baby showers, or having well-meaning people ask if she and Paul wanted to have a family. She told no one, not even the colleagues she'd worked beside for years (not least because they were mainly awkward, techy men). EastWest, the hedge fund she worked at, was delighted by the firebolt they'd hired. They didn't realise that the sadder she was in her personal life, the more it drove her to succeed at work. She was fast-track promoted, again and again. If she wasn't working, she was gambling, and sometimes she was doing both.

Gambling made everything easier. It was even easy to lose; sometimes she liked to wallow in a loss, luxuriate in it. That was a loss she could deal with. And she could just win it back anyway.

Jules wrinkled her nose as a series of notifications pinged in, obscuring her view of her cards.

*When in Paris*

**Nina:**
Are we still on for Paris in Feb? I've kept the apartment free. We should book our Eurostar.

**Alice:**
Yes! I need a break. Take me to Ladurée and stuff me with macarons :-)

**Jules:**
Sorry. I'm on a big transaction. They've said no hols for the foreseeable.

It didn't even cross her mind to go to Paris this year. She loved Alice and Nina, they were pretty much the only friends she kept in touch with these days – and the only ones who knew about her fertility struggles – but it was easier to stay at home, easier not to have to talk, easier not to have to pretend she was coping. That was hard enough at work and she was just about managing it.

Had Alice known that Jules was sitting alone, a fortress of her own construction, the only light from her phone, sunlight having long ago leaked from the room, she would have been there, arms open wide, turning on the lights, convincing Jules to speak to someone.

Had Nina known, she would have arrived with food: foil containers with marinated lamb and couscous and pomegranate; chicken tagine, bursting with preserved lemon and olives; sweet, sticky baclava and rose-water macarons. But they didn't know. That was the problem. Jules clicked back into her betting account and drifted further away.

# 13

## After Paris

*Nina*

Nina sat in her loft apartment, the steeples and rooftops of Spitalfields peeking over the window frame, and beyond that the City. She felt regal, her feet propped up on a silk cushion, a soft, thick fleece throw over her legs. Luca had set up the projector screen and together they were rewatching *Schitt's Creek*, with popcorn and hot chocolate, thick, like he had it at home in Milan. After much protesting, she had submitted to being looked after.

'I'm ordering you some vitamins,' Flynn called from the kitchen where he was making dinner, a chicken stew he used to eat with his family on Sundays in Colombia. *Sancocho*.

When Nina had stepped off the train in London, Flynn had been waiting for her just beyond the ticket barriers. He'd taken her straight to a private clinic in the City, where he'd paid for a scan. Afterwards, they'd walked back to the flat, him pulling her small case, their chatter fuelled with adrenaline: Nina was still pregnant. The sonographer had confirmed she had experienced early bleeding, but all was fine. They'd even heard a very tiny heartbeat from the sonographer's wand, like a rhythmic, frantic flapping of wings, transcending their hopes. They didn't know what the future would hold: they weren't even dating, they were friendly co-workers who occasionally slept together, but it felt exciting. It felt good.

Back at the warehouse they'd told Luca and Kai, their smiles indicating something was up the moment they walked through the door.

'How was your weekend with the girls?' asked Luca now, throwing popcorn aloft and catching it in his mouth.

'You could choke doing that,' tutted Kai from the kitchen, where he was removing packs of berries from a jute bag and stacking them on the concrete island. Kai was German, with close-cropped dark hair and sharp cheekbones.

'Fun,' Nina said, smiling at Luca, who was pulling an *I've been told off* face. 'But difficult, you know, too... I couldn't tell them...' She waved in the direction of her abdomen.

'You hadn't even told me!' Luca said.

'I only found out Thursday night and I couldn't tell you at the patisserie on Friday morning...' How was that only a few days ago? The Nina leaving the building that morning clutching her passport seemed like a different person altogether. 'And you're not trying to have a baby,' she said, nudging him.

A look passed over Luca's face and she noticed Kai, who was assembling an elaborate pudding, glance over in his direction too.

'Are you?' she asked, her head moving between the two of them.

'Hey,' Flynn said softly. He wiped his hands on a tea

towel and came over, sitting across from Luca, a hand on his shoulder. 'You okay, man? You never said.'

Flynn had known Luca as long as he'd known Nina and worked with him in the evenings sometimes. Nina felt so lucky to have these men by her side, but she ached as she thought of her girlfriends.

It was weird, now she thought about it, that she hadn't heard from either of them yet. Neither had checked in to see why she'd left so early, or if she was okay. She was relieved, in one sense, because she didn't have to lie, but she was also a bit pissed off. The fact is, she'd needed them, even if she wasn't able to explain it to them; knowing they were there for her would have helped, would have been a comfort on the train and now, sitting here, fearful of what lay ahead. It niggled at her, this assumption that her life was easy in comparison to theirs. Why should the obligation always be on her to arrange things and be in touch?

Luca stood and walked over to the kitchen to retrieve more popcorn. 'We've been looking into adoption. We didn't want to say anything until we had good news to share.' He blew a kiss to Kai, who grinned.

'Watch this space,' Kai said, waving a spoon laden with cream.

It was food that had brought the four of them together, Nina realised. She imagined a lifetime of Sundays like this one, cooking and sharing food and being together. They were a family already. Unconventional, but fully formed.

'You will be godfathers though, no?' Flynn asked. 'Good practice for when it does happen.' He had an arm outstretched to each as he caught Nina's eye and she nodded. She felt briefly caught off guard by how accepting of things Flynn was, when he'd only found out about the baby yesterday. It felt like they'd leaped from casual sex to a couple overnight. She didn't feel ready for that level of commitment to him yet, and it was disconcerting.

Briefly, she pictured them all in a church, her and Flynn and the godparents: Luca, Kai, Jules, Alice. Regardless of her current annoyance, Jules and Alice would have to be there, as they'd been for Alice's children's christenings. Her family – Joanie and Liam and Carey – and Flynn's sister, Luna. Perhaps her Aunty Niamh and Uncle Seamus and Erin and her family would travel over from Ireland. Erin was married now with three rambunctious little girls who liked to send Nina voice notes singing rude renditions of nursery rhymes (Nina enjoyed them immensely). But the picture still wasn't quite right... would it be in a church? Maybe more of a naming ceremony thing outside?

She pictured them on top of the highwalk at the Barbican, or in London Fields, but there was still something amiss. What was missing from the picture?

Oh, the baby! She'd forgotten about the baby.

*Old habits die hard*, she thought, mentally cutting and pasting a small baby into her arms, Flynn and her closest friends and family around her. How would it feel to hold a baby and know it was hers? Her heart quickened at the thought. She put a hand to her stomach.

Nina had never told Joanie about her abortion. Joanie wasn't anti-abortion per se – she'd joined Nina on a march in London to repeal the 8th – but it seemed to Nina she was conflicted. *She supported women*, Joanie had often said, *but she couldn't do something like that herself*. Nina felt the sting of her judgement each time. Felt a distance between her and Joanie as a result. Perhaps if she had a baby, it would be a chance for her relationship with Joanie to strengthen? Since Joanie had quit nursing and opened her floristry, she'd been a doting mother to Carey, and Nina knew she'd make a wonderful grandmother. Joanie loved babies and Nina knew she'd love hers.

*Her baby.* Every time she remembered, she felt a wash of wonder overwhelm the niggling doubt that was still worming its way through her body. She'd always been so sure she didn't want a baby, but almost losing this one had thrown everything into sharp relief. So why were her old feelings trying to resurface? *This was what she wanted, wasn't it?*

She pulled the fleece throw further up her chest and slid her arms under, reaching across herself in a hug, hands jammed into her armpits as a chill ran through her. *A baby.*

*Nina O'Connell was having a baby.*

*Alice*

Alice had expected the house to be quiet when she returned – Ted should have been collecting Wilf from the class party – but as soon as her key was in the lock, she heard scuffling. She opened the door and was engulfed by Wilf and Phoebe, shrieking 'Mummy! Mummy! Mummy!' She laughed, her pink paisley print scarf unravelling as she bent over to hug them.

'Hello, my darlings!' She crouched down, happy for their sweet-scented skin to be wrapped around her neck. She wobbled precariously, trying to balance within their embrace. 'How was the party, Wilf? You're back early.'

'I didn't go,' he said, running off back to whatever he was playing. 'Charlotte's fault,' he added crossly.

Phoebe looked between Alice and Ted fearfully.

Alice turned to Ted, eyebrows raised, a question playing out on her features.

'Hi,' she said, removing her coat, but it was clear she was waiting for an explanation.

'She's upstairs,' was all he replied by way of greeting.

Alice climbed the stairs quickly, a knot of anticipation working its way through her back. She felt guilty, already, that she'd gone away. She knocked softly on the door. Charlotte croaked out a hopeful 'Mummy?' and she entered. Charlotte had been crying. She was curled up in a ball on her bed, knees to her chest.

Alice sat down on her BTS quilt; it was a subtle pink with the band members on, and Alice had used some of their pastel hair colours – one was purple and one green – as accent colours, framing some of Charlotte's posters and painting the wooden frames to match. She'd repainted the room to complement the duvet and sourced some Kawaii-inspired pieces: a cloud lamp and a panda rug that she knew Charlotte would love. The room upgrade had only taken a couple of days, but she was really pleased with it.

'Are you okay, sweetheart?' Alice stroked her hair and then recoiled in alarm. The top of her arm was covered in an angry bruise, black and flecked with violet. 'What happened to your arm?' she asked.

Charlotte looked down at it as if she hadn't noticed. She shrugged.

'Charlotte, try to remember. It looks really sore. Were you and Phoebe fighting? Did you climb the Big Tree?'

She shook her head forlornly, her long hair matted. She knew without asking that her daughter wouldn't have showered, or washed her hair, or brushed her teeth, since Thursday. It required gentle coaxing to encourage her to do these things. Ted would have asked and then shrugged when she said no.

'I guess it was Daddy,' Charlotte said, matter-of-factly. 'He kept grabbing me and putting me in my room. He said I was being annoying. And he got really cross when I opened the present for the party.'

'Why did you open the present for the party?' Alice asked, although she knew. Anything wrapped, anything she couldn't see, any suggestion of a surprise, increased Charlotte's anxiety. That's why any wrapped gifts were kept out of sight, in the pantry, until they were about to leave. She'd explained it very carefully to Ted a number of times.

'It was on the table...' Charlotte said, her voice small. 'When I came down for breakfast, it was there...' She tailed off, her tone laden with shame. 'I'm sorry Mummy.'

Alice felt her heart pumping, her anger building. *Don't lose it in front of the children*, she told herself. She leaned down and kissed Charlotte's head. *What must it be like to spend all day apologising for who you are*, she thought.

'It's okay, sweetheart. It's not your fault. I'm just going to talk to Daddy, okay?'

Ted was waiting for her downstairs, his hopes that Charlotte wouldn't have said anything visibly departing as he crossed his arms in defence.

'I suppose she told you what happened?' he said sharply.

'Why don't *you* tell me what happened?' Alice replied, her voice scathing.

'Look, I lost my temper. I told her not to touch the present, but did she listen? Not only did she open it, she *built* it! I couldn't even wrap it back up!'

'I told you to leave it in the pantry until it was time to go.'

'I didn't want to forget it. I took it out the night before and left it on the table.'

'But you *knew* she'd open it. She can't bear for things to be wrapped up. That's *why* I left it in the pantry, so she wouldn't see it. Why don't you listen to anything I say?'

'It's ridiculous. Hiding things and pandering to her. She has to learn—'

'No!' Alice said firmly. 'No. *You! You* have to learn. You can't set traps for her to fall into and then get cross with her when she does! You've hurt her. Her arm is bruised!'

'I *had* to lock her in her room! She was attacking me! Scratching at my arm, kicking my leg!' He proffered his forearm to Alice, visibly marked. 'What was I supposed to do?'

'Not lock her in! She's not an animal. What's wrong with you?'

This questioning of him – rather than condemnation of Charlotte – only incensed Ted further.

'Because she's not *right*, Alice! There's something wrong with her!'

'She's *autistic*, Ted. When are you going to accept that?'

Ted shook his head angrily, breathing through flared nostrils.

'It's my fault, isn't it? Everything's always my fault. If only I could be as "good" as *you*. Or as "good" as *Mr Hough*.' He made air quotes with his index fingers, his face fixed into a sneer.

Behind them a door slammed. Charlotte had heard the whole thing.

Alice pressed her fingertips to her forehead and let out a deep and weary sigh.

'What are you talking about?' she asked, distracted. Wondering what she should be doing next. Her husband had hurt her daughter.

He slid her iPad over the table to her, where her text message exchange with Mr Hough was laid out. He stared at her, his blue eyes dark as he glared, a blaze of red slashed across his cheeks.

Her eyes widened as she stared down, Mr Hough's torso, and her messages, lying exposed on their farmhouse kitchen table. Mortification seeped out of her skin. It had never occurred to her Ted would be able to see them.

'I'm leaving,' he said. And she didn't try to stop him.


He began packing immediately, moving his things out to the car. He sat the children down and gingerly explained he was moving out 'for a little bit'. Alice was pleased to see he looked guilty, even if he showed no remorse towards Charlotte as he was leaving.

'And it's nothing to do with any of you,' Alice emphasised, trying to look at the three of them equally as she spoke. 'Mummy and Daddy both still love you very much.' But Ted stayed silent on the opposite couch.

Charlotte kept her eyes trained downwards on her iPad. Alice recognised the irrepressibly catchy 'Life Goes On'.

'Is it my fault, Mummy?' Charlotte asked at bedtime, not moving her eyes from the book she was reading, one she had created herself: *BTS ULTIMATE BEST EVER FAN GUIDE FOR SUPREME FANDOM!!!* 'That Daddy's gone? Is it because we don't get along?'

Alice put her hand on Charlotte's cheek. 'It's not your job to get along with Daddy, sweetheart. It's mine,' she said sardonically, and she pulled an awkward grimace, her eyes flaring. They both laughed.

## Jules

Jules strode into the office the next morning as though nothing had happened. As though her marriage wasn't over, as though her friends had been in touch, as though she hadn't received an email from the IVF clinic first thing confirming the cancellation of her procedure that week. Paul must have contacted them.

Jack, the team secretary, did a double take, spluttering into her coffee as Jules strode past.

'Change of plan!' Jules called airily, gripping her tote bag and trying her best to sound sunny.

'Jules?' Ralph said, emerging from his office with two women Jules didn't recognise close behind. They discreetly slipped away. Ralph rubbed his forehead at the exact spot where Jules would have worry lines if it wasn't for Dr Maryam. 'What are you doing here?' he asked, and added, before she had a chance to respond, 'You'd better come in come in to my office.'

\* \* \*

She sat down facing his mahogany desk, covered in oak-framed photographs of vaguely famous sportsmen. The panelled walls reminded Jules of an alpine ski resort.

He opened with: 'We need to talk about your performance.' *So this is rock bottom*, Jules thought.

She looked down at her lap. Noticed for the first time she was wearing her favourite red pumps. Oh dear, with her purple shift dress. Purple and red were not an authorised colour combination from her personal stylist. *Oh well*, she thought. *Shit happens.*

'We've had a number of red flag markers on your trades the last few weeks.'

She stared straight ahead at him. She knew the drill. An official telling-off so he could tick a box and then she could get back to work. But Ralph wasn't following the usual script.

'I'm afraid,' he said, and for the first time she realised how uncomfortable he looked, 'HR have recommended a period of leave…'

'HR?' She baulked. No one ever listened to *HR*.

He nodded, swallowing, squirming in his seat. 'Yes, but I explained you're off this week anyway. The spa trip?'

'It got cancelled,' she explained quietly.

'Well, look, they agreed you could take this week as annual leave and we were going to have this conversation next week when you're back. Okay?' He smiled as though he was giving her a two-hundred-grand bonus. She knew, because he'd done that once. She didn't want to dwell on where that money was now. The large sums at the fund were part of the problem. The movement of huge sums on a computer screen rendered *real* money meaningless.

'But I want to work,' she said, picking at her nails, drawing out small slivers of skin and niggling at them. 'I've come to work.'

'Take a break!' he said, as if it was the most obvious thing in the world. 'Put that bonus to good use! And Jules. Take this opportunity. *Recharge.* Come back fighting fit. We can't afford to let you go.' His tone was anodyne, but there was a threat there. 'Okay?'

'Would you be sending me home if I were a man?' she asked sharply.

Ralph tilted his head then, the forced camaraderie fading away, leaving in its wake a stilted formality.

'It's not just the red flags. Questions have been asked about your... internet usage.'

She froze, the colour draining from her face. She'd seen male colleagues bypass the firewall to watch porn in the office, but they'd checked *her* internet usage.

'A number of these red flags happened when you were... distracted,' he said plainly. He moved a sheet of paper across the desk. There were rows and rows of entries with time stamps on them: all gambling websites. 'We all like a flutter...' he said, 'but... if it's compromising your concentration...' He hesitated. Drummed his fingers quickly. 'HR asked me to give you this.' He passed a leaflet over to her: *GamCare*. 'It's nothing to be ashamed of,' said Ralph, who had been in AA for the last decade himself.

She pushed her chair back abruptly, light-headed as she stood in her heels. She grasped the table. It was too humiliating. The whole thing was too humiliating. She'd never been dismissed from anything, never failed, never not performed, in her life and in the space of a weekend she'd fucked up her marriage, her friendships, her job and any chance of a family.

'I'm not going to be lectured to by a man who spends his lunchtimes fucking his secretary in hotel rooms,' she snapped. It was a cheap shot and a well-known fact. This time the colour drained from Ralph's face: his wife was also in finance, a more successful version of Ralph, and often joined the team for drinks.

'I think you'd better go.' He looked thunderous. 'Oh. And Jules?' he called when she was halfway out of the door. 'You will transfer the money to the ASD charity after the auction, won't you? HR asked me to remind you.'

'I'm not going to dignify that with a response,' was all she said as she stalked out of the room.

Jules returned to her desk and unlocked her computer. There was another email from Aki Mantel complaining about Alice. She groaned. She wished she'd never recommended Alice to Elliott and Aki for their nursery wing. Never agreed to be a liaison between them since Aki was super paranoid about sharing her contact details.

Out on the street, she appeared lost. She was. Ordinarily, Paul drove her into the City – it made sense rather than taking two cars – and she got a work taxi home, but when she tried to order a car now, as she had done successfully that morning, her account had been suspended.

For a few bewildered moments, she had no idea how to get to Chiswick from the City. Then she remembered: the train. Her personal card was declined when she tried to buy a ticket. Humiliated, she withdrew her joint account card from her Balenciaga purse. Paul would know when he saw it show up on their account; he would know she'd lost the money.

She returned home and it occurred to her that for the first time in decades she had nothing to do. *I should eat*, she thought. That's what functional humans do. As light bathed her face from the fridge, she realised she couldn't remember the last time she'd bought food. She ate at work, in the canteen, most days, or had takeaway delivered to her desk and charged to a client in the evenings. When did she last cook? If anyone cooked at home, it was Paul. She felt a wave of despair, picturing him at the marble-topped island, chopping vegetables and steak and listening to jazz. She looked at the contents of the fridge: eggs, some blue cheese, tomatoes. How long could she make that last for? In the cupboard she found chickpeas, spices, rice and jars and bottles of Asian ingredients she wouldn't know what to do with. What was she going to eat? The enormity of her situation began to overwhelm her: Paul bought the food, along with doing the cooking and paying the bills. What was she going to do without him?

She opened her banking app and frowned in confusion. There was money in her account! Then she realised it was the ASD charity money, just transferred in. But she couldn't spend *that*. That money was to help children like Charlotte who weren't getting the support they needed. She'd rather starve than use that money when she'd had so many privileges in life. She transferred it into her savings, an account which once held a six-figure sum and was now empty. She couldn't think about it for too long. *She was a good person*, she reminded herself, blinking back tears.

The screen froze and a name flashed up as her phone rang: her personal bank manager. He'd been trying her for weeks. When it stopped, she deleted the notification and idled into her messages. She barely registered the lack of communication from Nina and Alice. They must be pissed off with her after the weekend and disappearing like that. *Who could blame them?* It was better, really, she couldn't face them. She couldn't face anyone. She thought only of Paul. His kind eyes, his musky scent, the way he wore a suit really well, even the trousers looking sexy, snug around his bum. *It's very difficult to look sexy in suit trousers*, she thought to herself, and then shuddered, her eyes glossed with tears. She wiped them away and squared her shoulders.

She put the contents of the fridge in a tote bag and went outside, climbing into her car. Her little red sports car. A classic Jag. Her father would have loved it. She wished he could have seen it. It was cool outside, but the sun had warmed the leather seats through the glass. There was no point in putting the key in the ignition. No point turning it. She hadn't been able to put petrol in the car for the last three months. She couldn't afford to. But she liked to sit out here sometimes. To feel, briefly at least, normal. As if she'd just returned from the shops or from meeting friends. She closed her eyes, tried to recall a holiday she and Paul had taken, wine-touring around California in a car similar to this. She tried to recall the feeling of the sun on her face and the wind whipping her hair. She willed her body, her mind, to be someplace else. But neither would cooperate.

*It's empty*, her brain whispered. Everything that represents your successful life – your car, your bank account, your house, your marriage, your friendships, your body – is empty.

She swallowed. Checked the time. She knew the routines of the street from the days she'd worked from home. Mrs Elvery from next door was due back from her daily Autumn Yoga class any minute.

*What was she doing?* The thought engulfed her, like poisonous venom shot into her veins. Her ears began to throb, a strobe effect, like standing too close to a speaker. *What had her life become?* She gazed at the beautiful thick-trunked blossom trees that lined her street. They were full and pink. The beauty of spring at its peak, which ordinarily would move her, make her feel optimistic and bright for the summer ahead, but she couldn't feel anything. There was *nothing* bright ahead.

She wondered how quickly she could accelerate, how fast she would need to go, for the impact against a blossom tree to be sufficient. *Not quick enough*, she thought, thinking instead of the huge Range Rovers jammed with sunglass-wearing mums and prodigious offspring that often shot down their street. How fitting it would be to be railroaded out of here by one of them. Her car was small, could it be crushed by a large family car? Would she need to get on to the arterial road, wait for a truck or a lorry? Would it happen quickly? She turned the ignition. Just in case. Just in case there was enough petrol in there to propel her away from this life and into oblivion. Oblivion is where she wanted to be. Oblivion, right then, felt like the only option. But there was no spark of life; the car struggled, the engine died. There was nothing.

Eventually, Mrs Elvery walked past. 'Lovely day for a drive!' she said as she passed, rapping her hard knuckles on the glass, as she always did, and Jules wanted to kiss her.

'Yes,' Jules called, 'I've just been doing a spot of shopping.' She retrieved her tote from the passenger well, waved a cheery goodbye to Mrs Elvery and went back inside the house.

# 14

## One Month After Paris

*Alice*

Alice sat on the mustard love seat in the drawing room, fresh from the school run in jeans and a jumper. She loved this room; *her Paris room*, inspired as it was by the sumptuous decor at Ladurée on rue Bonaparte. It was lined with books on one wall, built in around the wide-framed door that opened through to the light-filled open-plan living space beyond. The house was still and quiet, but for the odd burst of noise – birds through the window, a plane overhead, an alarm from a child's sports watch beeping upstairs – aftershocks in the dust of an earthquake. It felt strange to know that her marriage was over while Ted's things still littered the house. His clothes in the wardrobe. Photos of them together lining the stairs. How long would it take to unwind their lives? She felt exhausted at the thought of it. No, that wasn't it. She was exhausted already, and it was another mountain looming. The house, the joint accounts and memberships, subscriptions.

She didn't think of it as four weeks since Ted had left. She thought of it as four weeks since she'd last seen Mr Hough or her friends. She'd been ghosted by both. And she had no idea why. On the Monday morning, the day after she returned from Paris, Mr Hough left the school without notice. She'd tried calling him but it didn't even ring and she had to deal with a devastated Charlotte. For two weeks, she'd cried every day after school: 'I miss Mr Hough, Mummy,' she would sob into Alice's shoulder. 'He was nice to me.' And Alice would think, *Me too, my love, me too.*

There were rumours as to why he'd left. She learned from Vita (a mum from school; her son Fred was in Charlotte's class, and Alice loved her for her flamboyancy and genuine, rather than self-professed, lack of judgement when it came to Charlotte) that she was at the centre of them. 'Did you...?' Vita asked. '*No!*' Alice replied, mortified, because the truth was nothing had ever happened beyond a few text messages, but she couldn't miss the looks from the other mothers: some scandalised, some jealous, some impressed.

Perhaps there was a benefit in the misunderstanding around Mr Hough. There was a dignity in it, she felt, to be the one in the wrong rather than the one wronged. Maybe she was clutching at straws. Whatever, she'd listened to enough Brené Brown and Glennon Doyle in the last month to know that she – and her children – deserved better than this. And not just from Ted. She deserved more from her friends too.

When she returned home from school that Monday afternoon, after Paris, confused and bereft as to the disappearance of Mr Hough, she'd still not heard from Jules or Nina. What began as a bulb of anger grew and flared in her chest, growing roots, fronds of fire furling. Did she mean so little to them that they could stand her up and extend no explanation or apology? Was her life as small and unimportant as they made it out to be? Her husband had left her, so too had her friend (Mr Hough *was* a friend, right?) and Charlotte's teacher, rendering both mother and daughter distraught, and she had no friends to call and tell. She couldn't confide in Vita or the other mums about Mr Hough; what if he came back? *Please let him come back*. But it had been a month and there was still no sign of him. No response or call back. He had gone.

The truth was, though, she hadn't told Nina or Jules about Mr Hough either, had she? And why not? Was there something wrong at the core of their friendship that had stopped her? A sixth sense that below the surface she couldn't trust them? She was so cross, and felt so let down by them, she couldn't tell any more.

She wouldn't contact them, she promised herself, and when they eventually called, she wouldn't answer: let *them* feel rejected this time. She raced through to the kitchen and got a large black sack. She threw in any of Ted's things she could see: pretentious books, piles of discarded *GQ* magazines, his flat cap collection. She was taking out the trash: Ted, her so-called friends and anyone else who couldn't give her the respect she deserved. She got to work.


Alice's gusto after her ruthless clear-out lasted about a week. And then she started to feel guilty. Really, really guilty. Her husband had left her, after all. Her children were now from a broken home. Could she have worked at her marriage harder, as her mother had suggested? Supported Ted more when he was struggling with Charlotte? And what *had* she been doing, flirting with Mr Hough? As sadness enveloped her, she became convinced she had imagined the whole flirtation. But then she would go back to the photo of him at the beach. Stare again at his sea-splashed skin. Wonder where he was. Had the allure of Cornwall that weekend proved too much? Had he never returned to Oxford? Had he met someone there? Someone who wasn't saddled with three children and an angry husband?

Vita took pity on her as she slouched around the school gates one morning in her jogging bottoms and a manky old sweater she used to wear when she was a student. She'd uncovered it in her clear-out and barely taken it off since. 'Come, Alice, I need some help with the remodelling. Tomorrow? After drop-off is good?'

'I don't do that any more. I told you.'

'Of course you do! Look at your house,' she scolded. 'It's stunning. I need your eye. *Please*, Alice.'

Alice went along because it was easier to say yes to Vita than no. Which she suspected explained all the husbands.

She threw herself into the task, redecorating Vita's new master wing (with side-by-side bedrooms for her and Mr Vita #5 and individual en suites. *The dream*, Alice thought). 'I want my side to reflect me,' Vita laughed, 'sexy and passionate!' And Alice laughed too. The project was an effective distraction from her pain.

She tried not to think about the Mantels, put what had happened down to her still finding her feet with her work. The good thing about Vita was that she didn't lie. Alice knew that if she did a bad job, Vita would let her know about it.

Sometimes she worried she was trying too hard. She'd

hear herself speaking and her whole body would pulse with embarrassment. 'What you need are some really slutty flowers in the bedroom... Something juicy and alluring, like...' *Slutty flowers?* What was she talking about? *You're turning into a parody of yourself, posh-girl-cum-interior-designer.* But Vita loved the idea and that was why Alice was sitting at the kitchen table one Sunday afternoon after Ted had dropped the children off, in a comfortable shirt dress, flicking through wallpaper samples of flowers that looked like labias, when Phoebe said innocently, 'Daddy's new Mummy is nice.'

'I'm sorry?' she choked out, but she didn't need clarification. Daddy's Mummy had died when he was a child.

Under the table, Charlotte kicked Phoebe. 'Ouch!' Phoebe yelled.

'She's not pretty,' Charlotte said bluntly. 'Not like you.' Her cheeks flamed red and she glared at Phoebe again.

'It's okay, Charlotte,' Alice said, and she reached out and rubbed her shoulder.

*It's been a month!* her brain was screaming. A month!

She smiled at her children, quietly eating their sausages and mash, the air thick with tension. '*Sorry, no time for pudding tonight!*' she breezed tightly, and no one disagreed. She bathed them and put them in bed. Charlotte didn't even complain about washing her hair, moving around the bathroom compliantly. *Maybe I should have my heart broken every day*, Alice thought miserably. She waited until the house was finally quiet and then fell into a heap on the mustard love seat, pulled a thick teal blanket up to her chin and sobbed and sobbed until her throat felt dry and raw and her eyes were so bloodshot she could barely see.

She called him. 'Are you seeing someone?' she asked when he answered.

'So?' he responded churlishly. 'What did you expect?'

'I expected you to have a bit more respect. And not to introduce anyone new to our children so soon,' she said angrily. 'How long has it been? Five weeks? Six? When did you meet her?'

'I don't think that's any of your business,' he sneered. 'You were trying it on with Charlotte's teacher, Alice! And you didn't even have the decency to do it discreetly. Do you know what it was like to see those messages while you were in Paris with your friends having a good time?' She held her phone away from her ear as he berated her, clutching a tissue with her other hand. 'You've made your bed,' he spat. 'Now lie in it.'

He hung up and she sat for a long time holding her phone in the large, silent house. Her marriage was over and it was all her own doing.


*Nina*


Nina set their drinks down on the concrete island: water for her and a beer for Flynn. Summer was in full swing and the warehouse was hot and stuffy. She took a deep breath. She had thought about this so much; it had begun to dominate her every waking thought and eventually penetrated her subconscious ones too; she fell asleep easily, exhausted and overtired, but woke sweating, the following hours spent staring up at the ceiling, willing herself to find the courage she needed. She'd never wanted a baby. Had never pictured it as a moment in her future, not like she'd dreamed of her music being played on the radio, or a life filled with travel and adventure, or the patisserie being a success. She knew, close up via Carey, what it was like to raise a child, and that however much you wanted to believe having a baby wouldn't impact your life, it would. *If it doesn't, you're not doing it right*, she thought. And if she was going to do it, she would fully commit. Put the expansion plans for the patisserie on hold, decline the coffee-table-book proposal her agent had received. Pivot. Pivot to mum and baby groups and roughly chopping cucumbers for a teething child, rather than the neat triangles that went into her popular watermelon and mint salad.

Luca and Kai, and even Flynn, were so excited, and she had been swept along with them initially, but then she started to think, I can't have a baby *for them*. And I can't have a baby for Joanie. Or Jules. Or anyone else. I can only have a baby for me. And the baby wouldn't belong to her in any event. The baby would be a unique individual who would grow and move on and be their own person while Nina's career, her passion, might never recover in the same way. How old would she be when she'd be free again? To travel to new places; to work the hours she worked now? She had found her passion and that was no mean feat. *Be true to yourself*, she whispered to the ceiling. She was certain it was the right decision, and she was sure she would have come to it sooner, had it not been for what happened in Paris. As the days and nights had ticked on, unyielding, so too had her resolve. She knew she wouldn't change her mind. She had considered, briefly, asking Luca and Kai if they would adopt the baby but she knew she couldn't watch her child grow from afar. What would happen if she disagreed with their parenting approach? Or if they decided to move, to Italy or Germany, taking her son or daughter with them? The potential for disaster, for heartbreak and chaos, was too high.

'I'm not sure I'm ready, after all,' she said, watching Flynn intently for his reaction. His amber-flecked eyes flickered but gave nothing away.

'That's okay.' He said it softly, as though he were choosing his words carefully.

'What?' she probed, sensing there was more to be said. She hooked a finger under the wide collar of her blouse and gently scratched at her skin.

He smiled. 'I had a sense you... I don't know, you haven't seemed yourself.' He shifted his weight from one foot to the other. 'I was just getting used to the idea.'

'Me too,' she admitted, because she wasn't averse to scrolling through sweet little romper suits online, or mountain-themed nursery schemes. 'But I feel like I've been swept up in a fantasy of how perfect it could be, and now reality is setting in.'

He didn't say anything but he nodded, a sad smile playing out over his sun-weathered features. Her perception of Flynn had altered this last month. He had grown from being a man whose company she enjoyed to a man she saw most days and, when she didn't, would be checking in, making sure she was okay, offering to work longer hours at La City Pâtisserie so she could rest (which she always declined).

That was part of the problem. He had told her he was falling in love with her, that he saw a future for them together, had even hinted that they marry, if that's what she wanted. She'd dismissed it initially – just a month before, they'd been casually sleeping together – but had begun daydreaming about Flynn in a dark slim-fit suit, a thin black tie, sunlight flitting across a wedding band as vows were exchanged. She couldn't trust herself to know what she wanted any more, not since she was pregnant. She felt driven by a powerful concoction of hormones and this fear had begun to gestate that as her belly grew, so too would her feelings for Flynn and it would build to a heady, climactic finale when, in seven or so months' time, she could find herself with a husband and a child, and when the hormones wore off, and the mind-and-body-wrecking lack of sleep set in, would she feel like she'd made a mistake? Because she'd never wanted a baby. She'd never been sure she wanted a husband – she got the support she needed from her friends. But since she'd made her retreat last month, and not been in touch with them, *or heard from them, come to think of it*, Flynn had filled their space.

When *had* she last heard from her friends? She frowned, looking at her Eiffel Tower tattoo. It wasn't unusual for them to go a week or two without being in touch, before someone would drop a message into their *When in Paris* group (*'Please help me I'm going to die if I get one more ParentMail about head lice...!'*) and a burst of chatter would ignite, but it had been over a month, she realised. The time had whizzed past in a blaze of worry and information and *'what-next?'*'s.

She'd been annoyed not to hear from Jules and Alice at first, but as the niggling doubts she felt over having a baby grew louder, she began to feel grateful. Telling Jules she was pregnant would have been hard enough, telling her she was pregnant and considering not keeping it was unthinkable. As well as that, since being pregnant and spending that weekend in Paris, she couldn't shake the feeling that it was time to tell Alice what had happened with Ted. She wanted to move forward in her life, with her friendships, with a clean slate, not another secret.

'How long until you need to decide?' Flynn slid his hands into the pockets of his denim cut-off shorts and held his elbows close to his body.

'I'm still less than ten weeks, which makes it easier. It's just a pill...' She tailed off because they both knew it was so much more than just a pill. 'I've booked an appointment for Friday,' she added quietly.

Flynn's eyes widened. 'Oh. Okay.' He swallowed. 'Well, I can stay over that weekend, or if you want space I can be just a phone call away if you need anything...' His voice quavered.

Nina nodded and felt a rush of tears.

'Come here,' he said threading his arms around her waist and pulling her in to a hug. She resisted at first, mindful not only that she was hurting Flynn, but also of the way her blouse was sticking to her sweaty skin. But then she breathed in his scent, wood smoke and tangerine, and she melted on to his chest, her face tilted on his shoulder, a crescent moon, orbiting this man who in a short month had become her sun. *Did she love him?* Sometimes she thought she did. *But where did pregnancy hormones end and true love begin?*

She wasn't proud of what had happened but she was proud of one thing: that she'd brought Flynn in, hadn't gone through the process alone like last time. The situation was different in innumerable ways, but as she looked at Flynn's face now, his soulful eyes weighted by grief, she had to admit all that she had taken from Ted, without his knowledge. He deserved to know what had happened, just as Alice did.

\* \* \*

## *Jules*

It was a condition of her returning to work that she would have a weekly therapy session. On Wednesdays at 11 a.m. she left the office, turned right to avoid La City Pâtisserie, and crossed over London Wall, to a private psychiatrist. She marvelled that even at her lowest ebb she was being cushioned from her fall by the corporate machine. She had to hold on to her job. Not just for her salary, but for the other perks: food, transport, distraction. Her work had become her world. And she hadn't gambled. Not since that weekend.

Home was a trap: she couldn't watch TV without being bombarded by adverts for gambling; even daytime TV was sponsored by bingo. She thought of the women stuck at home without the options she had and shuddered. This wasn't her first time in therapy. At Paul's insistence, she'd started seeing a therapist after her second miscarriage. When she would return from work on Friday, get into bed in her suit, and not move again until Monday. She spoke about her loss, about the way it made her feel as a woman, but her gambling never came up. Why would it? Jules had grown accustomed to compartmentalising her life. She was good at it.

'I'm feeling a lot better,' she told Cindy. And it was true. After Paris she had spent a fortnight, for the first time in her life, without any money. Without access to food or the freedom to do as she pleased. She took long walks along the Thames Path, practised yoga via YouTube videos, cobbled together food with the random things in the cupboard and freezer. She didn't even mind; her overriding feeling as she glanced around her immaculate home was how lucky she was to have the four walls that surrounded her. It had been an invaluable lesson. She would never put herself in a vulnerable position like that again. She would never gamble again.

After the fortnight she'd been paid, thankfully. She transferred her share of the mortgage and bills into the joint account as usual and walked to her local supermarket, filling her trolley with comfort food; things not permitted under her fertility doula, Flora's, regime: rice pudding, fish fingers and thick crusty bread.

Cindy tipped her head, assessing her. 'How so?' she asked.

'Well, I've been paid.' She smiled. 'I'm looking after myself. I'm cooking and cleaning and doing all the things Paul used to do.' Now she was getting the hang of looking after herself, she recognised with some embarrassment the extent to which Paul had been molly-coddling her. No wonder he didn't want to have a baby with her.

'How are you feeling about therapy now?' Cindy asked, recalling Jules's fury at their first meeting that she had effectively been forced to come.

Jules smiled gingerly. 'I... Of course they were right to send me. Of course I needed to come. I'm so grateful for it now. I've started to see what happened as an opportunity, you know? It's been good for me. To stand on my own two feet again. I lost my grip on things for a while there but I've had this chance to *reset* and yes. I feel good.'

Cindy looked at her impassively, a tiny frown belying the *Are we really going to do this?*

'It's funny,' she said. 'I've met a lot of women in this room. Women who never want to show any weaknesses, women who will tell me exactly what they think I want to hear so I'll discharge them and they can get back to work. Put all the messy business behind them and get back to normal.' She wiped her hands over each other and flung them apart, like throwing away rubbish.

'That must be frustrating,' Jules responded evenly, but her interest was piqued. 'You've met a lot of women like *me*?' she asked curiously. There were so few women doing what she did in the City, she couldn't imagine anyone else having messed up so badly.

Cindy nodded. 'It's alcohol usually. Sometimes drugs. Porn. Sex. Love. Shopping. Painkillers.' She looked out of the window, which framed gleaming towers of glass and steel. 'There's a lot of addicts in the City. There's a lot of addicts everywhere.' She glanced up at the clock. 'I'm going to recommend you start going to meetings.'

'A meeting?' Jules snapped.

'It would help you to connect with other gamblers. To feel less isolated.'

'I don't feel—' she started, but she stopped. She absolutely did feel isolated but that's why she was doing all this. To get Paul back. That was why she was doing everything. 'Do I look like an *addict* to you?' she said, alarmed. 'Really? Is this how a *gambling addict* behaves? Getting their life back on track? I've not gambled in a month! Not since Paris. I told you, it was a blip and I'm feeling much better.' Her voice rose in alarm. She couldn't go to a *meeting*. Meetings weren't for people like her. Meetings were for people with real problems, people with nowhere to live, no one to help them. People who had lost everything. She was wearing a Chanel suit and was perched on a private psychiatrist's velvet chaise longue in the City. She was hardly in the gutter.

'I want you to go to one before our next session,' Cindy said firmly.

'But I'm very busy now I'm back at work. I've had to make up for my time off.' Which was true. Jules knew her fall from grace was a poorly kept secret. The rumour was she was an alcoholic, but she preferred that; somehow it felt less shameful than a banker who couldn't look after their own money.

'They run early morning, at lunchtimes, after work. You will definitely find time between now and next week.'


A few days later, on Friday night, Jules found herself entering a small loft room in Hampstead (she'd wanted to be far away from the City and Chiswick so there was no risk of bumping into anyone). This wasn't how meetings were meant to look. They were meant to be in vast church halls with chairs in a circle and tepid coffee and biscuits on a rectangular trestle table. This was an airless room above a coffee shop, with an assortment of chairs and sofas, all set at different heights, and a humid, tropical climate. There wasn't even a broad mix of people: they were all men, scruffy ones at that, men who looked like they'd had a hard life and not eaten many vegetables. This wasn't where Jules belonged, in her cigarette pants and silk vest top.

Her entrance caught the attention of the room, the murmured conversations drawing to a hush as she sat down. 'This is GA, isn't it?' she asked, self-conscious, as a pale man with a neat shock of red hair and an armful of tattoos nodded. She couldn't recall a time she had ever felt so out of place.

'Too much bingo was it, love?' a short, round man with grey hair and big bushy eyebrows asked her kindly and the others gently remonstrated with him.

'Don't mind him, he's new,' one said. 'Like you.'

'Right,' she said stiffly. She turned to the man. 'Poker, mainly,' she said. 'Hold 'Em; no limit and big tournaments, Omaha, Stud...'

He tipped his head in approval, weighing her up, and nodded.

Jules felt her heart pounding as the meeting opened. It was being led by Lane, a young man who didn't look old enough to have had a debilitating addiction and recovered from it. He wore a white shirt with his sleeves rolled up and a neat thin navy tie. Jules wondered where he worked. He looked like a good fit for the IT department at a bank.

An agitated-looking man spoke first, his knee trembling the whole time, his right hand clamped on it as if trying to stop the shaking. *That* was a person in the grip of an addiction, she thought. He hadn't gambled for two years but had come undone at his daughter's school fete, abandoning – and losing – his toddler son when he ran to collect his raffle prize. *Good grief*, she thought, her eyes widening, these were not her people. At that moment he turned and caught her eye. He addressed Lane, gesturing at Jules with his elbow.

'I don't feel like I can speak freely while she's here,' he said. Some of the group frowned at him and muttered words of disquiet, but Jules noticed others who were also starting to turn, restless, discomforted by this incongruous woman in this group of men.

'A bit like having the wife here, eh?' added another, pulling his bottom lip between his thumb and index finger.

Jules's face turned scarlet as Lane reminded the group of the guiding principles of GA; 'It's a fellowship,' he was saying, '*everyone is welcome*', a note of exasperation in his voice.

'Aren't there women's groups?' one asked.

'No, actually, there aren't,' Jules said, frustrated. 'There's two. One in London at 5 p.m. on a Tuesday, which I can never make because we have a weekly team meeting then, and one in Manchester!'

'I'm really sorry,' Lane said, turning to Jules. 'The truth is I've been running this group for three years and you're the first woman we've had.'

*How can that be true?* Jules thought. Shame stung her cheeks. She reached down, one hand on her bag, preparing to bolt, but she froze and without intending to, she began to speak.

'I'm a hedge-funder,' she said. Maybe she shouldn't be here, but that was her business, not theirs. Jules had spent her university and working life surrounded by men, carving out her own space, and she wasn't going to be railroaded out of her first GA meeting by this group of no-hopers. 'I've made £250,000 a year, and about the same in bonuses, for the last fifteen years, and it's all gone.'

There was a stunned silence. Lane nodded at her to go on.

'Last month, my husband found out. He knew the first time I got in trouble, and he bailed me out, but I did it again... I got a bonus, another seventy grand, and blew the lot. I was already in £80,000 debt by then...' The numbers floated above her head, dissociated with her in this room. What did they mean, anyway? 'So I spent a weekend winning it all back. I was in Paris with my oldest girlfriends, staying up all night online when I should have been enjoying myself with them. I even roped them into coming to a casino with me. In Paris! And I did it, too.' The pride she'd felt in the toilets of the casino had long since deserted her. Now it seemed unreal, something that she knew happened but couldn't properly remember. 'I won it

all back. And more. But it was too late. My husband left me.
He refused to go through with the IVF we had planned. So I
did it again. And I lost the lot. My friends haven't contacted
me since. My work found out. I'm just about clinging on to
my job.' A terrible realisation came to her now and she felt
the horror of it as she verbalised it: 'And the worst bit is, I
know I'd do it all again…'

The room was silent. Jules felt a weird mix of *Ha! I told
you!* and despair that she did share some similarities with the
men in this room.

'It was IVF with me too,' the quiet red-headed man said.
Jules stared at him in amazement. 'My wife was just… crying
all the time. If she wasn't crying, she was angry – those
hormones – and that's when I started gambling. I could be
there, beside her, but at the same time someplace else.'

'My daughter was unwell,' the man with the shaky leg
said. 'Leukaemia. And I'd sit by her bedside, in the hospital,
placing bets.' He shook his head. 'You can't stop when you're
winning and you can't stop when you're losing.' A murmur
of knowing acceptance reverberated around the room. Slowly
their stories began to resonate. The *whys* and the *you knows*,
because she did know. She knew how you could betray the
people you loved because in that moment it was the only
thing that made sense.

She was pensive as she made her way home on the overground.
It was cool outside now and she wished she'd brought a light
jacket. She hugged her bare arms in against her chest, wistfully
thinking of the corporate taxis she used to travel in. She still
couldn't quite reconcile herself with the men she'd met at the

meeting. These people didn't have a choice. They were mostly on low incomes, when they gambled it was *everything*; when she gambled, it was something to help distract her from her grief, it was temporary, until her next pay cheque and bonus. It wasn't *ideal* and she'd definitely gone too far, but she was putting it right now, wasn't she? Did that make her an addict? It was such a heavy word, she felt it slumber on her shoulders, lion paws, an anaconda, pinning her to the ground as she trudged home from the station. Could she really have made it this far in life if she were an addict?

It was a pound coin, glinting in the gutter, that did it. Illuminated like a star by the street lights. It felt like a sign. Certainly something to act upon. She could gamble with this pound coin, discarded in the street, and she could stop. She thought of Alice in the casino and her joy at winning her €5 bet. Maybe she needed to transition back to the gentle buzz she used to feel when she put money on the horses with her father? She held the pound coin in her palm. Rubbed her thumb along its edges and bumps in her pocket. There was something beautiful about its circularity, its promise. At home she placed it on her mid-century coffee table and sat back, flipping on the retro ball arc floor lamp. Alice had created a Mad Men-style den in here and Jules was used to gasps and exclamations when people saw it for the first time, as the Mantels had. Alice had a flair for marrying textures and colours, that was obvious, but Jules had always thought that Alice's true skill was in taking something mundane, or ordinary, like the small nook in the corner, and making it shine, as she had with the inclusion of a vintage cocktail trolley. As she had when she first met Jules at *le Bal* and with a few small adjustments had transformed her from an awkward spotty teen to a woman ready to dazzle. It was the exquisite little details that Alice noticed, which others might miss, and brought to life. Combining things that shouldn't work, at least to Jules's mind, like the orange-and-brown geometric rug under the coffee table and the plum-leather wing-backed chair in the corner, but did. It was a gift. She'd probably have gone to university having never been kissed, were it not for Alice. *Oh Alice.*

She tried not to think of her friends. Tried not to let her sorrow burrow into her heart because it was so hard to shift. Alice and Nina. Her two best friends. Where were they now? What were they up to this Friday night? She thought of noodles washed down with Asahi beers in Chinatown, nights on squishy Moroccan sofas eating tagines in Paris. She felt the familiar knot of betrayal. Why had neither of them got in touch? She could be pregnant now, for all they knew. Was her behaviour in Paris that weekend so bad she deserved to be excommunicated? It was a blessing and a curse all at once. Their absence meant she didn't have to tell them what she'd done, but it also made her feel impossibly empty. As though she could never be whole again. They were the only friends who truly got her. Her only friends she could be herself around. Jennifer had dropped out of contact long ago when she was on to her third child and living out her free-range chicken fantasies in the suburbs, but Jules had grown tired of their friendship long before that. She hated the competitive side of her that emerged when they were together.

She stared at the pound. Eventually, at 21.55, just before it was due to close, she walked to the newsagents and bought a scratch card. The tingling through her forehead as she slowly peeled off the layer of silver, the glimpse below of fragmented numbers and cash signs. It rippled through her, waves of excitement. It was just like the first time. She felt giddy. She'd *missed* this feeling. Missed this rush.

An hour later and she could no longer think straight. Since the scratch card, she'd already gambled the remaining money in her personal account, maxed out her overdraft and reactivated the accounts that had been flirting with her ever since Paris, offering her free stakes if she returned, all of which she'd used and lost. She stared at the numbers for a long time: £10,300. The money she'd raised for the ASD charity. It had already been match-funded by the bank and the charity had emailed her politely a number of times asking where her portion was: *Could she have transferred it under a different name? Did she have the correct account details for them?* She'd held on to the money like a crutch. It was proof she was a good person. It was proof she didn't have a problem. And it was a final, last-resort cushion in case she urgently needed some cash.

Thoughts swirled around her head. She could double the money for the charity, couldn't she? Triple it, maybe? She wasn't sure she even believed that herself any more. Had she ever believed it? *But look what happened in Paris. Look how much you made there...*

She closed her eyes and took a deep, steadying breath. Then she put it all on red.

# 15

## Three Months After Paris

*Nina*

Nina woke and for the first time in months didn't feel sadness pinning her under her duvet as she tried to muster the energy to begin the day. Instead, she felt a flush of intention, like the first rush of spring: it was time to speak to Ted.

She was off-kilter, had been since she discovered she was pregnant. There was a long road ahead to feeling back to herself and she felt like speaking to Ted was a necessary part of her recovery; delaying it would only prolong the pain.

Nina dressed as she would for a business meeting, in wide-leg khaki-green trousers and a black sleeveless roll-neck. She slung the matching jacket over her arm, still warm, despite the chill in the air, from her morning run.

She almost went alone to the appointment. Flynn had offered to come but it didn't seem right, this being her decision rather than his. She wished she could have been with Erin, like last time, but she couldn't ask her to leave her family and travel over from Ireland, although she probably would. Luca was on hand for any work-related emergencies. The people she wanted by her side the most, the women she could sit beside and not need to say a word, were Jules and Alice, but that was out of the question. Not least because she still hadn't heard from either of them.

The day before her procedure, feeling restless and tearful, stabs of doubt arresting her, she'd hopped on her bike, cycled from East London to Essex, and arrived at her mother's floristry, sobbing. Joanie, dressed as ever for a night out in a fifties diner in a pale pink cardigan and white skirt with blue flowers, looked up in alarm from behind the counter and ran over to embrace her. '*Nina*,' she'd gasped. 'What's wrong?' And tearfully, over a cup of tea and a Mars bar at the little wooden table out the back of the shop, the 'CLOSED' sign on the door, Nina had told her everything. About what had happened with Ted, and what was happening now. 'And I know you're ashamed of me,' she'd sobbed, turning a small square of chocolate over so many times that it had begun to melt on to her fingers.

'Ashamed of you, Nina? Why?' her mother had said, eyes wreathed with concern.

'For having an abortion,' Nina said.

'Am I now?'

'*Yes*. I've heard you say you don't know how people can do it.'

'*Nina*,' she said. 'Didn't we go together to the march to repeal the 8th?'

'Yes, but I've heard you say it: *I could never do it myself.*'

'Oh Nina,' she said, shaking her head. 'Nina, Nina.' She cast her eyes around the room then, her lips rolled inwards as though weighing something up. 'Lookit. When I told Samir

I was pregnant, what do you think he suggested I do?' Nina gulped. She'd always known a termination would have been an option for Joanie, had never known Samir had suggested it. 'And when I've said, I couldn't do it myself, it's because I've been thinking of you. I could never not have you, Nina. And I'd be saying it in anger at himself. That good-for-nothing...'

'Okay, okay...' Nina put her hands up, in a 'stop' gesture.

'Well, you get the picture,' Joanie concluded, her eyebrows riding high on her forehead as she admonished Samir.

Outside someone rattled the door and, finding it locked, moved on.

'But to do it twice?' Nina said, as though she wanted her mother's condemnation. 'I feel so reckless and foolish.'

'But last time you used a condom? And even if you didn't. It's what? Two mistakes. Fourteen years apart. It's not ideal, Nina, for the emotional toll on yourself, but it doesn't make you a bad person, if that's what you're getting at.' She rested her chin on her cupped palm, looking thoughtful. 'Your Aunty Niamh had one, you know. Before Erin. Before she was married. She had to come over here. I came with her. I would never judge another woman for what they wanted to do. And I would never judge *you*. Nina, I'm so proud of you. I know we're not good at talking, you and me. But it can't have been easy for you when I was nursing and you were with your aunt and uncle. I do get it, you know. I'd come home and you'd always been busy baking with Niamh. Those neat little rhubarb tarts you loved. I knew you'd laboured over them for hours, your little tongue poking out in concentration. I can't so much as look at a stick of rhubarb without feeling sad. I missed out on a lot. And I regretted it. That's why I didn't want to make the same mistake twice with Carey. It pushed me to change. Kind of like what happened with you and Alice,' she said, gesturing her hand, recalling Nina's earlier admission. 'That was when you stopped getting drunk all the time, wasn't it? And did that course? I wondered what started all that off.'

Nina nodded. Hands clasped round her mug. 'Do you think I'm making another mistake now?' she asked.

Joanie considered this carefully.

'I think you could be happy whichever path you chose. And I think what you're doing takes courage.'

Joanie stood then and walked around to Nina, and Nina tipped her head against her mother's torso as she hugged her. It occurred to her that falling pregnant had brought them closer together, but not in the way Nina had expected.

It was Joanie who went with her in the end, and then took her back to the house in Essex where Nina, Joanie, Liam and Carey watched Netflix, Nina clutching a hot-water bottle to ease her cramps. Joanie kept a record of painkillers administered and delivered the best nursing of her life. Alone in her room Nina cried, but deep down she knew she'd made the right decision. And for the first time as she sat in her family's semi-detached house in Hornchurch, it felt like home.

Ever since then, she'd buried herself in work. She'd missed a couple of weeks on the expansion project and had catching up to do; the pace was picking up as they neared another opening, in Manchester, and she was increasingly being asked for interviews in magazines and podcasts and for her food-styling service at weddings and industry events. Her social media presence had grown and she was nearing fifty thousand followers.

She had swung from feeling relieved at not having heard

from Alice and Jules to aggrieved; yes, they had stuff going on, but so did she. A month or so ago she'd found the note she'd written in the apartment, a barely coherent scribble on the back of a receipt, telling the girls she had to leave. It fell out from her sherbet-striped jumper, which she'd moved from her case to her chest of drawers on her return. *How odd*, she'd thought. Her friends hadn't known she'd had to go but she still hadn't heard from them. She couldn't have seen them, of course, or told them what she'd been through, but knowing they were at the end of the phone if she needed them would have been sustaining. She was starting to feel like she'd been ghosted but that brought a wry smile. *They would never ghost each other.* It had been three months though, the longest they hadn't been in touch. It would be so easy for her to send a message over WhatsApp. Why did she keep putting it off? She wasn't sure. Was it the guilt towards Alice that had resurfaced when she was pregnant? Was it guilt that she'd not wanted something that Jules was so desperate for? Occasionally, she wondered whether Jules would ever be able to forgive her if she knew. And although that would be unfair, she understood and before getting in touch with Jules and telling her what had happened, she needed to be sure she was ready to say goodbye to their friendship.

Ted's company was housed in a tall City building with a sushi restaurant on the roof. The front-desk team were enthusiastic patrons of La City Pâtisserie since they'd been issued with discount cards by Ted's firm. Alex smiled at her as she approached. 'Up to see Ted?' they asked, handing over a visitor's badge.

Nina checked Jules's social media while she waited for a lift, as she did most days now, hoping for a photo of a scan or a discernible bump, but she still hadn't posted anything since Paris. In the lift she struggled to find a suitable distraction, her phone signal cut off and her social media feeds frozen as the lift climbed higher, stopping at each floor.

*Was she doing the right thing?* Raking up something that had happened over a decade ago? *Yes*, she told herself, *yes*. It can't be a dark secret festering away in your past any more. You need to confront it. Tell Ted, tell Alice. Make peace with them both if you can and *move on*.

Ted's firm was arranged with an open-plan area in the centre and offices for the partners lining the outside glass walls. Nina passed unhindered towards Ted's office, the bank of secretaries who usually occupied the middle space (and always asked her how she was and if she was seeing anyone) thankfully all out at lunch. Ted's door was closed. *Make peace and move on*, she urged herself as she knocked, not wanting to disturb him if he was mid-meeting or conference call, although she suspected he was most likely eating lunch at his desk. Behind the door she heard a kerfuffle, a chair pulling back quickly and a muted '*shit!*'

'Ted?' she called, knocking again, concerned she'd startled him and he'd fallen over or something.

*How naive*, she thought moments later, as Ted opened the door, flustered, and a woman she recognised from the group of secretaries (*Sarah?*) emerged from behind him, rearranging her red dress. She shot a quick, awkward smile at Nina before walking over to her desk, picking up her handbag, and bolting out of the office. Nina followed her trajectory across the floor and turned back to Ted, open-mouthed.

'What the—?' she said as Ted ushered her into the room by her elbow, his face hot and panicked but, hideously, bearing the tiniest trace of a smirk. 'Are you fucking serious?' Nina said, not bothered that the door wasn't yet fully closed. She thought of how Alice was that weekend in Paris, the degradation of her confidence during the course of her marriage. It was like soil erosion, small particles of earth slipping into the sea so slowly that you don't realise until it's too late how much has been lost.

He closed the door behind her and folded his arms across his chest.

'Hi, Nina. Good to see you too.' The way he said it recalled a Ted of the past, a Ted from before he got together with Alice. Aside from that one terrible night, before the wedding, all interactions between them since had been purely platonic. He was being flirtatious and it made her stomach flip with nausea.

'Don't do that,' she said, short.

He paused thoughtfully, looked her up and down and a feeling of revulsion shuddered in her temples. Something was deeply wrong. It occurred to her she hadn't been alone with Ted since that night. For a long time she had avoided him, then there had been the christenings and birthday parties during which she was always careful to stay out of his orbit, and then, after more than a decade, there were the business meetings with him and the other partners, but they had never been alone.

'Does it offend your moral compass?' he asked, his head inclined towards Sarah's desk.

'Yes, it does, as a matter of fact, because you're married to my best friend and you have three children, Ted. What on earth are you doing?' To her horror Ted remained indifferent, moving over to his desk, opening a drawer and retrieving a bottle of Scotch and two tumblers.

'As I'm sure you know, Nina…' He slid a glass of Scotch across the desk to her, but she ignored it. 'I'm separated. So I can do whatever the hell I like.'

'What are you talking about?' She suddenly felt unsteady; she sank into one of Ted's square tan-leather chairs, which looked over the City. *Oh my God*, she thought, and felt her face crumple. *Did Alice know about what happened on the eve of her wedding?* Is that why Nina hadn't heard from her? She'd always known she needed to tell her, but she thought she had time; she never dreamed Ted would tell her first.

'Don't worry,' he said, reading her. 'It's not about that.' It hung between them, a revolting truth they were both ashamed of. He watched Nina slowly processing, shock moving over her face. The bravado he'd shown when she first entered the room dissipated. He softened and spoke again. 'Haven't you spoken to her? I thought you girls were always jabbing away on WhatsApp?'

Nina mouthed a 'no', her hands sweating against the soft leather. She *had* been ghosted by her friends.

'Oh. So you don't know about—? Well. She—' He became agitated then, his tumbler shaking in his hand. 'We— We're not together any more.' Ted appeared to freeze, his eyes darting left to right.

'You got caught out?' Nina asked and he shrugged, a flicker of relief glancing over his face at being spared having to spell it out.

'How long have you been shagging Sarah?' Nina asked.

'About a year.'

'You're a fucking cliché,' Nina said, and he couldn't help but agree.

'Tell me about it, Neen,' he said, crashing into his desk chair, his head in his hands. 'Why do I always fuck up?' He gestured wildly with his right arm, knocking his tumbler over. It spilled its sweet, smoky contents across the papers on his desk, the glass rolling to the floor. He growled angrily, swiping at the papers with some tissue and holding them aloft.

All his swagger had dissolved, leaving a residue of melancholy, as though Ted had found himself in this impossible position of fucking his secretary and he hadn't meant for it to happen and what was poor Ted going to do now? It reminded her of sitting with him outside Le Sacré Coeur; it reminded her of the night before his wedding.

'You always fuck up because you only think about yourself,' Nina snapped. She felt an agitated energy building inside her. 'Because you don't *care*, about *anyone else*.' Her voice was tight but with a slight wobble, like a guitar string being twanged. 'Because ever since you were a child, people have made allowances for you. *Including me*. But you're just not a very nice person.'

Ted rolled his eyes, as though he'd been hoping for an ally, not a dressing-down. 'I thought you'd understand,' he said.

'Why would I understand? I don't have a wife or children.'

He pulled a *go figure* face and she strode over and slammed her hand down on his desk.

'*Fuck. You*,' she shouted.

He looked instantly chastised and wiped at his eyes as though tears were budding. 'I thought you'd understand because you've never followed the herd! That's one of the things I always liked about you. When we were younger you weren't obsessing over boys, you were consumed by your music, writing songs and—'

'Ha,' Nina scoffed, her index finger rigid and stabbing at his desk. 'I was the *most* obsessed, but it was boy singular. It was just the one boy.' *Life in general and love in particular*, she thought, cringing at the memory. 'I was obsessing over *you*,' she said simply. 'I wasted so much of my life obsessing over you.'

His face clouded, as though this was new information, and Nina was momentarily thrown. This wasn't the first time she'd shared her feelings with him, she'd told him so outside Le Sacré Coeur that day, and later in bed that evening, but he was rubbing a hand across his temple and frowning, as though confused. Maybe it was possible that his feelings had once been as deep for her as hers were for him.

*What a mess*, she thought. She felt sad at Alice and Ted's separation, at her friendship group imploding. They had built something together, the four of them, from that chance encounter in a hotel restroom, and seeing Ted like this gave her a dizzying sensation of the foundations of it crumbling, the scaffolding coming loose. It would make it easier, at least, to tell Alice what had happened.

'I'm going to tell Alice,' she said. He raised his head and met her eyes, a sense of reckoning in the room. 'And, there's something else you need to know.'


## Jules

Jules would marvel later that she thought she'd reached rock bottom that morning in Ralph's office after Paris. She still had her home then. She still had her job.

It hadn't taken long for the charity to email the fund, chasing up Jules's share of the ASD money. They'd assumed they had the wrong email for her, or their emails were slipping into her junk mail. It wasn't the amount of money that was the problem for Ralph, it was the glaring evidence that Julia Frey-Jackson was totally out of control.

And it hadn't taken long for news of her demise to reach Paul. 'I'm putting the house up for sale,' he said. 'I can't watch you do this to yourself. I need a clean break.' And that was that. The house was under offer within a week. Jules had no savings for a deposit elsewhere, no income to secure a mortgage.

'It's theft, Jules,' Ralph said flatly.

'I reinvested it,' she insisted.

'Where is it then?' he asked impatiently, and she stared down at his desk. For the first time she realised her actions could be construed as a crime.

'HR wanted to contact the police,' he continued. She gasped and he raised a placatory hand. 'I've convinced them not to. The money has been taken care of, the charity has it now so they're none the wiser, and I could do without the police or an internal investigation. But…' He looked down at himself now and Jules felt dismayed, returning her eyes to the swirls of wood beneath her fingertips. Ralph had hired her as a graduate. Had always had her back. She knew he wouldn't be enjoying this. 'You can't keep working here, Jules. Please resign, so I don't have to…'

Her head flew up. She needed to keep her job. She had to work. It was all she had left. 'How about a different role?' she suggested, desperate. 'A non-risk-based role?'

She could feel the sweat gathering around her hairline and bulbing on her forehead; trips to Dr M were no longer a possibility. Her skin was breaking out too, she couldn't afford the medication or the laser treatments and facials she had come to rely on. *She would have to sell all her clothes,* she thought suddenly. *Her accessories collection!* It must be worth a fortune. Ralph pushed himself back in his chair. He couldn't look her in the eye.

'I'll take a pay cut,' she added. *'Please.* You can trust me.' *I'll keep your secret* was the subtext, and she hated herself for it. She wasn't in the business of blackmail or meddling in other people's affairs. *What had she become?*

He glared at her then with a steely expression. 'It's none of your business, Jules, but for the record, Samantha and I have an open marriage. I'm fairly certain, although we don't exchange details, that she's fucking her hairdresser. Don't bring my wife into this again.'

Jules couldn't speak, could feel her face twitching and contorting, beyond her control. She nodded and shakily made her way to the door. *She'd blown it.*

*'For fuck's sake!'* Ralph muttered behind her. 'Look. Jules.' He sighed loudly. 'I can't make any promises, but I'll speak to HR. I'll see what we can do.'

She turned, disbelieving. 'Why?' she croaked.

'I don't fucking know,' he said, scratching the back of his neck. 'Because we've worked together for eighteen years. Because you've been my best ever hire. Because, you don't deserve *this.*' And he gestured at her, his pity flooding her heart with shame. 'But Jules, please. Go to a fucking meeting, will you?'

'What happened at work?' Paul asked the following week,

when he was at the house collecting some documents he needed for the sale. 'Actually, don't tell me. I don't want to know.' She'd never seen Paul look like this. He was thin, his visage drained. He looked unwell.

'I'm going to meetings,' she said in a small voice.

'Are you?' he said wearily, in a tone that precluded it being a question.

'A women's one,' she said. As part of her change in role at work, she'd requested to leave at 4 p.m. on a Tuesday so she could make the meeting. 'There's only one a week. Would you believe it? There's hundreds for men! And try watching TV without being bombarded by adverts. It's impossible! Even those nice northern lads you like on Saturday night TV are at it.'

He shrugged. He wouldn't be drawn. She watched him run his hand along the door frame, distracted.

'You've spent the last five years trying to outrun our problems in an app, Jules, but I've felt it all: every shock, every tremor. I've felt it enough for us both and it's still so hard to leave. But I'm so *tired*, Jules.' He sank to his knees in the hall. Bent over himself as he sobbed, his long overcoat covering the beautiful geometric tiles so carefully selected by Alice. Jules rushed into the hall and crouched beside him, a hand on his shoulder.

'*I'm sorry. I'm so, so sorry,*' she whispered into his ear. Eventually, she felt him stiffen, his shoulders crunched together. He rose slowly, his hands rubbing his eyes. He groped in his coat pocket for a tissue and blew his nose. 'I'm going to do it this time, Paul. I'm really going to do it.'

'Good luck,' was all he said as stepped out softly into the night and out of Jules's life.

She sank down to the floor herself, wrapping her arms around her legs as her whole body shook.

She needed her friends. Still on the floor, she leaned over to her handbag in the hall, retrieved her phone and opened their WhatsApp group, *When in Paris*, but time had brought with it an awkwardness she didn't know how to navigate. What would she say to them now? How could she explain? Where would she begin? They had ghosted her after her terrible behaviour that weekend and she didn't blame them. Who would?

A familiar feeling began to vibrate in her head; a buzzing in her ears. Without giving it any chance to develop, she swiped out of WhatsApp and searched for a meeting, her eyes quickly scanning places and times until she found one.

*I will suffocate you*, she said to the impulse, the part of her that was running ahead to apps and races and games: anything that might blur the edges of the pain caused by Paul leaving.

She heaved herself upwards, pulled on her trainers over her work tights, a look she would have hitherto *died* rather than replicated, and ran, as fast as she could, to the meeting.

*Alice*

Vita gazed round the room approvingly. The labia-flower wallpaper, in an ochre-yellow and midnight-blue colourway, looked opulent and vivid in Vita's bedroom. The ceiling had been painted a metallic gold, which shone, iridescent, as the subtle ceiling light, a square of gold, was dimmed. Real flowers in shocks of electric blue and violet sprang from a vase in the shape of a woman's torso, love handles and voluptuous buttocks included. 'Very, very nice,' she purred. 'Seriously, you should be doing this as a job. I have two friends who've already asked me for your details.'

'Will they pay me?' Alice joked, because Vita knew all about what had happened last time Alice tried this for a living. To Alice's immense gratification, Vita had paid Alice the day she had finished, a pre-agreed amount ('*Charge me the same as the Mantels!*' Vita had instructed) and she still said she felt like she was ripping her off. 'I should be paying you double that,' she had grumbled.

'*Yes*, they will pay you,' she said now. 'And those Mantels should too. Richie, my last husband, sees them at these City functions, presiding over everyone like Jesus! I told him. Those women are *cheap*!'

Alice smiled. Everyone loved the Mantels. They were the darlings of the philanthropy scene. That's what made their rejection of her work sting so much.

'I know what your USP is,' Vita said, a finger tapping on her bottom lip. 'You make things sexy. But not in a black-satin-sheets way, you know. Your look is very *sumptuous*. You notice the little details,' she said approvingly, her fingers in a chef's kiss. Jules had said something similar to Alice once. Something about the little details, making the best of a unique feature, be it a person or an interiors project. Alice knew what she meant. She'd grown up self-conscious, had learned from an early age how to accentuate something she liked – like her arms – rather than something she disliked – like her middle. And that had made her feel sexy, self-possessed, in a way that she hadn't really felt since having the twins. She'd been too tired to notice any of the attention to details of herself, Alice Digby (she was definitely going to change her name back to Alice Digby formally when she had the energy to). She'd allowed herself to fall into a rut, accepted the pitifully small affection she had received from Ted as part of parenthood, but she felt the stirrings of change, of new beginnings, as she looked around at her work.

'I would love to do more of this, but I don't think I can,' she said. 'I have the kids, and I'm still finding my way with Charlotte...'

Charlotte's diagnosis had been helpful, because it forced the school to put in place more support for her, but beyond that Charlotte remained a puzzle for her parents, or in this case Alice, to figure out. Even her privately funded paediatrician had suggested she 'look up some groups on Facebook for ideas'. She shook her head at the memory. There were so many girls – and boys – like Charlotte not getting the help they needed, and it wasn't right. It made her think of Jules. The charity auction she set up. She wondered what was happening with that now. She hadn't heard anything from Jules. She looked her up on social media every now and then but there'd been no posts, no updates. Alice was sure if Jules had fallen pregnant there'd have been a reference to it on Instagram by now. She didn't think Jules would be able to resist after all those years of having to trawl through other people's pregnancy announcements. *Or maybe for that reason she wouldn't post about it?* Alice mused. Jules was a good person, after all. A good person who couldn't be bothered to let Alice know why she'd abandoned her in Paris.

She hadn't heard from Nina either and she'd come so close to messaging her a few days ago. She'd have loved the conversation Alice had had to endure in the playground. She'd been standing behind Chernoble, who was waxing lyrical to the Glossy Mums about apples. She'd lowered her voice, as though 'apples' were a dirty word:

'I've tried to kick Percy's apple habit, but he's still having three a day,' she'd confided. 'They're like crack to him!' she cackled. 'But no wonder, their sugar content is *sky high*.'

'I had a friend at university who would have an apple instead of a coffee when she was revising late at night,' crowed Philippa, nodding vigorously.

Alice had clocked Chernoble tipping her head and eyes in her direction mischievously, so she knew what was coming. 'How many apples a day does Charlotte have, Alice?' She raised her voice imperiously, a glint in her eye. Alice had simply laughed, much to Chernoble's chagrin. Where once this sort of thing would have paralysed Alice, since her life had fallen apart she found she was a lot less bothered about playground antics. Which could only be a good thing.

Vita's dogs – small, yappy things – barked downstairs and Vita went to open the door, shushing and babying them in Greek.

While she was waiting, Alice walked over to Vita's mirror. She turned, looking at her neck: her Eiffel Tower tattoo. *What had happened with her friends?* She opened *When in Paris*, her finger hovering as she considered leaving the group once and for all, but her heart jump-started. Nina was online. Jules was online! Her finger moved tantalisingly over the text box, tempted to type 'hello?' But the last message in the group, *her* last message, hung above it:

That was such a good night! I love you ladies! I just did somthing stuuuupid. I'll tell you in the morning. Love Alice x

x x x x

She'd sent it from her room, while they slept behind walls either side of her. They'd felt so united then. Anger, which had recently begun to dissolve, flared again in her chest: *They didn't even want to find out what I'd done.* She meant so little to them and they meant so much to her.

She glanced around the room again as she considered what to do. When she looked back down at her phone, Nina and Jules had disappeared. They were no longer online, a passing eclipse. *That's that then*, she thought, the window of opportunity slamming shut.

Alice didn't know that Jules had just said goodbye to Paul and had also been sitting staring at their group, wondering if she should try to reconnect before the shame of the last few months came cascading over her. Or that Nina had left Ted's office and was willing herself to call Alice: *Call her and tell her now!* All she knew was they'd abandoned her long ago without an explanation and she couldn't forgive them.

Vita called up. 'Come! Lunch has arrived!' and Alice descended the stairs to a Greek feast: triangular pastries stuffed with feta and mint, freshly grilled lamb and soft, doughy pitta bread.

'Do you get this delivered every day or just the days I'm here?' Alice asked.

Vita shrugged. 'I hate cooking. Christos and the boys love food. What can I do, I can't spend my whole day at the stove?' For each husband Vita had gained a son and they all lived here with her and Christos. 'Have you thought about an interior design course?' Vita asked with sudden interest. 'Maybe it would give you a much-needed *boost*?' She looked her up and down. Alice was wearing a pink floral dress with a chunky blue jumper and boots. 'At least we got you out of that stinky sweater,' she winked.

A month later and Alice strode confidently out of the first day of an interiors short course at an art school in Chelsea. It was only a six-week course one day a week and with no entry requirements, but it suited her perfectly. She had some experience – her own home, Jules's, the Mantels and now Vita's new wing – but she needed help pulling it into a '*compelling proposition*' as her tutor, Ashley, had indicated all the students needed to do. This was what Alice was lacking but the course would provide: business direction. She needed to learn how to work with clients, to be clearer from the outset on their objectives so she could deliver. Her work wasn't for everyone and that was okay too. She felt shot through with motivation as she boarded a bus up to Paddington station to get the train back to Oxford. She replayed Ashley's feedback on the photos she'd brought with her:

'What are these?' Ashley had asked, drawing a photo out by its corner. It was a photo from the Mantels' nursery project: the ceiling of the bedroom. Spurred on by their wish that it be a sensory calming space, Alice had taken the nursery mobile concept one step further and fixed a thousand origami cranes, in different pastel shades, to the ceiling. She remembered how peaceful it was to lie on the tatami mats below and watch them shift with the gentle breeze through the window. 'Did you work on this?' Ashley asked.

'Yes,' Alice sighed, quickly trying to push it back under the pile of other photos. She thought she'd removed all the photographs of the Mantels', fearing it wouldn't impress.

'It's beautiful,' Ashley said, holding the corner down with her thumbnail and scrutinising it carefully. 'The use of light is very clever, the contrast of materials... this is professional level, Alice.'

'Thank you,' Alice said sincerely. It was gratifying to hear that someone liked it, after all the time she'd put into it. She opened her mouth to say 'The client didn't agree', but stopped. Ashley didn't need to hear about that. It was enough that she appreciated it.

The course finished at four. Lilly, Vita's nanny, had agreed to collect the children from school and bring them home. In preparation, she had done the school run with Alice the last two Mondays – Charlotte needed to spend time with new people before Alice could leave them alone. Fortunately, they hit it off. Lilly was totally relaxed, taking Charlotte's behaviours in her stride. 'Fred told me you were into K Pop,' Lilly said. *I bet he did*, thought Alice. She imagined it was all Charlotte mentioned in school. 'And is this Dimples? What does he fancy for dinner today?' She had a low, calm voice and Charlotte warmed to her immediately. It was the first time Alice had been able to leave the children with anyone since they were small. Even her parents hadn't been able to cope with Charlotte, didn't understand why she was so 'difficult'. *And I thought you were hard work*, her mother would mutter. And the last time she'd left her with Ted, to go to Paris, had been a disaster on so many levels. She felt lighter by an afternoon out the house; less weighed down by the relentlessness of parenthood.

She watched London pass by through the bus windows. For the first time in a long while she didn't feel stress clamped to her heart like a vice. It was a beautiful day, russet and amber leaves spiralling from the sky as the season turned, and she impulsively pressed the bell as the bus drew towards Hyde Park.

She crunched through the drifts of leaves in the park, tuned in to the small interactions around her. Children laughing and asking for ice cream despite the cold, parents asking what had happened to their left glove – *Did you drop it? Over there?* – and personal trainers motivating their clients, who puffed scarlet-faced, performing burpees on the hard ground. And then she heard her favourite voice of all, deep and earthy; it drifted into her consciousness like a warm and welcome breeze.

'Sure, I can do four days next week, no problem.'

She stopped in her tracks and looked around, instantly blushed as she realised her mistake. There was no sign of Mr Hough. *Why would he be here in London?* she scolded herself. He was last spotted on a beach in Cornwall.

She walked on but the hairs on the back of her neck stood on end. She felt like she was being watched.

'Alice!' a voice called, and she turned. *Mr Hough.* 'I was sitting on that bench over there,' he said. 'You walked right past me.'

She felt her heart rocket, colour flooding her skin. She took in his grey beanie and thick padded navy jacket, his broad, firm chest still discernible beneath the layers of T-shirt, hoodie and scarf. With his glacier-blue eyes and defined cheekbones, he looked like he'd stepped out of a luxury casualwear brochure. A fox-red Labrador stood by his feet. *Just when you thought he couldn't get sexier.* A dog!

They stood taking each other in. Alice noticed sunlight flittering over his face as above them the wind moved clouds across the sky, conkers fell and split, dodged by frantic squirrels in pursuit of something unseen, and gulps of swallows soared noisily overhead. She was aware of the world moving around her, moving *on*, but all she could see was him.

'How have you been?' he asked as she blurted out, 'Where did you go?'

# 16

## Six Months After Paris

*Nina*

It had been three months since Nina had seen Ted and determined to tell Alice and she still hadn't worked up the courage. She was so confused: why had Alice and Jules cut her off like that? She understood that Alice would have a lot on her plate, going through a separation, but wouldn't she have needed her friends more than ever? And where did Jules fit in? She had been checking Jules's social media more frequently; once a day was now two or three times a day. Still no news of a baby. Was she in a blissful bubble, her pregnancy dreams having finally materialised and made it past the twelve-week milestone? She had never made it that far previously. Or was she in a pit of despair, her final chance at IVF dashed? Were she and Alice angry with her? For leaving that way? She should have messaged them, she knew, but she had so much on her mind and... she threw down her tea towel in frustration and began making herself an oat milk flat white at the barista machine.

'Can you make two of those?' called a voice, and she turned to see Ted standing at the counter sheepishly.

'With oat milk?' she asked, raising an eyebrow, a hand on her hips.

'You can't milk an oat,' he replied, deadpan.

She smiled in spite of herself. She hadn't seen Ted since the encounter in his office. She'd emailed her team afterwards and requested Ted be removed from the account and replaced with his partner, David, instead. In a sign that the power dynamic had shifted since she'd acquired an investor, it was done immediately and without comment. She'd half expected an irate email from Ted, but she hadn't heard from him at all.

'Do you have five minutes?' he asked.

She nodded. It was the sweet spot between the lunchtime rush and the mid-afternoon sugar-fix run. She finished their coffees and brought them over to a quiet table near the back of the café. She didn't need to work in the patisserie any more, the staff were fantastic, but she insisted on doing a day a week in the City. She liked to don a *La City Pâtisserie* T-shirt (black with a discreet white logo, modelled on the girls' simple, matching Eiffel Tower tattoos) and see for herself the reaction to a new product or hear the sort of off-the-cuff feedback you would never get from a focus group. It was coincidence that her day in the City – Wednesdays – coincided with Flynn's regular shift.

'What can I do for you?' she said, setting down the coffees.

'I never said sorry. For what happened before the wedding. And I never explained to you what happened after I left that day.' He spoke in a measured tone, as though this was something he had been rehearsing.

'We don't need to talk about that,' she said. 'It was a long while ago. It's fine.'

He looked down at the table in his grey suit, lightly drumming his fingers on the marble-effect top. 'It *was* a long while ago,' he agreed, 'but it's not fine. My behaviour. Not fine at all.' He sighed and looked up, meeting her eyes. 'I did go to tell Alice. I know you probably think I got what I wanted and scarpered, but it wasn't like that.'

He looked into her eyes and all the layers fell away. He was briefly returned to the young man she met at *le Bal*, confident but newly so, still half-glancing in her direction when he spoke, desperately hoping he was sounding cool, meeting Nina's approval.

'I ran into Dickie, outside the hotel. He was furious with me, slapped me, said I had to do the decent thing and marry Alice and figure out what to do later. Said I couldn't jilt her *in Paris* of all places, with all our family and friends having travelled there.' His voice wobbled, uncertainty flashing over his features. When he resumed speaking his tone was crisp, as if he was back on script: 'And he was right, I suppose. All her brothers there... Mind you, I was more afraid of her mother's wrath than theirs.'

He smiled wryly at Nina but she was deep in thought, her brow furrowed.

'The next morning, Alice told me she was pregnant and I thought, "well, that's that then". And ever since... I've tried to forget it happened. To put it behind me. But the truth is, I've been a rotten husband. I've been a rotten father. I've let everyone down.'

Pride, Nina thought, was something she could relate to. Cowardice too.

'Did you sleep together that night?' Nina had always wondered but never wanted to ask. She had read once that very few newlyweds had sex on their wedding night.

'I don't think so,' he said. 'I think she tried to, but I was too drunk.' All the arrogance and swagger he'd worn like a badge of honour the last decade or so had gone now. It was like talking to him on the phone, back in her bedroom in Mile End.

'Me too,' said Nina, closing her eyes at the memory.

'That was my fault as well,' he said. 'You getting like that. I was watching you nervously and thinking, *what have I done?* It was almost a relief when you passed out and Jules took you upstairs so I didn't have to worry about you falling over and hurting yourself.' He shook his head ruefully. 'You really took a tumble on the dance floor. And poor old Jules...' They each cracked a smile then, in spite of themselves.

'I hate what I did that night, Nina, the night before my wedding. I hate the position I put you in with Alice. I hate what sort of man that makes me.' He raked his hands through his hair, twisting the ends. 'I did love Alice. I was just so confused.'

Flynn moved easily around Nina and Ted now, wiping down tables and regrouping chairs with tables. The friendship between Nina and Flynn had deepened over the last three months, and they were hanging out together again, but no longer slept together. He caught her eye and gave her a 'you okay?' look and she gave a confirmatory nod and shifted her attention back to Ted.

'I had this silly idea when we were younger, after we met. I thought we were soulmates,' he said.

She cupped her coffee and shot him a quizzical glance. She

imagined her teenage self giving her current self a high five and yelling, *I knew it!*

'There's always been something about you, Nina Laurent.'

She rolled her eyes then, unable to suppress teenage Nina entirely. 'Nina O'Connell,' she corrected.

'See! There!' he said, triumphant. 'You've always been able to cut me down to size with just one look. How is your father, anyway?'

'Fine, I think. I never hear from him. But I see something about him every now and then in the paper and know he's alive.'

Ted nodded but looked preoccupied, his mind elsewhere.

'There *was* something between us though, wasn't there? We shouldn't have done what we did but...' He trailed off. 'I've been doing loops in my head since I last saw you. Did I spend my whole marriage burying my feelings for you? Was that what the affairs were about? But I truly believed I loved Alice when we were dating, when I asked her to marry me, right up until the wedding and I panicked. And I broke your heart!' He was sobbing now, tears falling from his eyes, snot trailing from his nose, and it crossed Nina's mind that he'd probably never spoken to anyone else about this before. 'Am I a monster?' he asked.

She reached over the table and took his hands. They felt cold and clammy as she squeezed his fingers. 'No, Ted, you're not a monster. You just need a really good therapist.' She smiled at him to show the interaction was friendly, but firm. 'For what it's worth, I thought we were soulmates too,' she added. 'For a long time. I had to have, I would never have done what I did otherwise... and then I hated you for a long time too.' She gave a short, sad laugh. 'I think the truth is, we recognised something in each other. Even when we were young, we knew what it was like to feel alone, *abandoned*, in a way that Jules and Alice didn't. Maybe they do now as adults, but it's different when you're younger. You were the first person I'd ever met who'd experienced anything similar to me. And yeah, I got wrapped up in that too. But then I realised you can't have a relationship based on pain.' She shrugged.

'You sound very wise all of a sudden.'

'I've had a lot of therapy myself,' she said pointedly. 'And don't worry about my broken heart. That wasn't what needed fixing.' She tapped a finger to her head.

'Do you remember the name of your album, Nina? *Life in general and love in particular*?'

Nina covered her face with her hands. 'I do.'

'Were there any songs about me?' He peeked up at her from beneath his fringe, which had become floppy and tousled in his distress. He reminded her so much of teenage Teddy.

'There were. That's all I'm saying.' She smiled as she pictured teenage Nina and teenage Teddy punching the air and chest bumping: *We knew it!*

Around them, La City Pâtisserie was filling up and Nina saw Flynn nobly trying to make headway with the queue alone, not wanting to disturb them. 'I'd better go,' she said, standing up.

'Indeed,' Ted said, pushing back his chair. 'I saw the figures last week, Neen. You're smashing it. I'm really happy for you.'

'Thanks,' she said and beamed. From the devastation they had wreaked, Nina had carved out a life for herself and she was proud.

Ted hesitated. 'One last thing: why haven't you told Alice

about us?' he asked. 'She hasn't tried to bludgeon me to death with a frying pan yet, so I assume you haven't...'

Nina held on to the back of her chair. 'Honest answer? I'm scared I'll tell her and she'll never speak to me again.'

He nodded, his hands in his pockets, his suit jacket flaring behind his forearms.

'How's she doing?' she added.

'Okay, really. Desperately worried about Charlotte, of course. She's not coping at school at all since that Mr Hough left.'

'Mr Hough *left*?' Nina asked. She knew how much Alice had sought his counsel. 'It was thanks to him Charlotte got any support in school in the first place!' she exclaimed.

Ted leaned back on his heels, chewing on his bottom lip. 'It would seem so,' he said. 'Hang on. Why don't you know about that? You've been in touch with Alice? Since Paris?'

Nina shook her head, as bewildered as he. 'No,' she said. 'Nor Jules. I can't explain it. They ghosted me. I had to leave early that morning, and I just never heard from either of them again. I had a lot going on, so I didn't contact them either and then, I don't know, it became a thing.' Something occurred to her. 'I suppose they could think I ghosted them. Alice has certainly had a lot on her plate and Jules, I don't know what happened with her IVF...'

'I'm sure I heard something about Jules...' Ted said, face briefly wrinkled in thought before he shook his head.

Nina was lost in her own thoughts: she still had to fight the impulse, whenever a song came on the radio they all liked, or had memorably danced to, to press her phone against the speaker, recording a voice note and singing along, sending it to their WhatsApp group, *When in Paris* like she used to.

Just before he left, Ted turned back. 'Do you think things would have been different, Neen? If we'd dated first? I often wonder, if I hadn't gone on my gap year, might it have set us on course, for us to end up together?'

So many scenes played out in Nina's mind: meeting Ted for the first time at *le Bal*; him at her little terraced house in Mile End; him and Alice and a tangle of sheets. Sacré Coeur, Montmartre, the night before the wedding. They began to blend and meld in her head, a jumble of fleeting looks and moments but all of them grounded in one thing: pain. They were all edged with sadness and worry, anxiety and despair.

'No,' she said simply. 'I just don't think we were ever right for one another.'

Hi Alice

It feels weird to even write that. We've not emailed each other in about ten years, have we? But I've got too much to say for WhatsApp and it felt even stranger, too formal, to write a letter. But I've got something to tell you and I think it's best I lay it out here and you don't have to see me – ever again if you don't want to, although I really hope you do – while you think about things. Because what I've got to say is going to come as quite a shock.

There's no easy way to say this, Alice. The night before your wedding, I slept with Ted. It's the biggest regret of my life, by a mile. The truth is, I thought we were meant to be together. Obviously that seems ridiculous now – and it was ridiculous then – but I was young and stupid and as you know, back then, quite reckless. It's why I'm not so reckless now. It's why I finally got my act together: started therapy, did my course, opened the patisserie. I had betrayed you and I couldn't live with myself like that. I had to change.

I didn't see Ted for a long time after the wedding. I made sure I only saw you when I knew he wouldn't be there. The next time I did was at Charlotte's christening, but we didn't speak that day and we didn't speak for a long time after, probably not until Jules' wedding, and we barely spoke then. I don't want you to think there were looks or glances behind your back; there weren't.

By the time you suggested us working together, it felt like we'd all moved on. I knew – I thought at least – you two were happy together. In a strange way I had convinced myself that it was in the past and it didn't matter any more but as I write this now I realise how foolish – and selfish – that was. I had moved on but I'd not given you the same opportunity.

I'd decided to tell you after that last weekend in Paris. I had to leave early, I had an emergency. (Why did you never check I was okay, Alice?)

Nina paused. Tears had been cascading down her face since she typed 'Hi Alice' and her throat felt swollen. This was the hardest thing she'd ever had to do. She deleted the last line: ~~(Why did you never check I was okay, Alice?)~~ She was supposed to be begging forgiveness, not feeling sorry for herself. She took a deep breath, and continued:

And then, I don't really know what happened. When I didn't hear from you or Jules at first it was a relief. Because I could put off telling you. I wanted to tell you, that's what you have to understand. I wanted to, but I was so, so afraid. And it affected my judgement. And now, I'm worried that I've left it too long, but I have to try.

Nina decided not to tell her about the baby or the abortion. She didn't want Alice to think she was trying to elicit sympathy. Her fingers hovered above the keyboard, the light from the screen illuminating the café, which had dimmed into darkness.

I miss you Alice and I'm so, so sorry. I'll do anything to put things right.

Please forgive me. If you can't – if you don't want me in your life any more – then I respect your decision. I won't contact you again.

Love Nina x

~~PS – we'll always have Paris.~~

*Alice*

Alice sat in her car after morning drop-off and stared at the email for a very long time. Then she deleted it, sniffed and checked her make-up in the mirror. The look she was aiming for was business-but-keep-it-creative: she was wearing a long pink-and-yellow leopard-print dress, knee-high leather boots and a blazer. As she drove into London, it zipped into her head intermittently: *Ted had sex with Nina. Her husband slept with her best friend.* It seemed impossible. How could it be true? But more and more was emerging about Ted that hadn't seemed like it could be true, like the message she'd received from Sarah, a secretary at his work, explaining they'd been having an affair for a year before Ted had recently called it off. How could she have known so little about her own husband? And had Nina – and maybe Jules – known about the affair too? Is that another reason they hadn't been in touch?

She parked and gazed down the street. Ordinarily, this row of houses in Notting Hill, painted in pastel tones of marshmallow, blossom and biscuit, made her soul sing, but today she saw only the grey sky, a weighty band of drizzle hovering above. The only positive about the email was its neutralising effect on her nerves. She couldn't feel anything.

'Alice?' the woman said, opening the door. 'Samantha. Please come in. Ashley speaks so enthusiastically about your work.'

Alice entered the beautiful Georgian house. It was light and airy, layered in different shades of cream and beige. She went through the motions, accepting a coffee and wincing when she noticed a shining bean-to-cup machine, pulling out her portfolio on the white kitchen counter.

'We've recently moved in,' the woman said, 'and it's fine,' – she gestured around – 'but all this cream,' she grimaced. 'I want to inject some colour, some character, into the place.'

'I would love to help,' Alice said, which was true. She'd enjoyed her course in Chelsea so much that she'd taken a further course since then and Ashley, her tutor, had started recommending her to clients. Alice knew she wasn't doing that for the other students and it meant an enormous amount to her. She was finally starting to feel valued.

'These are gorgeous,' Samantha said, flicking through Alice's portfolio.

'Oh.' She frowned. She'd reached the photos from the Mantel project and Alice inwardly swore. Ashley had insisted she include them, but Alice should've known better. 'I know this room...' Samantha said. 'You worked on the Mantels'?' she asked, and then, '*Oh*, you're *Alice*.' She looked up at her in bemusement. 'So if I give you this job, you're not going to do a runner on me, are you?'

'I'm sorry?' said Alice.

'I'm just kidding. But whenever I see Aki, she's always bemoaning how you're too busy now to work for her. So you went back to college instead? No offence, but odd decision – you could've made a fortune working on Aki's last launch. She said no one has the same sense of style as you.'

'I think you must be confused...' Alice said. 'I did work for the Mantels but—' What could she say? She couldn't bad-mouth the Mantels, it would reflect badly on her. People didn't like to talk about money. 'I didn't hear from them again after I did the nursery.' *Not even to get paid.*

Samantha frowned again, setting down her coffee cup. 'Really? How strange. Maybe I got confused,' she said, looking embarrassed. 'The woman I'm thinking of was good friends with a colleague of my husband, Ralph. Julia Frey-Jackson. Do you know her?'

'I do,' Alice said. 'I am that person.' She waved her hand in the air to signify she was the elusive Alice, friend of Julia Frey-Jackson. 'But I never heard from Aki or Elliott after I completed the project and I was...' The shock of Nina's email had left Alice disarmed and defensive. '… quite disheartened, to be honest with you. No. Actually. Pretty well *pissed off.*' *Lordy, she'd blown it now, but fuck it.* She laughed at herself, appearing, no doubt, quite mad.

Samantha tipped her head to one side contemplatively. 'I must have made a mistake,' she said quickly. She gestured at her watch – a neutral pink-diamond-studded affair – 'Sorry, I must dash!' she said. 'I'm booked in with Antonio at Zed in ten minutes. These roots need attention!' she laughed. She said it with a wink, as though Alice should know who Antonio was, and it reminded her of the way Jules and Nina used to speak, how excluded she felt. Perhaps it was the secret, she thought bitterly, perhaps it was Nina having slept with her husband. Not only had Nina blown her marriage, but she'd also blown her shot at this commission with the timing of her email.

'Look, the job's yours if you want it,' Samantha said, surprising her, as she shoved items into a large blush-leather tote. 'Send me your rates and we'll discuss. I can't wait to tell Aki I've bagged her favourite designer for my revamp!' Her face clouded over. 'Actually, I'd better not. Ralph will kill me if I piss off his biggest client!'

'Er, excellent,' Alice said brightly, forgetting for a moment about Nina's email. 'Thank you.' She could feel her eyes shining with tears embarrassingly as she gathered up her things.

'Hold on, I'll head out with you,' Samantha said, wrapping a scarf around her neck. 'Terrible business with Julia,' she tutted as she set the alarm. 'How's she getting on?'

'To be honest, I don't know. We've not been in touch for a while,' Alice said.

'I thought she and Paul were rock solid,' said Samantha, locking the door behind them.

'*Jules and Paul?*' Alice gasped.

Samantha's head whipped back round. 'They're separated, Alice. Didn't you know?'

Alice shook her head slowly, trying to process. *Jules and Paul.*

'Goes to show, you never know what goes on behind closed doors. Poor Julia. And having to switch jobs like that. Anyway, gotta run. Send me that quote!' she called, striding off to her date with Antonio and his famous highlighter brush.

'You look like you've seen a ghost,' Nate (formerly known as Mr Hough) said when she turned up.

'I have,' she joked weakly. 'I've been visited by the ghosts of friendships past.'

Nate slid a wine glass in front of her and began to fill it. She noticed the bottle – one of her favourites – and smiled. Nate had suggested this pub in Notting Hill for lunch when she told him about her appointment.

'I'm driving,' she said, 'so I can only have the one.'

'Don't worry. I'll take the rest home. We can finish it when you stay over.' He caught her eye meaningfully and she looked away. It had been three months since she had bumped into Nate in Hyde Park and they'd walked for an hour, as though they hadn't spent any time apart, but it was more intense because he was no longer her daughter's teacher and she was separated. This fantasy she'd harboured for so long was theirs for the taking, but it didn't seem right to jump into something so soon, she didn't feel ready. And Nate had his own reasons for holding back, thanks to Ted, but as time had moved on the connection between them was undeniable and they were finding it harder and harder to contain themselves in each other's company. It was the headiest, most potent foreplay Alice had experienced, and it had lasted three months and counting.

'I was going to ask, do we have something to celebrate, but instead I'll say, do you want to talk about it first?' His eyes were so clear and calm, his face open and kind. She wanted to reach over the table and kiss him, to act finally on the impulse they had both been repressing, but she knew she'd be doing it as a response to Nina's news, and Nate deserved more than that.

'I got the job,' she said sadly. 'Yay me.' Her mouth was the reverse of a smile. They sipped their wine quietly.

'What exactly did Ted say to you, at school that Monday morning, after I got back from Paris?' Alice asked.

Nate sighed and rubbed a hand over his stubbled chin as if he had hoped to avoid the topic of Ted for a little longer. 'He said if I didn't leave the school, he'd report me and I'd struggle to work again. He said you two were working on your marriage and if I had any decency, I'd leave you alone and never contact you again. When I agreed, I didn't know he'd already moved out. I thought that's what you wanted too. But—'

Alice shook her head furiously, one hand up to indicate he stop speaking and one hand rubbing her forehead. She'd been resisting her attraction to Nate, even as her body refused to deny it; tiny jolts of electricity fizzed over her skin whenever their arms bumped or their hands grazed. Even her mother, hitherto Ted's chief cheerleader, had been encouraging her to 'move on' since she'd learned of his affair with Sarah, but it had seemed inappropriate; disrespectful to her marriage. But who had she been kidding? Ted had slept with Nina the night before her wedding, when they were already legally married. Her marriage vows had been violated long ago.

'Ted slept with my friend Nina. The night before our wedding.' Saying it aloud didn't make it seem any more real. She was in shock, she supposed.

'*What?* How did you find out?'

'She emailed me today. A confession,' she said tartly. 'Thirteen years too late.'

'I'm sorry, Alice.' He reached over the table and held her hand. Her skin crackled beneath his touch. 'How are you feeling?'

'Fine. Just dead inside.' Her jokes weren't landing today at all. 'It's weird, it's like, it's a surprise and it's not a surprise. When we were younger, they really fancied each other. It was so obvious. And I thought it just fizzled out. I thought... I thought he'd chosen me. But he was hers all along.'

Nate frowned in disbelief. 'Did it happen more than once?'

'I don't think so. Nina says it didn't. Says she couldn't live with herself afterwards, she had to change her life, so she had therapy and became a famous entrepreneur. As you do,' she said angrily. 'I can't open Instagram or read a magazine these days without a piece about La City Pâtisserie and its success and Nina's coffee and her aesthetic and her fabulous, irritating life. She got to live that life after she'd destroyed mine.'

'Fucking hate that coffee,' he said, and she laughed in spite of herself.

'I bet she knew, when we were in Paris. About Ted's affair. She was snappy that weekend, not her usual self, and I can see it now. *She knew* and she didn't want to tell me.'

'You don't know that,' Nate reminded her. 'I do need to tell you something about Ted though, Alice,' Nate said, suddenly serious. 'I was hoping we could have our celebratory lunch first but we're here now.' He played with the beer mat in his hand, sliding it through his fingers. 'Ted emailed me. He must've got my email from the educational consultancy website.' Burnt from the fiasco with Alice, Nate hadn't wanted to commit to another permanent role. He had been doing supply teacher work and, motivated by his work with Charlotte, private Special Educational Needs consultancy work with families.

Alice's forehead wrinkled in shock so satisfyingly she was grateful she'd never been to Dr M. 'What did he say?'

'He... apologised. He said he acted like a dick and he was sorry and he wouldn't make a formal complaint about me. Regardless of "what happened in the future". He stopped short of saying, if we got together, but that seemed to be his intention.' Nate shrugged. 'He actually seemed to be encouraging me to go back to Holsbrook. He said how much Charlotte had struggled since I'd left and asked if I would consider meeting him some time to talk through ASD strategies with him.'

'No! "*Strategies?*" He used that word?' Alice exclaimed.

'Yeah,' Nate nodded, as perturbed by this as Alice. 'And then he asked me if I could recommend any books or things he could read!'

'*To read?!*' Alice screeched, as though Ted were incapable of such a thing.

Nate nodded. 'It was a far cry from the angry man who waited for me outside school on that Monday morning and threatened to ruin my career if I ever spoke to his wife or daughter again.' He took a contemplative sip of wine as Alice fanned herself with a coaster, overcome. 'I think you should talk to him.'

Alice pondered what to do on the drive home. She had no intention of replying to Nina any time soon. She needed to process what had happened. It was too much. It was a lie that had penetrated the very foundations of her marriage, a marriage that had since disintegrated, and who knew what part Nina's betrayal had played in that? And there was more that bothered her. It was the abrupt tone of: '*I had to leave early, I had an emergency.*' So what? Alice had an emergency brewing too, fell face first into it when she returned home. But she would never have just left her friends like that without a word or a note.

And what had happened to Jules? Had Paul been abusive as she and Nina had suspected; perhaps not physically but emotionally, leaving a deeper, more indelible scar? Had they attempted that final round of IVF and were unable to fix themselves back together in the aftermath? There had been a time when Jules had allowed the girls to support her after her miscarriages. Not fuss over her as such, as she could never tolerate it, but they would sit together and watch TV, or order takeout, or eat leftovers from La City Pâtisserie. Ordinary acts, executed in silence. Sustenance and support. Had Jules needed them and they weren't there? And there was something amiss with the Mantels.

Why not pay her but then talk her up like that? Was that some rich person's power play? Should she confront them? She wouldn't know how to get in touch with them; Jules had been their go-between and their PA was legendary for withholding all but the most essential information from them.

It was that twinkly time of year, darkness falling earlier, candelabras glowing in windows; ten-foot-high piles of Brussels sprouts and turkeys gliding along the motorway. The loss of her closest friendships remained a raw, open wound. She swung between cursing herself for her stubbornness, for leaving it so long to get in touch, to anger at the way they had left Paris without her and not a backward glance – or text message – in her direction. But she ached for them too. Ached for the easy shorthand between them, the lack of formality when they were together, they way they *fitted*. Part of her had known, instinctively, that while she might not always have Ted in her life, she would always have those women. They had known each other before, and they would know each other after. That was the creed at the heart of their friendship. They were bonded for life, from that very first moment in the toilets at Le Crillon. And how apt was that? A luxury hotel but the three of them in the loo. *That's just us!* She smiled to herself even as tears streamed down her cheeks but her smile faded to a frown. How had they let this happen? Why had they abandoned her? And she hadn't had to cope with just them, there was Ted, leaving her as soon as she got home; Mr Hough leaving school the next day. But the biggest loss of all had been her friends. She hadn't seen it coming and she'd never understand.

She was almost home when a call came through via the

car's audio system. She recognised the number immediately: it was the school.

'Mrs Astor?' The headmaster's voice was grave and Alice instantly felt the cold that surrounded the car sink into the interior and into her bones. 'There's been an incident at school today. Charlotte kicked a chair and knocked over a table following a simple request. Fortunately no one was injured but I'm afraid we're going to have to exclude her for the rest of the week.'

She called Nate on the hands-free, not with the hysteria that had gripped her when Mr Sharp had threatened Charlotte with exclusions in the past, but with a deep sense of dread in the pit of her stomach: this was how it would be for Charlotte now. The roundabout of exclusions and reduced timetables, all designed to fit her unique, beautiful, diverse, square-peg daughter into an inflexible, mainstream round hole. Every time it happened, its message to Charlotte was the same: you are not enough. What can it do to a person being told that by the very system that should support them to flourish and grow?

'This world isn't built for her,' she whispered, tears leaking from her eyes, the raw gutting pain of that statement overwhelming.

She would never forget his voice in the car, the way it soothed over her anxieties and gave her hope for the future.

'So let's build a new world,' he said.

Later, she would recall that as the very moment when she knew she had fallen for him. And the flush of hope that that thought too had provided: despite everything, she hadn't yet given up on love.

★ ★ ★

*Jules*

'I think I'm autistic,' Jules announced to her therapist, 'and I think I have ADHD.'

When she'd shared this with her mother last week, Nancy had laughed: 'Don't be ridiculous,' she'd scolded. 'You're not a five-year-old boy.' So Jules was prepared to list her reasons, which of her behaviours supported her theory, but Cindy simply tilted her head and nodded. 'Oh, right,' Jules said. 'When did *you* know?' she asked.

'I was pretty sure after your first session and I'm completely sure now,' she said.

'Oh, okay.' Jules smiled. 'You could have shared that and saved me a lot of agonising,' she said in a friendly tone. She was wearing a charcoal knitted wrap dress and Chelsea boots, but she had retrieved one of her old handbags from storage – a crystal-embellished predominantly gold clutch in the shape of a croissant, with red and white crystals studded on its underside to resemble a napkin (her personal stylist had deemed it '*too garish*') – and was twisting its metallic chain around her fingers.

'What would your response have been if I had?' Cindy asked.

'Fair point,' she acknowledged. 'It's strange,' she said. 'It's like I always knew but I didn't know. When Alice, you know, one of my old friends, would talk about her daughter Charlotte, who's autistic, I would really tune in. Like it meant something. And at the time I thought it was just because I wanted to support Alice – which I did – but at the same time, I knew there was something more there, and I wanted to ignore it.'

Her therapist nodded. 'The subconscious is extremely powerful,' is all she said.

'I think that's why my performance was patchy at work. When I was in hyper-focus, I was all over it, but I couldn't sustain that for long periods. Even at school, if I struggled at something, like French, I had to work *so hard* at it, but I wouldn't admit it to anyone, I went to extreme lengths to prove to myself – and my family, I suppose – that I could do anything. What teenager begs to work in a pharmacy in Paris to improve her French?' She laughed. 'I should have been snogging boys at youth club,' she added wistfully. 'And that weekend, the study drugs, for people with ADHD, I could notice the difference. It wasn't good taking them like that, the wrong dosage, and I'm lucky I didn't experience any side effects, but I think they could help me if I was prescribed them properly. I've got a referral from my doctor to be formally assessed,' she added.

'Lots of addicts have ADHD. You're doing really well.'

Jules nodded. She wasn't afraid of the word 'addict' any more. It was part of her story. In fact, she now introduced herself in GA meetings as a 'recovering compulsive gambler', no longer ashamed.

'Have you thought any more about contacting Alice, or your other friend, Nina?'

Cindy was keen for Jules to *reconnect*. That's why Jules had found herself in Guildford a few weeks ago, to tell her mother everything. She'd expected denial or derision from Nancy, she hadn't expected her to burst into tears and blame herself. Jules had been confounded until her mother explained that Jules's father had had a gambling addiction too, which had started shortly after he'd sold his business and retired. 'His busy brain got bored,' her mother said. They'd protected Jules and her brother from it. That was why they downsized and moved, why they never decorated, why her mother would roll her eyes when Jules would sit with her father placing bets for him. He couldn't do anything by then, after his stroke, but the damage had been done. She'd sold the house after he died and moved to a small flat back in Guildford, near her friends, where she'd never wanted to leave. 'I should have warned you,' Nancy said. 'I didn't think...' She didn't need to finish that sentence. No one, least of all Jules, would have thought that could happen to her. But it did.

As well as Cindy being keen for Jules to connect with Nancy, she wanted her to find a way back to her friends. 'Perhaps you should discuss this with them? Among other things,' she said now, her eyebrows raised.

Jules shook her head to indicate 'no' but answered, 'I do want to explain. I feel like I'm ready, or close to being ready – are you ever totally ready, I don't know? But also I still feel let down by them. I look back and I was acting *so strangely* that weekend and didn't they notice? Didn't they wonder what was going on? I think they *had* to have noticed and it must have pissed them off and that's why I've not heard from them since. But can twenty years of friendship come undone in one weekend?' She was animated now, because this was something she thought of often, something she pored over in meetings with other addicts who had wiped out decades of friendship and family ties.

'Maybe they had their own things going on that weekend?' Cindy asked.

'Hm,' Jules frowned. It seemed unlikely they were experiencing anything on the same scale as Jules, but then

Alice had seemed worried about Charlotte and Nina wasn't quite herself either, come to think about it. A small thought burrowed its way up from her subconscious: *Nina wasn't drinking*. She was stressed about work. Stressed enough that it had irritated her IBS. Jules googled Nina most days and there was always something new: a profile piece or expansion to the La City Pâtisserie product range: her cutlery and glassware was now being sold at Anthropologie. Work stress still didn't seem like enough though. It wasn't very Nina, to have cut her off because she was busy at work.

'What does Paul think?' Cindy asked.

'He doesn't like to talk about it. That weekend. He changes the subject.'

Jules and Paul were separated now and he was subletting a flat near to the house while they waited for the sale to go through. They were at the whim of their buyer, the capricious Mr Legg, who every few weeks would come up with another issue with the house that bothered him and try to use it as leverage to negotiate a reduction in price (which Jules and Paul would politely refuse). They could have called his bluff and given him a deadline to exchange but neither was in any hurry to. They were still married and Paul hadn't asked her to divorce, as a favour to her really, she supposed, since it made it easier for him to be in control of her finances. It was her idea, to put Paul in charge, something he initially resisted, but when she had been in therapy for two months, and was regularly attending meetings, he agreed. She lived on an allowance and if she needed anything extra she emailed Paul and the money immediately appeared in her account. She didn't feel controlled or subjugated, as she might have expected to; she felt empowered. She had sold her car, which had cleared a large chunk of debt, and taken out a consolidation loan to pay off the rest. The first thing she tried to pay back was the ASD charity money to Ralph but he refused to take it, looking embarrassed. 'What?' she pressed. 'Jules, it was Paul,' he said sadly. *Of course,* she thought, *of course.* It would take a long time to clear the rest of her debts on just her base salary, but she was enjoying the lower demands of her new role box-ticking in compliance, and the extra time it afforded her to think and piece her life back together; the things she had been running from all along.

They had dinner together once a week, trying a different restaurant each time, alternating whose turn it was to pick. It was like dating, but at the end of a relationship rather than at the beginning; a wind-down in feelings, rather than a ramping up. Not that her feelings for Paul had ever dissipated, nor did she believe they ever would. She loved him and that's why she had to let him go. She had hurt him too much. She'd read an article about twin brothers; one had died and the remaining twin's heart was so broken, so bruised emotionally, that it had left physical scarring, evident on a scan. But hearts could be fixed, apparently. A few years on and a scan detected that the bruising had subsided. She often thought of Paul's heart, and the damage she had inflicted, and whenever she was tempted to lay a hand on his over the table, or look at him in a certain way, she thought of his heart instead and she imagined it healing, scars melting and fading, the colour returning. She wanted his heart to be the way it was when she met him: healthy and whole, strong and open, walking into the ocean beside her with his arms held wide.

'I found some recovery podcasts, like you recommended. There's one run by two women. I wrote in to thank them, marvellous what they're doing, and told them a bit of my story. They've invited me on as a guest – how it's going, six months on.'

'That could be interesting,' Cindy noted.

'Hm,' Jules agreed. 'Interesting and available for the whole world to download. I know it's common knowledge in my old team, my immediate contemporaries, but no one knows the details and a lot still assume it was drinking rather than gambling.' She grimaced. 'I'm not sure I'm ready to tell the full story.'

'When are we ready for anything?' Cindy asked with a smile, her palms flat in the air.


After her session Jules walked home, rather than catching the bus, winding along the river, through Barnes, and along the river path, past empty gasworks and squat urban buildings and wider long-grassed sections that made you forget you were in a city. It was sunny despite the chill and small groups of people were sitting along the river, their legs kicking against the stone wall lining the Thames, cupping mugs of mulled wine from the riverside pub.

She went inside to the bar, ordered a single whisky, and found a bench outside close to a heater, her gold crystal-croissant bag on her lap. She tuned in to the hubbub of conversation around her, the reports of bad dates and husbands not pulling their weight and irritating colleagues. She missed her friends. It was a deep, whole-body ache. Like wanting a child, but worse. She had grown with these women; they had been a part of each other's lives for so long. How could this have happened? She opened their WhatsApp group. Silent, still.

*What would happen if she sent a message?* she wondered. Would anyone respond? But what could they possibly say, what could any of them say to explain their absence? How could Jules, without telling them all what she'd done? They'd abandoned each other, hadn't they? Was it too painful for their friendship to have continued?

She wasn't ashamed of being an addict, but she was ashamed of how she'd behaved. Did she owe them an explanation? She couldn't decide.

She pulled up the list on her phone. When she had begun confronting her debts and paying them off, she'd made a list. It was long – longer than she'd realised or wanted to admit to. Most were on credit cards, which she'd swapped from zero interest to zero interest until she'd run out of options and the repayments had ballooned. With the consolidation loan she was paying them off slowly each month, but there were others that she was still working her way through.

She scanned down the list until she got to 'Alice: £5,000.' Then she pulled up Aki Mantel's number. She closed her eyes and exhaled deeply. She knew what she had to do.

# 17

## Nine Months After Paris

Alice was having the strangest day. Earlier, she'd received a deposit for £5,030 into her bank account, from an account she didn't recognise. The reference was 'Mantel Nursery'. Finally, almost a year since she'd completed the project, she'd been paid! It was the amount she was due, plus, she suspected, a little extra for interest.

She had crossed over the leopard-print-carpeted drawing room, her blue puff-sleeve maxi dress billowing around her, and into the study where Nate was working with Charlotte. He tutored Charlotte in the mornings, working with other families in the afternoons. Alice worked in the morning and then swapped with Nate. She and Charlotte did things to ease her anxiety in the short window before her siblings returned home: cycling, swimming, skateboarding. Sometimes they cooked (always Korean, although Charlotte had recently shown an interest in a Norwegian singer and Alice was hopeful they might try some Scandinavian food next). Charlotte was learning Korean on an app and Ted had bought her some Korean comics, which she enjoyed translating. If Alice needed to work then Nate, or Lilly, stepped in. Ted had Friday afternoons with Charlotte before collecting Wilf and Phoebe from school and had them overnight. It wasn't perfect but it was progress.

This morning, Charlotte had been learning maths by way of BTS sales (*If BTS sold X records at £X, how much money would they make in Korean won?*). Alice was relaying the curious incident of the mystery payment to Nate, when a WhatsApp notification pinged on to her screen:

*When in Paris*
**Jules:**

The shock was such that she spluttered mid-speech, half-choking. 'What the...' she said as Nate looked up curiously. 'You okay?' he laughed.

'Yeah, I just got a WhatsApp from Jules,' she said, lifting the phone screen for him to see.

It was weird to see her name there, like that. As if the last nine months hadn't happened.

'So open it?' Nate said quizzically.

'I don't know.' Alice bit her lip. 'I feel like I should just delete it. What could she possibly have to say that will put things right?'

'Just read it,' he said, ever the voice of reason. 'She was your friend for twenty years. That's important.'

'Hm,' she said. 'I guess.'

Nina was abroad, styling a food shoot in Milan for a leading women's magazine. She was reliably informed by Carey that she was now a multi-hyphenate, which she liked the sound of.

Her dark hair was newly cropped, back to how she wore it in her teenage days, but with one of her trademark scarves – a floral yellow print today – knotted over the top. She'd dressed carefully, a fine-knit halter-neck top beneath her black *La City Pâtisserie* apron, her arms bare but for her scattering of delicate fine-line tattoos and a single bracelet, a gift from the girls, because she knew today's photographs would also be featured in her lifestyle book, *With Nina,* which was themed around seasonal entertaining. She had been delighted when she signed the contract but couldn't miss the note of irony that she wasn't able to share the moment with her oldest girlfriends. Her favourite Adele album was drifting through the room's state-of-the-art speakers, while Luna, Flynn's photographer sister, discreetly snapped away, when her phone pinged and she glanced at the alert.

*When In Paris*
**Jules:**

She dropped the prosciutto she was artfully draping and snatched up her phone, crossly rubbing it over her apron to remove the resulting smear across the screen, ignoring the jerk of Luna's head to check she was okay. Without hesitating, she opened the group. There was a link and a single word: 'Sorry.' She clicked on the link and her phone opened her podcast app. 'Rolling in the Deep' stopped abruptly and was replaced by a jaunty soundtrack.

'Do you mind?' she asked Luna, indicating the speakers, as Luna shook her head in a *no, she didn't* and a woman introduced the podcast: a recovery podcast. Nina knew immediately – she'd been right! Jules was an alcoholic! – but she gasped as the woman's introduction revealed the truth. Jules was a recovering compulsive gambler. *What?*

She checked her watch. She only had an hour before she had to leave for her flight. But she couldn't wait. She continued to style cornichons and edible flowers, Luna focusing on her hands, no doubt her dark blue nail polish and Eiffel Tower tattoo forming a better background than her frowning face as Jules's voice filled the room. Each admission drew a fresh gasp from Nina: *Jules had broken up with Paul! She'd lost her job!* She listened to her former friend detailing their weekend in Paris but adding colour to the story: how she'd stayed up all night gambling (*that's why she fell asleep on the boat!*), how she'd ignored Paul and he'd eventually turned up and told her he was leaving her (*my God, that was the man she was speaking to!*), how she'd fractured her most important friendships and feared they could never be recovered.

At this, Nina paused the recording and she stood in the bright room, daylight streaming through the windows, with her hand to her chest to steady herself. *Jules!* she thought, *Jules!* Her heart ached that she hadn't been there for her friend. *How had they let things get this far?* she thought, crossly. What were they all playing at, not speaking? It was ridiculous.

She resumed the recording, resolving to message Jules back the minute it finished, but there was more: *She'd stolen money from Alice.* Shit. That project Alice had done that she'd been so anxious about. She'd never been paid. Jules had amended the account details on Alice's invoice to her own. Wow. That was... grubby. Underhand. That was... *She's an addict, Nina. Come on. Have some compassion. Haven't you done some grubby things yourself?* But she wondered how Alice would feel, hearing what Jules had done. She knew how much it had knocked her confidence, not being paid.

She picked up her phone to call Alice and stopped, her finger hovering over the call button. She hadn't heard from her since she'd sent her email. She'd promised her she'd leave her alone if she didn't hear back. The podcast didn't change things and Jules was in recovery, wasn't she? She should leave things where they were. But as she stared at her phone, it began to ring.

'Alice?' she said, snatching the phone close to her ear.

'Have you listened to it?' Alice breathed.

'Just now. Have you?'

'Yes, I was with Nate and—'

'*Nate?*' Nina enquired before she could stop herself.

'Um, Mr Hough to you,' Alice said. Both women paused, the enormity of the last nine months hanging between them. Nina couldn't repress an admiring laugh. 'Good for you,' she said, and she could hear Alice smiling as she replied, 'I know, right?' Tentatively, she stepped a foot back into their friendship.

They all met three days later, on neutral territory: the South Bank. It was almost the end of winter. The sky swirled with glacial blues and moody greys, clouds heavy in the sky.

'I'm so sorry, Alice,' Nina said as soon as they began walking. She was wearing a long camel coat over a pale blue sweatshirt, with a black cross-body bag.

Alice pulled her faux-fur coat around her tightly, burying her neck in its collar. A flippy gold skirt, tights and chunky boots peeked out below. 'He was cheating on me. When we were in Paris. Did you know?'

'No. I promise I didn't know then.' Nina looked nervous.

'*Then?*' Alice asked quickly. That's what had been bothering her the most; that her friends had known Ted was having an affair and hadn't told her.

Nina sighed. 'I found out later,' she admitted. 'Accidentally. I walked in on them in his office in London.'

'Why didn't you tell me then?'

'I planned to,' Nina said. 'About everything. But I hadn't heard from you both – it had been three months since Paris then – and I suppose I used that, not hearing from you, as a justification for not getting in touch myself. It was cowardly and I'm sorry.'

'I really need to get some new friends,' Alice replied quietly, a half-joke that fell flat as she whimpered on the inside. She'd promised herself she'd never cry over Ted Astor again and actually, she realised, right now she wasn't tempted to. Perhaps it would have been different if they'd had this conversation while they were still married, while she was still pretending, but as it was it merely confirmed that she had been right all along to leave him – or rather, not kick up a fuss when he left her – even though her family, as it was then, had fractured. Because they felt like a family now. Her, Nate and the children, and even Ted, in a strange way.

'Please don't,' Jules said. She was wearing a long red puffer coat and sporting a large Gucci tote: it bore the classic Gucci fabric with a cherry print over it. Alice remembered her buying it in Le Bon Marché after she'd received her first bonus. It was nice to see Jules in her old clothes, like colour returning after a long winter.

'It's your turn to fuck up,' Nina added.

They walked a little further in silence, under the next bridge and towards the Hayward Gallery, a space Alice loved. She stopped, jamming her hands in her pockets. 'In some ways, I fucked up too... Not being honest about what matters to me, or what's going on, or... Nina. I hate your coffee. I'm sorry. I know you've won awards for it but all I want is a decent cup of tea, or the branded one in a jar I'm used to. That probably makes me basic, but honestly... *I don't even know what that means!* And my children...' Jules's betrayal over the invoice emboldened her to lay her feelings bare. 'I feel like I can't mention them around you, because Jules, you'll be offended or Nina, you'll be disinterested and...' She saw her breath in the cold air. 'And... also, when we were in Paris, I was texting Nate. And I didn't tell you both. So, I had something going on too. And, if I'm being really honest...' She looked up to the sky. Dusk was falling on the South Bank and strings of bulbs lined the Thames. 'At some level I always knew you and Ted had feelings for each other, Nina, but I tried to pretend to myself it wasn't a big deal. I knew you'd fancied each other when we met, it was obvious, but then it seemed to fizzle out and I suppose I hoped it was because he'd fallen in love with me. I thought he'd *chosen* me and the insecure part of me was just so *amazed* that he'd choose me over you that I didn't stop to think whether that was fair... but maybe, now, looking back, maybe it wasn't.' Her friends stared at her, open-mouthed.

'He *did* choose you, Alice, he loved you. The thing with me was him panicking. Pre-wedding nerves.' Nina reached her hands out to Alice. 'But yes, *I* had remained embarrassingly in love with *him*. I did my best to forget about him. As you know, I was half-cut most of the time,' she smiled wryly. 'And we were friends. Good friends. That was it, until that day before.'

'Did you know about them?' Alice asked Jules.

Jules nodded ruefully. 'Nina wanted to tell you, Alice, straight after the wedding, but I'd noticed you swapping your full champagne glasses with Ted's empty ones. I guessed you were pregnant, so I told her not to.'

Alice chewed on her lip. Jules put a hand on her shoulder. 'I'm sorry,' she said. 'I wanted to protect you.'

Alice looked skywards, exhaling, as gulls swooped against the clouds. 'We were already married.' She shook her head as the other two gasped. 'We married the week before, officially, in London. It's a pain marrying abroad. But we didn't tell anyone. We didn't want to spoil the romance.' She sneered at *romance*.

'Fuck,' was all Nina said. She'd slept with her best friend's *husband*. She felt the colour drain from her face. Even a few months ago, in the patisserie, when Ted had the chance to confess all, he hadn't taken it, omitting this important detail. Was it because he always wanted people to see the best in him? Shame? Arrogance? Was it, as she suspected, knowing Ted, that he always *wanted* to do that right thing but just couldn't quite manage it? She couldn't say. All she knew was that she didn't want her closest relationships to have omissions at their heart. She knew it was now or never. 'There's something else,' she said.

'Seriously?' Alice snapped, as though both she and the final threads of this friendship were close to breaking point. Her eyes searched Nina's.

'I fell pregnant too,' Nina whispered. 'When you... when you all went back to London after your wedding and I stayed in Paris, I found out I was pregnant. And I couldn't tell anyone.'

'What?' Jules said.

'What happened?' Alice asked.

'I had an abortion,' Nina said. 'My cousin Erin came with me. And...' It was coming out in a rush now, there was no stopping it. 'I was pregnant again, that last weekend in Paris.'

Jules's eyes widened with shock, then she exclaimed, '*I knew it! You weren't drinking!*'

Nina nodded. 'And I had another abortion,' she said, her voice cracking, 'and that's also why I didn't get in touch. I didn't want to break your heart, Jules, I didn't want you to know...'

'And you couldn't tell me, because of what had happened with Ted...' Alice concluded correctly.

'Yeah,' Nina mumbled. 'I only found out the night before we left and I spent the weekend in a tailspin, trying to decide what to do, but when I woke up that Sunday morning – after we'd had that brilliant night out – *well, we thought it was brilliant,*' she said to Jules with a weak smile, 'we didn't know what you were going through... I woke up and I was bleeding. I panicked. In that moment I thought, *I want this baby.*' She bit her lip. 'So I went straight to London and Flynn took me for a scan and when everything looked okay, it felt like a sign.'

'But you changed your mind?' Alice asked gently. She added as an afterthought, 'And that's why *you* left without telling me.' She pieced the events of that Sunday morning back together.

'I don't think my mind ever changed. I always knew I didn't want to have children. I got swept up in that weekend, being in Paris and thinking of the future. I knew I couldn't give that baby everything it deserved. And you know, honestly, I think there's enough people on the planet. No offence!' She grimaced at Alice.

'None taken,' Alice said. She'd been thinking about how it must've been for Nina, pregnant at the same time as her, in love with the same man. She was thinking how it would have been for Nina as Charlotte had grown older. It was Ted she was angry with, not Nina.

'It's a fair point,' Jules said, storing it mentally to mull over later. Jules had a long way to go but through her sessions with Cindy she was starting to imagine a time when she might come to terms with not having children of her own, might be able to imagine herself living a full life, nonetheless.

'You loved him first,' Alice said. She tipped her head to the side as she processed this and Nina nodded, squeezing her fingers over Alice's warm hand.

'He didn't deserve either of you,' Jules said. She'd love to give Ted Astor a piece of her mind. And a good hard slap.

'I'm not defending him,' Nina said. 'But.'

'A big but,' Jules said.

'Yes, a big but. He's had his own stuff going on, hasn't he? Losing his parents like that, growing up with his grandparents. He never saw where he fitted in, and I think that's been a problem for him.'

'You're so forgiving, Nina. There's the value of ten years of therapy.' Jules smiled. 'Although I do see what you're saying.' She thought of some of the friends she'd made in recovery. The woman who started playing FIFA with her teenage son and spent £15,000 in one week, eventually selling his console and games without his permission to cover some of her debts. The woman who'd stolen from an old lady she did shopping for to play bingo (and was now paying back). 'None of us can judge, can we?'

'You sound like Nate,' Alice added.

'How's it going with Mr Hough then?' Jules asked. 'I thought you had a twinkle in your eye whenever you mentioned him.'

'I think she had a twinkle in other places too,' Nina laughed as they slotted back into a line and continued walking.


'This has been so nice,' Jules said a few hours later. They'd stopped to eat in a Mexican restaurant under a railway arch and the time had passed by in what seemed like minutes. When they emerged the sun had set, dropping the temperature a few degrees and shading the sky fuchsia. 'I really mean that. I've missed you girls so much. Let's never mess up like this again.'

'I don't think we could if we tried!' Nina marvelled. She smiled at Alice tentatively. She wouldn't blame Alice if she didn't want to see her again, but she held hope tight in her heart like a blanket that she would. That she could forgive her, and they could rebuild their friendship.

'Shall we grab a drink?' Alice asked. She knew things couldn't be fixed overnight but she couldn't deny that being back with the girls felt like chicken soup was being infused into her veins.

'I've got to run. I'm going to view a flat,' Jules said. 'My first one.' She was finally coming to terms with leaving her home with Paul, had reconciled herself to a fresh start.

'I can't believe you broke up with Paul,' Nina said, a note of awed wonder in her voice: how was that possible?

'Me neither,' said Jules. 'I don't blame him. It was all me. I'm lucky I still have him in my life as a friend.'

'Really?' Alice said. 'You can do that?' She couldn't yet envisage a time when she could be friends with Ted, despite Nate's insistence that she give it a go for the sake of the children. He liaised between them, was a sounding board for Ted and his struggles with Charlotte. Frustratingly, Ted would listen to Nate in a way that he never would with her, but at least it meant Charlotte was getting the support – and love – from Ted that she needed. And it gave her relationship with Nate a chance to breathe, meant she could pursue her new job with gusto, now Ted was sharing parenting duties. 'It's best for everyone if you two can get along,' Nate often said, and she had been trying, she really had, but today had brought a whole new can of worms to chew on.

Jules shrugged. 'Yeah. I don't know how it will be when he meets someone else.' She swallowed. Anxiety fluttered in her chest. She didn't want to think about it.

Jules stood on the pavement outside a beautiful Victorian house, only five minutes from her own, which had recently been converted into two flats. *I could live here*, she thought, noticing the reflections from the street lights in the choppy waters of the Thames. It was Jules who had loved their old house at first sight; Paul needed some convincing. If it were left to him, they'd have bought a swanky penthouse with floor-to-ceiling glass and a good view, no doubt the sort of place he'd be ending up in next. She smiled at the thought, happy for him. He was walking lighter recently, looking healthier, happier. He was recovering, *from me*, she thought gingerly, but she was happy it was so. Her biggest regret wasn't all the money she'd lost, it was the love she'd lost. It was the trust – and friendships – she'd gambled with that still kept her awake sometimes, but she was learning to accept what had happened; learning to accept herself. *Perfectly imperfect*, as Cindy liked to say. She stomped her feet to keep warm, watched her breath flare in the cold air. Above her was a clear and star-studded sky. She was content.

The estate agent, Laurie, pulled up in a flurry, angling his head out of the window to shout 'Sorry!' from a small branded mini, stalling and reversing a number of times in his attempt to parallel park. 'Hectic start! It's my first day! Listen, I hope you don't mind but my colleague was supposed to be showing the flat above at the same time and she's stuck in traffic...'

He finally parked and exited his car as Jules became aware of someone striding up behind her. She stepped to one side politely. 'Hello!' Laurie said cheerfully as he locked the car. 'Mr Frey-Jackson, I presume?' Jules's head snapped around. One of the things Jules loved about Paul was his insistence when they married that they would *each* take the other's name. She grinned as he reached her now, a spring in his step having spotted her. 'I was just explaining that Daniella can't make it, so I'll be doing both viewings. I've just got to send an email. Won't be a moment...'

'You're joking?' Jules laughed, turning to face Paul.

'Hello,' Paul said, smiling at Jules, his cheeks pink with cold.

Laurie looked up from his phone, running his hand through his curly mop of hair. 'You two know each other?'

Paul nodded, not moving his eyes from Jules. 'We go way back.' The air between them crackled.

Laurie looked between them, as if trying to read the situation, then back to his phone. Jules saw him pull up their email exchange and click on her name. *Julia Frey-Jackson.* He glanced up again, his nose screwed in concentration, as though he should know more about them but couldn't recall what, then went back to the email he was writing.

'I didn't think this would be your style,' she said, gesturing at the house behind them.

'Neither did I,' he said, 'but this crazy English woman put some sort of spell on me and now I can't help looking at these draughty old English houses and thinking that they're kinda cosy.'

Jules grinned. 'I told you so,' she said, shaking her head. 'So you're top floor?'

'Of course. Best views.' He lowered his voice. 'I like the sound of you being underneath me,' he added huskily, dipping his head so only she could hear.

'Shall we go in?' Laurie asked, still one eye on his phone as he opened the gate.

Jules and Paul looked at the neat garden and the large bay windows. Jules noticed crocuses, impatient for spring, pushing up through the soil, and felt this was a good omen. Paul kept looking up at the house and then back at Jules.

'Actually, I think we've got this.' He held a hand out to Jules.

'Are you sure?' she said as she took it, tiny jolts of electricity fizzing between them as their skin touched.

'Sure I'm sure,' he said.

He turned towards Laurie. 'I'm sorry we wasted your time,

man. Could you pass on a message to Daniella, please? Ask her to tell dear old Mr Legg we're out, will you?' He squeezed Jules's hand. 'Shall we?'

Together they turned and began walking back home.

# 18

## One Year After Paris

*The Amalfi Coast, Italy*

'Everyone say "formaggio!"' instructed the photographer, looking in the viewfinder and back up at the group. The balcony of Villa Cimbrone's *terrazza dell'infinito* curved behind them, sun-bleached terracotta, framing them either side with sprays of magenta petunias and pale stone busts, weathered by centuries of sun and wind, witnesses to love.

'Formaggio!' shouted Nina, Alice and Jules, grins wide across their faces, the colours of their dresses – brilliant yellow, purples and pinks, white and green – a striking contrast to the deep blues of the sea and sky behind them.

'One more time!'

'*Formaggio!*'

Luca lunged forward as Ezra, his and Kai's newly adopted toddler, wriggled free from his grasp. He scooped him up, tickling him under his chin, and Ezra's chuckles reverberated over the air. 'Sorry!' Luca called.

'Let's try again! No eyes closed this time... *Uno, due, tre...*'

'*Formaggio!*' they chorused, Wilf and Phoebe eliciting a chorus of '*ah*'s with their pronunciation: *madge-ee-oh!* Delighted with this response, Wilf began to run round in circles excitedly. 'Madge-ee-oh! Madge-ee-oh!' he chanted, only running and shouting louder when Alice and Nate tried to calm him down. They exchanged glances as Charlotte observed shrewdly, 'I think he might have ADHD, like me.'

Nate and Alice laughed. Nate was wearing navy chinos and a white shirt, Alice a midi dress in tiers of colour: violet and hot pink, fading to lilac and blush.

'What?' Charlotte asked.

'Nothing,' Alice said, ruffling her hair, which hung in loose waves. She was allowed to touch it now. Each month that Charlotte was home-schooled brought a reduction in her anxiety-driven meltdowns. A new person was emerging, a different future.

'I think you might be right,' Nate whispered in her ear as he thought, *And I think your dad might have it too*, recalling his conversation with Ted last week when he admitted how difficult he had found school, getting assignments in on time and trying to focus. *Everyone assumed it was grief*, he had said sadly, *but my brain had always operated like that.*

'And like me,' Jules said loudly (and proudly), a hand on Charlotte's shoulder. 'We're going to rule the world one day, aren't we?'

*She mightn't be wrong*, thought Alice. She was now a creative consultant for Aki Mantel's chain of hotels. Since having their first child, the Mantels had decided to focus their philanthropy on education. Alice and Nate were in discussion with them about funding a different sort of school, transposing a successful Silicon Valley model that better suited autistic children over to the UK. 'It's really, really exciting,' Alice had gushed when she told Jules, who promptly called Elliott Mantel and begged to be on the school board. It was a win-win for them all since Jules's profile was soaring since her podcast appearance. Shortly after listening to the podcast herself, Alice had sent the link to Ted, not knowing that all over the City, phones were lighting up with a similar message: *Listen to this now.*

Last week she'd googled 'Julia Frey-Jackson gambling' and a list of hits came up. Alice had watched a video, smiling, Jules in vibrant mismatched clothing, looking like she had when they were younger, speaking to other women about neuro-diversity. *She'll be doing a TED talk next,* thought Alice, not knowing an email invitation was already sitting in Jules's inbox.

'You bet,' Charlotte beamed up at her Aunty Jules. Since Charlotte's stress levels had reduced, a fierce intellect had emerged. She could hold a short conversation in Korean now, certainly enough to get by if she travelled to Korea, as she planned to. She frequently implored her parents and Nate to take her but so far only Ted had responded with a tentative 'maybe'. 'Let's not be *too* hasty though,' he'd said quickly, when she immediately pulled up a flight comparison website.

'One of the benefits of home-schooling,' Nate had said amiably. 'Flexibility.' And Ted had grimaced. Nate had become a listening ear to Ted the last few months. In fact, Alice might go so far as to say that they seemed like friends. She smiled at Nate now as he chatted to Phoebe, answering her questions about whether there were dolphins in the ocean and what their names might be.

\* \* \*

After the ceremony beneath the pergola, lushly adorned with a fragrant ceiling of white and blue wisteria, and after they'd all stopped crying, they returned to the *terrazza dell'infinito*, perched on the edge of the cliff. The water was calm, iridescent with sunlight in the gaps between small boats in the distance. Waiters circulated with trays of electric orange and rosemary Aperol spritzes and freshly squeezed peach bellinis, while others shaved slices of Parmesan and prosciutto on to delicate white plates in the shade. A small band played music.

*So beautiful*, thought Nina as 'Beyond the Sea' began in Italian, apt as she gazed at the brightly coloured houses covering the surrounding cliffs like wildflowers, cascading down to the sea. She propped her head on Flynn's shoulder as he slipped his arm around her waist. Her slim-fit yellow dress, with billowing sleeves, was cinched in with a cabochon-encrusted belt in blues and greens. They were tentatively exploring a relationship together, perhaps building a life. On Monday, when the others returned home, they were travelling from Ravello along the coast, to Positano and Capri, a much-needed break before her book launch next month.

Jules was resplendent in a Dolce & Gabbana white silk dress emblazoned with a green banana-leaf print, pointed cerise shoes and a clutch bag by her favourite designer: a yellow crystal-studded lemon. It didn't work but it worked.

'Things are really taking off for you,' Nina said, as they walked further along the terrace to the ancient crypt where they could already see a long table, laid for dinner.

'It's because I'm a woman. A white woman in a smart

suit with a big job and a house in West London. People are fascinated.' She shrugged. 'But whatever, I'm happy I can be useful.'

Jules had had what Nina would refer to as a therapy 'breakthrough', terminology Jules wasn't ready to embrace just yet. She had moved from her father's philosophy – to work hard and be the best – to Paul's philosophy – to work hard to enjoy life – but she'd never stopped to consider what her own philosophy was. It wasn't until the offers began flooding in – consultancy work at the investment banks (*'How can we harness women's neuro-diversity most effectively, Julia?'*), speeches at conferences and universities – that she realised this was where she thrived: helping others. She wanted to reach a hand down and help the neuro-diverse women below her climb on to her shoulders. When she stood on a stage and looked out across an eager audience, women who had grown up like Charlotte being told she was different, or masking like Jules, afraid to be her true self, she saw hope. She saw the future. She saw it as an evolving pyramid of cheerleaders, each pulling the next generation up and – when needed – letting her climb to the top with a megaphone, to get their point across.

'I think it's a little more than that,' Paul said, sitting beside her in a sky-blue Tom Ford linen suit.

'That was a beautiful ceremony, man,' said Flynn, smoothing his shirt as he sat down. Paul, ever the gracious host, said that the beautiful thing was them all being there together. Jules's mother, Nancy, joined them at the table, along with her brother William, his wife Gilly and their son Jasper, who was transfixed by one of Charlotte's fidget spinners.

The table looked out to the sea and mountains beyond,

exposed to the elements, which today were warm and mild. It was adorned with grey tapered candles, fistfuls of white blossoms, fresh herbs and small green apples. White plates were placed on blue-and-yellow Mediterranean tiles and replaced with dish after dish: red snapper carpaccio with melon, lobster ravioli, beef stuffed with mozzarella and porcini mushrooms, millefeuille layered with cream and wild berries, washed down with rich Tuscan wine and crisp flutes of Prosecco.

'You two are so sweet, renewing your vows,' Alice said. She was finding it hard to concentrate as Nate worked a finger slowly around the curve of her bum. After three months of teasing, foreplay had finally ended; the months since had been worth it.

'It felt like the right time.' Paul gazed at Jules, who put a hand on his cheek affectionately. Later, they were going to ask Luca and Kai for advice on beginning the adoption process. He raised his glass. 'God knows the last few years haven't been easy,' he said. 'For any of us. But I would marry you a thousand times, Julia Frey-Jackson.' He stood, his glass high. 'To love!' he shouted, his deep voice carrying into the balmy air and out to sea.

They all grinned and stood, eyes and hearts beaming.

'*To love!*' they cheered.


Dusk fell, bruising the sky shades of coral and lavender, and a canopy of stars exploded above them. The terrace was festooned with lights, the ancient busts cast bronze from the glow, flares of gold spilled out from the houses lining the cliffs like fireflies. After a break for dinner the band had returned, its music more uptempo.

'Is this our best ever dance floor?' Alice said, shimmying her shoulders and her hips, not quite in time to the music.

Jules nodded, swishing her arms and rolling her hips around in circles: 'The Ocean', she joked.

Alice strutted over to the band and leaned in. 'Do you know "Disco 2000"?' she asked, and the frontwoman – a dazzling burst of energy with flaming red hair – frowned, leaning backwards to consult with her bandmates.

'Hey, you know what next year is?' Jules said as she returned. 'Our fortieths. What do you think? A weekend in Paris for old times' sake?'

'Hm. I'm a big fan of Lisbon these days,' said Nina.

'I quite fancy Berlin,' chipped in Alice.

'But Paris...' said Jules, and images of low-lit restaurants and crisp coupes of Kir royale and the Eiffel Tower hung in the air between them like a jet trail as the frontwoman shot a thumbs up to the group and the opening bars of 'Disco 2000' electrified the evening air. 'Seriously though, we should do something to mark it?'

'I think one Eiffel Tower tattoo's plenty,' Jules laughed.

'I don't think we need anything,' said Nina. 'Just us is enough.' She reached her arms around them both, the sea behind them midnight blue, shards of moonlight glittering over its surface, all the people they loved moving and dancing around them. 'We made it,' she said.

They grinned at each other for a moment before Alice and Jules spoke in unison.

'We really did.'

# Author's Note

CHARLOTTE DIGBY is autistic, with a demand avoidant profile. Essentially this means that the more overwhelmed she becomes, the more she says 'no' to the everyday demands of life. Extreme demand avoidance such as Charlotte's may be diagnosed as Pathological Demand Avoidance or 'PDA', a part of the autism spectrum (I say 'may' because the route to diagnosis is complex and, relative to autism in general, understanding of PDA is in its infancy).

Because I love Alice I gave her a hot SEN-teacher-boyfriend-cum-Ted-whisperer, a flexible job, oodles of money and the prospect of a specialised SEN school on the horizon, so that she can best support Charlotte. In reality this is a highly unlikely scenario. It is very difficult to obtain support for autistic children in the UK (and especially those with PDA) - a situation which has worsened since Covid - and yet it profoundly impacts a child's experience of school and accordingly their sense of self-worth and their future prospects.

If you do not have experience with autism I hope that Charlotte and Alice's (and Jules's) stories resonate with you nonetheless and help you to, like Charlotte, see the world a little differently. Not better, not worse, just different.

To better understand autism I recommend the book 'Uniquely Human: A Different Way of Seeing Autism' by Dr. Barry M. Prizant Ph.D with Tom Fields-Meyer.

For an introduction to PDA I recommend listening to episode 121 of Neurodiversity Podcast: Understanding Pathological Demand Avoidance with Harry J. Thompson.

# Acknowledgements

A book is a collaborative effort: thanks to Laura Palmer, Anna Nightingale, Bianca Gillam, Kate Appleton, Ayo Okojie, Nelle Andrew and the teams at Head of Zeus and Rachel Mills Literary Agency respectively who have worked to publish this book and help it find its way into readers' hands. I am enormously grateful.

Thanks also to my readers and the champions of the publishing world: book bloggers. I don't like to have favourites but especially those of you who have recommended one of my books to a friend, posted on social media or written a review. Such efforts warm my antsy writer's heart.

I had the idea for *After Paris* when I was writing *Everything's Perfect* in 2017. It had been at the back of mind, gestating, from then until I came to write it last year. I knew that Jules was an addict, and struggling with undiagnosed neurodiversity, but I couldn't quite figure out what she was addicted to until a friend, Chris Gilham, bravely shared the story of his gambling addiction online. As I read – with surprise – his account, I realised this was the missing part of Jules's story: she was a compulsive gambler. I'm hugely grateful to Chris not only for sharing his experience – which both educated and enlightened me – but also for reading a draft of *After Paris* and sharing his thoughts. While researching this book I listened to a number of recovery podcast episodes, notably from All Bets Are Off (which Chris Gilham co-hosts) and Hooked: The Unexpected Addicts, both of which I highly recommend. I am awed by the strength and courage of the hosts and contributors.

Many of Nina's baking creations were fantasies of my own imagination but those that were not were inspired by Claudia Roden's *A New Book Of Middle Eastern Food*.

Thanks to Billy Thomas for a crash course in poker and reading through the poker scene many, many times; John McGinley for odds-calculations; Rupert Beecroft for help in the planning stages of this book; Christopher M. Hawkes Esq. who is always on good form; Tom Butterworth, for his enthusiasm and support; Olivia Berreen for checking my rusty French; and to my early readers, Rebecca Keane, Claire Bushell and Katie Butterworth.

In 2005 I had the good fortune to meet Mattias Johansson at a bus stop in Cañas, Costa Rica and to spend the next few days with him, before he abruptly left this world for his next *solo aventura*. On the bus he showed me his journal where he had written '*life in general and love in particular*'; matters, he explained, he enjoyed discussing with his best friend Jimmy Högberg. It struck me then as a cool phrase, so I have borrowed it here as an album name for my cool girl, Nina, with permission from Jimmy. *Tack*.

Thank you to Paul Bradley Carr and Ashley Strong, who donated to Care International (via Books For Vaccines) and to our children's PTA respectively, to each have a character named after them.

One of the joys of publication has been connecting with

other writers. Thanks especially to Clare Mackintosh, Sarah Turner, Lia Louis, Holly Miller, Louise Hare, Katy Collins, Jennifer Saint, Frances Quinn, Andrea Mara, Suzanne Ewart, Lucy Vine and Laura Marshall for their support.

Thanks as ever to the family and friends who have travelled with me on my writing journey, particularly my husband Tom and my sons Dylan, Arthur and Felix.

To many Paris is the city of love, to me it is the city of friendship: of nights out and big dreams and trying to find yourself, in your twenties, in a new city without a map (followed by hen do revisits in our thirties). Thank you to the friends I have been fortunate to spend time with in Paris, the memories of which inspired this book. I enjoyed writing *After Paris* immensely in part because it allowed me to escape there briefly – in my imagination – while grounded during a global pandemic. Thanks especially to Nicola Lloyd Martin, who not only shared a whole mille-feuille with me once in Paris, but also provided investment banking insight for Jules's career trajectory; and to Cara Pannell, Jemma Thomas and Katie Butterworth who have been by my side since our childhood in Essex, via Paris, and beyond. It felt only right that this tribute to friendship is dedicated to you.

# About the Author

NICOLE KENNEDY grew up in Essex and studied Law at Bristol University. She has always loved to write but her efforts were waylaid by work as a corporate lawyer in London, Paris and Dubai. During Nicole's second maternity leave she began writing poems on motherhood and family life. She completed her first novel during her third maternity leave (by then it was easier than leaving the house) and her second during the pandemic (by then she wasn't *allowed* to leave the house). Nicole lives in Kent with her husband and three sons. You can find her on Instagram (@nicole_k_kennedy) and Twitter (@nicolekkennedy).